FOREV

(THE INN AT SUNSET HARBOR—BOOK 5)

SOPHIE LOVE

BOOKS BY SOPHIE LOVE

THE INN AT SUNSET HARBOR
FOR NOW AND FOREVER (Book #1)
FOREVER AND FOR ALWAYS (Book #2)
FOREVER, WITH YOU (Book #3)
IF ONLY FOREVER (Book #4)
FOREVER AND A DAY (Book #5)
FOREVER, PLUS ONE (Book #6)

CHAPTER ONE

"Dad?" Emily repeated.

She stared at the man on her porch step, a man she barely recognized anymore. Silver hair where once before it had been black. The shadow of stubble on his chin. Creases and furrows lining his face. But there was no mistaking it. It was her father.

Words failed her. She couldn't catch her breath.

The crinkles at the sides of Roy's eyes deepened as he smiled. "Emily Jane," he replied.

That's when Emily knew it was real. He was real. It was her dad.

She ran as fast as she could up the porch steps and threw herself into his arms. She'd imagined this moment so many times, wondering how she would behave if he ever came back to her. In her imagination she'd acted cool, been aloof, had risen above it all by not letting him see the pain his disappearance had caused her, nor the utter relief she felt knowing he was safe. But of course the reality was completely different. Instead of being standoffish, she wrapped her arms around his neck and held him like she was a child again.

He was warm, solid. She could feel him breathing hard, each expansion of his lungs betraying his emotions. Her tears came almost immediately. As though in response, she felt his own tears wet her cheeks and neck.

"You came back," Emily managed to say, her voice cracking as she spoke. She sounded as young and vulnerable as she felt.

"I did," Roy replied through deep sobs. "I'm—"

But he stopped short. Emily knew instinctively that the only word to conclude that sentence was "sorry" but that her father wasn't yet ready to deal with the torrent of emotions such an utterance would unleash. Emily wasn't either. She didn't want to go to those painful places yet. She just wanted to stay in this moment. Bask in it.

She lost track of how much time passed as she and her father stood there holding each other, but she felt a sudden change in the way her father held her, a tensing of his muscles, like he was suddenly uncomfortable. She moved away from him and looked over her shoulder to see where Roy's gaze was now affixed: Chantelle.

She was standing in the open door of the inn, a look of bemusement on her face as though trying to comprehend the strange scene before her. Emily could read all the questions in her eyes. Who is this man? Why is Emily crying? Why is he? What's going on?

"Chantelle, honey," Emily said, extending a hand. "Come here."

Emily saw in Chantelle's hesitation an uncharacteristic shyness.

"There's nothing to be scared of," Emily added.

Chantelle took a few paces toward Emily. "Why is he looking at me like that?" she said in a stage whisper that Roy could clearly hear.

Emily looked at her father. His damp eyes were wide with confusion. He wiped the wetness from his lashes.

"You have a daughter?" he finally stammered, his voice thick with emotion.

"Yes," Emily said, reaching for Chantelle and pulling the girl to her side, into a half embrace. "Well, she's Daniel's daughter. But I'm raising her like a mother would."

Chantelle clung to Emily. "Is he going to take me away?" she asked.

"Oh no, no, sweetie!" Emily exclaimed. "This is my father. Your grandpa." She turned her gaze then to meet her dad's. "Papa Roy?" she suggested.

He nodded immediately. He seemed bewitched by the child, his pale blue eyes sparkling with intrigue.

"She looks so much like her," he said.

Emily understood immediately what he meant. That Chantelle looked like Charlotte. No wonder he'd assumed she was Emily's child; Emily herself sometimes struggled to believe that those were not Charlotte's genetic characteristics expressed in Chantelle.

"I see it too," she confessed.

"Who do I look like?" Chantelle questioned.

Emily felt like this line of questioning was far too much for the child to handle. She wanted to shut it down right away. Even though she felt like a trembling lamb she knew she had to step up and take command.

"Someone we used to know a long time ago, that's all," she said. "Come on, Papa Roy needs to meet Daddy."

Chantelle brightened suddenly. "I'll get him." She beamed, bounding off back inside.

Emily sighed. She understood why her dad had been so shocked by Chantelle, but having a stranger stare at her like that—like she was a ghost—was the last thing the child needed.

"She's really not biologically yours?" Roy asked the second the child had disappeared.

Emily shook her head. "I know, it's crazy. She's sensitive like her too. And kind. Funny. Creative. I can't wait for you to get to know her." Her voice hitched then, with sudden fear at the thought that Roy wasn't staying, that this was just a flying visit. Perhaps she wasn't even supposed to have known he'd been here. Maybe his plan was to avoid her altogether, to swoop in and out before she'd had a chance to realize he was back, like his covert trips in his beat-up car that Trevor had witnessed from his spying window. She rubbed behind her ear awkwardly. "That is, if you have the time."

"I have the time." Roy nodded, a small flutter of a smile appearing on his lips.

Just then, Chantelle returned, dragging Daniel along behind her. He stopped at the doorway and glanced at Roy.

"Papa Roy?" he said, raising his eyebrows, clearly repeating the name that Chantelle had so innocently relayed to him.

Emily saw the look that crossed between them and remembered how Daniel had told her about that summer back when he was a teenager and had needed a friend, how Roy had been there for him, had helped him get his life back on track. She could tell in that moment that Roy's safe return to Sunset Harbor meant almost as much to Daniel as it did to herself.

Roy offered his hand for Daniel to shake. But to Emily's surprise, Daniel took the hand and pulled Roy into a bear hug. She felt a strange clench in her chest, a peculiar emotion that was somewhere between joy and grief.

"I think you've met Daniel," Emily said, her voice cracking once again.

"I have," Roy replied as he was released by Daniel, taking him instead by the shoulders. He seemed overwhelmed with emotion, treading that fine line between weeping tears of joy and bursting into relieved laughter.

"We're getting married," Emily added, somewhat dumbly.

"I know," Roy said, grinning from ear to ear. "I read your email. I'm so delighted."

"Are you coming inside?" Daniel asked Roy, softly.

"If I may," Roy replied, sounding concerned that he may not be accepted back into Emily's life.

3

"Of course!" Emily exclaimed. She clutched his hand tightly, trying to tell him that everything was okay, that he was wanted here, accepted here, that his return to her was a joyous occasion.

Roy's face seemed etched with relief. He visibly relaxed, as though a hurdle he'd been worried about jumping had been accomplished.

As they walked toward the door, Emily became suddenly aware of the fact that the house her father had abandoned over twenty years ago in no way resembled its former self. She'd taken over, changed it all, changed its purpose from a family home to an inn. Would he be mad?

"We've made some renovations," she said quickly.

"Emily Jane," her father replied in a kind, firm voice, "I know you've been living here. That it's an inn now. It's fine. I'm delighted for you."

She nodded, but still felt anxious about letting him inside. Chantelle led the way and one by one they filed into the reception hall, Roy taking the tail, his gait slower and stiffer than Emily remembered.

He stopped in the hall and looked around him, his mouth open with surprise and awe. When he saw the reception desk, his eyes widened.

"Is this...?"

"The same one you sold to Rico?" Emily said. "Yes."

The inn had been a guest house originally before the owners abandoned it. Roy's story with the home mirrored her own in reverse. He'd wanted this place to be a family home, a haven for summer vacations. Emily had turned it back into a guesthouse, a business.

"I can't believe he kept it all these years," Roy said with surprise, still looking at the desk. Then he turned his eyes to Emily. "Do you remember the day I sold it to him?"

Emily shook her head silently.

"You were quite adamant that I shouldn't sell it," he said with a chuckle. "You'd put a Barbie in every one of the drawers. Said it was a hospital for your dolls."

"I think I do remember," Emily replied, feel⸍   ⸌⸍ melancholy.

"Rico was very kind about it," Roy added. "⸍ 'transfer' your 'patients' to another location. I thi⸍ cupboard under the sink." He, too, became som⸍ tore his attention away from the reception d⸍

4

renovation work. "This really is incredible. You've done a fabulous job."

The sound of pride in his voice made Emily's heart jolt. This moment was so much more than she could have hoped for. It was perfect.

"Do you want a tour?" she asked.

Roy nodded. Emily led him to the kitchen first. Inside, they could hear the sounds of the dogs barking from the laundry room.

"I don't know what to take in first," Roy exclaimed, glancing around him at the fully restored kitchen with its original retro appliances and decorations. "The amazing renovation work or the fact you have pets!"

"This is Mogsy and her puppy Rain!" Chantelle announced, opening up the utility room door and allowing the two to run inside.

They rushed up to Roy, sniffing him and trying to lick his cheeks. Roy laughed, the fine lines around his face becoming more pronounced, and scratched them both behind the ears.

"We don't usually let them run around the kitchen," Emily explained. "But since it's a special occasion—"

Her voice cracked as that pang of melancholy she'd felt earlier returned. Being with her dad shouldn't be "special"; it had been made that way by him leaving.

From his crouched position, he looked up at her, his expression filled with regret.

All at once, Emily felt a surge of anger. Some of her deeply buried hurt was beginning to bubble upward.

"Let's go to the dining room," she said, hurriedly, not wanting it to surface.

They went into the room with the large oak table. Straightaway Roy noticed that the heavy drape curtain that had once hung over the ballroom door was no longer there.

"You found the ballroom," he said.

Something about the comment irritated Emily further. This wasn't a game of hide-and-seek. She felt hotness creep into her cheeks.

"Found it. Restored it. Soon to be getting married in it," she said, as they passed along the low-ceilinged hallway and emerged into the huge ballroom.

She could hear the snappiness in her voice and took a deep breath to calm herself.

"Well, it looks beautiful," Roy said, either oblivious to her mounting anger or not yet willing to confront it. "I'm surprised the d glass looks so good after all this time."

"Daniel's friend George renovated it," Emily explained.

"George?" Roy said, raising his eyebrows. "I remember him when he was this big." He gestured with his hand to his waist to indicate a child's height.

It occurred to Emily then that Sunset Harbor was more her father's town than it ever had been hers, that he knew people from this place better than she did, that in the years he'd lived here he'd planted more roots than she could ever hope to. A new emotion of jealousy wormed its way into the complex mixture of feelings she was already trying to keep at bay. She tried her hardest to keep a neutral expression on her face.

They went upstairs next and Emily showed Roy the master bedroom, the room that had once been his and Patricia's, then, presumably, his and Antonia's when she'd visited, before finally becoming hers and Daniel's.

"This is fantastic," Roy exclaimed. "The colors are so fresh."

He'd been far more into his dark colors, the sorts of crimsons and navy hues that she'd decorated the guest bedrooms in. The crisp white and eggshell blue had been far closer to her mother's tastes, and Emily realized for the first time as she looked at her room that her style was a perfect blend of them both. Roy's penchant for antiques—seen in the huge bed, the vanity desk, the ottoman—and Patricia's cleanliness in the white colors. Emily felt like she was looking at the room anew.

"My room is next door," Chantelle said.

Emily was relieved for the distraction. She guided Roy out of the room and into Chantelle's, where he took in the delightful animal-themed furniture Emily had purchased for her. Chantelle waltzed around the room, proudly showing off her shelf of books, her wardrobe filled with dresses, her pile of cuddly toys, her wall of artwork.

"Chantelle, you have quite a lovely room," Roy said kindly, reminding Emily of that soft way he had with children, of the gentleness he'd spoken to her with back when he'd been in her life.

Chantelle beamed with pride.

"You chose not to put her in the room you and Charlotte shared?" he said. "The play room with the mezzanine?"

Emily felt a little jolt of pain in her chest to hear him refer to her childhood room. He'd locked it up after Charlotte's death, forcing Emily to switch rooms. That had been the first sign, Emily realized now, that her father wasn't going to process Charlotte's death, that her dying was going to become the catalyst to him abandoning her.

6

"That's the bridal suite," Daniel explained, taking over while Emily remained mute. "The mezzanine was a great selling point. Plus, we wanted Chantelle close to us."

The emotion was getting to be too much for Emily. She had no idea it was possible to feel so many conflicting, complex things at once. It suddenly dawned on her that once this tour was over, once they sat down in the living room face to face, she would release an explosion of rage at her father.

She felt her father's hand on her arm suddenly, steadying her, reassuring her. She looked into his blue eyes, saw the grief and regret within them, mixing with utter relief. He was silently telling her that it was okay, he understood her anger. She didn't need to keep hiding it.

They traipsed through the rest of the floor, glancing into a few of the guest rooms so that Roy could get a taste of the decor. He hovered briefly beside his study door. The last time he'd been here he was two decades younger, his hair black instead of gray, his body slimmer and more agile instead of the slight paunch that now sat above his waistband.

"It's the same," Emily replied. "I haven't changed it."

He nodded, but didn't say a word. She wondered if he was thinking about the myriad of documents he'd locked inside his desk, ones she had now read. The letters and secrets she'd found of his. Emily knew there was no way of knowing what Roy was thinking. The man was as much a mystery to her now as he always had been.

They went to the third floor and Roy lingered for a while beside the stairs up to the widow's walk. Was that New Year's Eve evening on his mind? Emily wondered. The one where he'd told her not to be scared, to open her eyes and look at the fireworks? Or had he forgotten all those memories like she once had?

Chantelle skipped around, showing him into all of the empty guest rooms. She seemed excited to have him here, and so proud to show him her home. Emily wished she could feel as light as the child clearly did, but there was so much going on in her mind it filled her to the brim with anguish.

"I'm really amazed by the work you've done here," Roy said. "It can't have been easy getting all these en suites in."

"It wasn't," Emily replied. "We only had about twenty-four hours to do it as well. Which is a long story."

"I have time." Roy smiled.

Emily didn't even know how to respond to that. Time was not something she could take for granted with him. She couldn't trust his sentiments.

"Let's head to the living room," she said, stiffly. "Have something to drink?" Then, realizing her slip-up in suggesting alcohol to an alcoholic, she added quickly, "Coffee."

With each step down the staircase, Emily felt her anger growing stronger. She hated the feeling. She wanted this reunion to be a joyful one, but how could it be, really, when she had all this resentment inside? Her father had to hear about the pain he had caused her.

They reached the downstairs hallway. Daniel headed to the kitchen to make the coffee as Chantelle showed Roy into the living room. He gasped when he saw the renovations, the way Emily had blended new styles and old styles, the way she'd incorporated modern art and Kandinsky glassware.

"Is that my old piano?" he asked.

Emily nodded. "I had it restored. The guy who did it, Owen, he plays here sometimes. He'll be playing at our wedding, actually."

For the first time, Emily felt a sense of triumph. Having not lived in Sunset Harbor long, Owen wasn't someone her father had known before her, for longer than her, or knew better than her. There were people here who were her own, who weren't tainted by the unpleasantness of that shared past.

"Owen helps me with my singing," Chantelle said.

"Oh, you sing?" Roy replied. "Can I hear a bit?"

"Maybe later," Emily cut in. "Chantelle promised me she'd tidy up all of her toys today."

"Can't I do it later?" Chantelle wailed.

She clearly wanted to spend more time with Papa Roy and Emily couldn't blame her. On the surface he was like a gentle giant, a Santa Claus of a man. But Emily couldn't keep plastering a pretend smile on her face forever just for Chantelle's sake. It was time for her and her father to talk like grown-ups.

Emily shook her head. "Why don't you get it done right now, then you'll have the whole day to play with Papa Roy, okay?"

Chantelle relented and left the room with a stomp in her step.

"You've opened up the speakeasy," Roy noted, looking at the sparklingly renovated bar. He seemed impressed by the way Emily had kept the period of the place in the same way he had, an homage to a time gone by. "You know it's original."

She nodded. "I figured as much. Except the liquor bottles."

Without Chantelle to buffer the situation, a tenseness rose between them. Emily gestured to the sofa.

"Will you sit?"

Roy nodded and settled himself in. His face had blanched of color as though sensing that the moment of reckoning was upon them.

But before Emily had a chance, Daniel appeared with a tray containing the coffee pot, cream, sugar, and mugs. He set it down on the coffee table. Silence swelled as he poured the drinks.

Roy cleared his throat. "Emily Jane, if you have questions to ask me, you can."

Emily's ability to remain polite and cordial broke. "Why did you leave me?" she blurted out.

Daniel's head snapped up with surprise. His eyes were as wide as saucers. He probably hadn't realized Emily's joy at having Roy back had dragged up her anger as well, that she'd been carrying her emotion with her throughout the whole tour of the house. He stood then.

"I should give you both some time," he said politely.

Emily turned her eyes up to him. He looked so awkward standing there, as though suddenly encroaching on a private matter, and Emily felt a little guilty to have turned the conversation sour so quickly in his presence, without giving him the chance to excuse himself in a more polite manner.

"Thank you," she said as he hurried out of the room.

She turned her gaze back to her father. Roy seemed hurt by her evident pain but he breathed calmly and looked at her with gentle eyes.

"I was broken, Emily Jane," he began. "After losing Charlotte I was a broken man. I drank. I had affairs. I alienated my friends in New York City until I couldn't bear to be there anymore. Your mom and I split, though that was a long time coming. I came here to put my life back together."

"Only you didn't," Emily replied, hotly. "You ran away. You left me."

She could feel tears prickling in her eyes. Her father's were growing red and misty too. He looked down into his lap, his expression one of shame.

"I was ignoring things," he said sadly. "I thought I could pretend everything was okay. Even though it had been years since Charlotte had died, I hadn't really let myself feel anything. I never went in the room you shared, moving you to a different one if you recall."

Emily nodded. She remembered vividly her father blocking access to parts of the house, making certain areas out of bounds for her during her summer visits—the widow's walk, the third floor, the garages, his study, the basement—until she'd all but forgotten they ever existed or what they contained. She remembered his increasingly erratic behavior, his obsession with collecting antiques that seemed to her like less of a hobby and more of a compulsion, his hoarding behavior. But moreover she remembered the diminishing contact, the way she'd spend less and less time with him in Maine until she reached fifteen and, one summer, he just never turned up to collect her. That had been the last time she'd seen him.

Emily wanted to be understanding toward her father's actions. But though one part of her understood he was a broken man who had one day cracked, the torment his actions had caused her could not just be explained away.

"Why didn't you say goodbye?" Emily said, the tears falling down her cheeks in torrents. "How could you just leave like that?"

Roy, too, seemed to be becoming overwhelmed with emotion. Emily noted that his hands were shaking. His lips trembled as he spoke. "I'm so sorry. I've been haunted by that decision."

"You were haunted?" Emily cried. "I didn't know if you were dead or alive! You left me wondering, not knowing. Do you have any idea what that does to a person? My whole life was on pause because of you! Because you were too much of a coward to say goodbye!"

Roy took her words like repeated punches to the face. His expression looked as pained as if they really had been physical blows she'd laid upon him.

"It was inexcusable," he said, barely more than a whisper. "So I won't try to excuse it."

Emily felt her heart racing wildly in her chest. She was so furious she couldn't even see straight. All those years of emotions were flooding out of her with the force of a tsunami.

"Did you even think about how it would hurt me?" she cried, her voice rising in pitch and volume even more.

Roy seemed gripped with anguish, his whole body tensing, his face contorted with regret. Emily was glad to see him that way. She wanted him to hurt just as much as she had.

"Not at first," he confessed. "Because I wasn't in my right mind. I couldn't think of anything or anyone but myself, my own pain. I thought you'd be better off without me."

He broke down then, sobs juddering through his body until he was shaking from the emotion. Watching him like that was like a stab to the heart. Emily didn't want to see her father crack and crumble before her eyes, but he needed to know. There would be no moving on, no reparation without getting this all out in the open.

"So you thought leaving would be doing me a favor?" Emily snapped, folding her arms protectively against her chest. "Do you know how messed up that is?"

Roy wept bitterly into his hands. "Yes. I was messed up back then. I stayed messed up for a very long time. When I realized what damage I had done, too much time had passed. I didn't know how to get back to where it had been, how to undo the hurt."

"You didn't even try," Emily accused him.

"I tried," Roy said, the pleading in his tone irking Emily even more. "So many times. I came back to the house on a number of occasions but every time the guilt of what I had done overwhelmed me. There were too many memories. Too many ghosts."

"Don't say that," Emily snapped, her mind immediately going to images of Charlotte haunting the house. "Don't you dare."

"I'm sorry," Roy repeated, gasping with anguish.

He looked down into his lap where his old hands were trembling.

On the table in front of them, the undrunk mugs of coffee were turning cold.

Emily took a long, deep breath. She knew her father had been depressed—she'd found the pill prescription amongst his belongings—and that he wasn't himself, that the grief was making him behave in unforgivable ways. She shouldn't blame him for that, and yet she couldn't help it. He'd let her down so badly. Left her with her grief. With her *mother*. There was so much brewing anger inside of Emily's heart even if she knew that blame had no place there.

"What can I do to make it up to you, Emily Jane?" Roy said, his hands in a prayer position. "How can I even begin to heal the damage I caused?"

"Why don't you start by filling in the blanks," Emily replied. "Tell me what happened. Where you went. What you've been doing all these years."

Roy blinked, as though surprised by Emily's line of questioning.

"It was the wondering that killed me," Emily explained, sadly. "If I'd just known you were safe somewhere, I could have dealt with it. You have no idea how many scenarios I cooked up in my mind, how many different lives I imagined you were living. I spent years not being able to sleep because of it. It was like my mind wouldn't stop conjuring up options until it found the correct one, even though there was no way for it to do so. It was an impossible, futile task, but I couldn't stop. So that's how you can help. Start by giving me the truth, by telling me what I didn't know for all those years. *Where were you?*"

Roy's tears finally slowed. He snuffled, dabbing his eyes with his sleeve. Then he cleared his throat.

"I split my time between Greece and England. I made a home for myself in Falmouth, Cornwall, on the coast of England. It's a beautiful place. Cliffs and wonderful scenery. There's a fantastic artists' scene there."

How fitting, Emily thought, remembering his obsession with Toni's artwork, the way in which he'd hung one of her lighthouse paintings up in the New York City home he'd shared with Patricia, and how angry Emily herself had felt when she'd realized how brazen he'd been, how disrespectful.

"How did you afford it?" Emily challenged. "The police said there'd been no activity in your bank accounts. It was one of the reasons I thought you were dead."

Roy winced at the word. Emily could tell how bad he felt to be confronted by the pain he'd put her through. But he needed to hear this. And she needed to say it. It was the only way they could move forward.

"I didn't sell any of my antiques, if that's what you mean," he began. "I left all of that for you."

"Am I supposed to thank you?" Emily asked bitterly. "It's not like a diamond can make up for years of neglect."

Roy nodded sadly, taking the brunt of her angry words. Emily began to accept that he was acknowledging her, that he was no longer trying to explain his actions but to listen instead to the hurt they had caused her.

"You're right," he said quietly. "I didn't mean to imply that it could."

Emily tensed her jaw. "Well go on, then," she said. "Tell me what happened after you left. How you supported yourself."

"At first I lived from one day to the next," Roy explained. "I made money doing whatever I could. Odd jobs. Car and bike repairs. Tinkering. I found my feet making and repairing clocks. I still do that now. I'm a horologist. I make ornate clocks with hidden keys and secret compartments."

"Of course you do," Emily said, bitterly.

The look of shame returned to Roy's face.

"What about love?" Emily asked. "Did you ever settle down?"

"I live alone," Roy replied sadly. "I have since I left. I didn't want to cause anyone any more pain. I couldn't bear to be around people."

For the first time, Emily began to feel sympathy for her father, imagining him lonely, living like a hermit. She started to feel as though she had released as much pain as she needed to, that she had blamed him enough to finally be able to hear his story. A cathartic wave washed over her.

"It's why I don't really use any modern technology," Roy continued. "There's a phone booth in town that I use to make my calls, which are few and far between. The local post office lets me know if anyone's responded to my horologist ad. When I'm feeling strong enough, I go to the local library and check my emails to see whether you've been in touch."

Emily paused, frowned. This was surprising to her. "You do?"

Roy nodded. "I've been leaving clues for you, Emily Jane. Every time I came back to the house I left another crumb for you to find. The email address was the biggest step I took because I knew as soon as you found it, it would provide a direct line from you to me. But the anticipation, the waiting, it was unbearable. So I limited myself to only a few checks a year. When I got your email I flew right here."

Emily realized then that this was the reason for those additional months of anguish he'd put her through after she'd learned he was still alive and then had contacted him. He hadn't been ignoring her or avoiding her, he simply hadn't seen her email.

"Is that true?" she asked, her voice straining as tears filled her eyes. "Did you really come here as soon as you saw I'd been in touch?"

"Yes," Roy replied, his voice barely a whisper. His own tears had begun to fall again. "I've been hoping and wishing and dreaming for you to get in contact. I figured that one day you would come back to this place, when you were ready. But I also knew you'd be angry with me. I wanted the ball to be in your court. I wanted you to be the one to make contact with me because I didn't want to intrude on your life. If you'd moved on without me I thought it would be best to keep it that way."

"Oh, Dad," Emily gasped.

Something, finally, was released from within Emily. Something about this last, final, heartbreaking admission from her father was what she'd been needing to know all along. That he was waiting on her to make the move. He hadn't been avoiding her, keeping himself hidden, he'd been dropping crumbs for her, trusting that once she put all the pieces together she'd make her own decision about whether or not she could forgive him and allow him back into her life.

She stood and hurried to the opposite couch, throwing her arms around her neck. She sobbed against his shoulder, deep sobs racking through her body. Roy clung to her, shaking too from the outpouring of grief.

"I'm so sorry," he choked, his voice muffled by her hair. "I'm so, so sorry."

They stayed like that for a long time, holding each other, shedding every tear they needed to, squeezing out every last drop of pain. Finally the crying ceased. Everything became silent.

"Do you have any more questions?" Roy finally said quietly. "I'm not going to keep secrets from you anymore. I'm not going to hide anything."

Emily felt exhausted, spent with emotion. Her father's chest rose and fell with each deep breath he took. She was so tired she felt as if she could fall asleep right here in his arms. But at the same time, she still had a million questions burning in her mind, but one more than others.

"The night when Charlotte died..." she began. "Mom filled me in with some stuff but she only gave me one side of the story. What happened?"

Roy's arms tightened around her. Emily knew it was hard for him to remember that night but she desperately wanted to know the truth, or at least his version of it. Maybe she'd be able to plaster together the three parts—Patricia's, Roy's, her own—and create something that made sense.

"I'd taken you for Thanksgiving and Christmas," Roy began. "Things weren't going well with your mom so she stayed home. But then you both came down with the flu."

"I think I remember," Emily said. She'd flashed back to some childhood memories of fevers. "Toni's dog, Persephone, was there. I collapsed in the hall."

Roy nodded, but he looked embarrassed. Emily knew why; this had been a turning point in his affair with Toni, the point when he'd been brazen enough to have his mistress's and his children's lives intersect.

"Do you remember your mom turning up unannounced?" Roy said.

Emily shook her head.

"She'd wanted to be there to look after you both since you were so sick."

"That doesn't sound like Mom," Emily said.

Roy laughed. "No, it doesn't. Maybe it was an excuse. She suspected the affair and it was her way of turning up unannounced and catching me in the act."

Emily let out a subdued nod. That was more her mother's style.

"You must have blocked out the argument because I'm sure we were shouting loud enough for them to hear at the harbor." He shrugged. "I don't know if it was that that woke Charlotte up. She was on medicine that made her groggy. You both were. But she woke up and I suppose she got confused looking for us, or was just generally feeling unwell and on medication. She ended up in the outhouse with the pool. I suppose you know the rest."

Emily did. But what she didn't realize was how little of a role she'd had to play in it all. It wasn't her fault for not waking when Charlotte did and stopping her sister wandering away. Nor was it her fault for speaking so enthusiastically about the new pool and planting the excitement in her sister's mind to go and see it. She'd been ill, confused, possibly even terrified by their parents' fight. None of it had been her fault. Not a single bit.

Emily felt a sudden sense of release. Weight she hadn't even realized she'd been carrying lifted from her shoulders. She'd been clinging onto her guilt over Charlotte's death, even after her mom had clarified that it hadn't been her fault. Now she felt as if her father had given her permission to let go of that guilt.

She snuggled in to him, feeling a new sense of peace settle over her.

Just then, the quietness was broken by the sound of soft knocking on the door. Daniel peered around.

"Daniel, come in," Emily said, beckoning him. She wanted him here now that she and her dad had gotten everything out in the open. She needed his support.

He came and perched on the edge of the couch opposite them. Emily wiped the tears from her lashes, but remained clinging to her father, curled up like a child beside him on the couch.

"Does anyone need anything?" Daniel asked softly. "A tissue? A stiff drink?"

It was just what the moment needed to cut through all the heaviness. Emily hiccupped out a laugh. She felt Roy's rumbling laugh in his belly.

"I could do with a drink," she said.

"So could I," Roy replied. "Is the bar stocked?"

Daniel took the lead. "It is. Come on. It's so fantastic in there. I'll make us drinks."

15

Emily hesitated. "Dad, is that a good idea?" she said.

"Why wouldn't it be?" Roy replied, looking confused.

Emily lowered her voice. "Because of your drinking problem."

Roy looked astounded. "What drinking problem?" Then his face paled. "Did Patricia tell you I was an alcoholic?"

"You *were* an alcoholic," Emily replied. "I remember you drinking. All the time."

"I drank heavily," Roy admitted. "We both did, your mom and I. It's one of the reasons our relationship was so volatile. But I wasn't an alcoholic."

"What about the eggnogs for breakfast on Christmas?" she asked, remembering how testy her father had been when she'd kicked his drink over.

"That was just Christmas!" Roy exclaimed.

Another piece of Emily's past realigned itself. She'd fallen for Patricia's bitter, skewed version of events, had allowed them to replace her own memories of her father. She felt a surge of fury at her mother for making Roy into the villain of their most traumatic experience.

They went into the speakeasy and took seats at the bar. Daniel got to work on the cocktails.

"We have a bartender in the evenings to do this," he explained to Roy. "Alec. He's fantastic. Better than me anyhow."

He poured them each a margarita. Roy took a sip.

"That tastes fantastic," he said. Then, a little coyly, he added, "I must say what a fine young gentleman you've turned out to be."

Emily felt her heart soar. She smiled, elated finally, feeling like everything was how it ought to be.

"I have you to thank for that," Daniel replied, shyly, not quite looking Roy in the eye. "For introducing me to things I cared about. Fishing. Sailing."

"You still sailing?" Roy asked.

"I have a boat at the harbor. Restored thanks to Emily. We take it out as a family. Chantelle loves it too. She's great at fishing."

"I still sail a lot as well," Roy said. "When I'm not working on a clock I spend my time out on the boat. Or in the garden."

"Do you remember that day you taught me how to grow vegetables?" Daniel asked.

"Of course," Roy replied. He smiled, reminiscing. "I'd never seen such a scruffy punk of a kid work so hard with a trowel."

Daniel laughed. "I was eager to learn," he said. "To take the opportunity. Even if on the outside it looked like I hated the world."

Emily found it strange to see them joking and laughing. There was so much less hurt between them. It was more like a camaraderie. Daniel had been forever thankful for the man who'd given him a chance when he needed it, even if that same man had disappeared on him as well. Maybe it was just a surprise to Emily to realize how close they had been once, knowing, also, that the summer they'd spent together had been a summer she and her father had spent apart.

Her phone buzzed then and she saw a text from Amy about their scheduled arrival that afternoon. She and Jayne had some urgent business stuff to attend to and were making a stop so would be arriving later than planned. Emily realized, guiltily, that she'd completely forgotten they were on their way. She'd been so caught up with her father everything else had gone out of her mind.

She quickly texted back and then returned her attention to her father and Daniel. They were laughing breezily again.

"I'm so glad that the boat managed to hold," Daniel was exclaiming. "Who'd have thought the weather would turn like that? A storm in the middle of summer."

"It was unfortunate timing," Roy replied. "Considering it was your first ever boat ride."

"Well, I had the best teacher so I wasn't that scared." He smiled, his eyes far away in reminiscence. "Thank you for introducing me to boats, to the water and sailing. I can't imagine my life without them now."

Emily watched on as Roy smiled along with Daniel. Now that she had released her anger she felt an overwhelming sense of peace, of rightness. This should always have been how it was. Her dad hanging out with her fiancé, enjoying one another's company, looking forward to soon becoming part of the same family.

It may have come a little late, but she was going to do everything she possibly could now to enjoy it.

*

As the evening wore on, Daniel made another batch of cocktails. He set a glass down in front of Emily just as her phone buzzed with an incoming call.

"It's Amy," she explained. "I'd better take it."

"Amy? From high school?" Roy asked, raising an eyebrow.

Emily nodded. "We're still friends," she informed him. "She's a bridesmaid. She's helping with a lot of the wedding preparations."

Emily dashed out of the speakeasy and took the call.

"Em, we're so sorry," Amy began. "The call took ages and now we're both too exhausted to drive. We're going to have to stop here over night. Don't hate us."

"I won't," Emily told her, secretly relieved that her friends weren't going to interrupt the reunion with her father.

"We'll leave first thing in the morning," Amy added.

"Honestly, Amy, it's fine," Emily said. "Some stuff's come up here anyway."

"What stuff? Wedding stuff? Daniel? Sheila?" She sounded concerned.

"It's nothing like that," Emily explained. Then she took a deep breath. "Amy, my dad is here."

There was a long silence. "What? How? Are you okay?"

Emily didn't know how to answer that, and she really didn't want to go into it too much now. She hadn't fully absorbed it yet. She needed time to untangle her emotions and make sense of it all.

"I'm fine. Let's talk about it when you get here."

Amy didn't sound convinced. "Okay. But if you need someone to talk to, call me right away. See you tomorrow."

Emily ended the call and went back to the speakeasy, to the joyful laughter of Roy and Daniel. Old bosom buddies back together again.

"Well," Roy said, draining the last of the liquor from his glass. "I think it's probably time for me to make myself scarce. Looks like you have guests to attend to."

Emily felt panicked at the thought of Roy leaving. "I have staff, they're covering everything. It's fine for us to spend time together. You don't have to go."

Roy noticed her panic-stricken appearance. "I just meant that it might be time to retire. To sleep."

"You mean you're staying?" Emily said, surprised. "Here?"

"If you have space?" Roy said meekly. "I didn't mean to be presumptuous."

"Of course you can stay!" Emily exclaimed. "How long are you planning to be here?"

"Until the wedding if it's not a problem. I could help out a bit with preparations if needed."

Emily was stunned. Not only was her father here, but he was planning on being here for over a week! It really was a dream come true.

"That would be wonderful," she said.

They went upstairs and checked Roy into the room beside his study. Emily knew he'd want to go in there at some point, probably alone.

"Will this room be okay?" she asked.

"Oh yes. It's quite lovely," Roy replied. "And right beside my secret staircase."

Emily frowned. "Your what?"

"Don't tell me you never found it," Roy said. There was a glint of mischief in his eye, one that revealed the brush with madness he'd once had, the spiraling downward that had turned his playful nature for treasure maps into secrecy and locked vaults with hidden combinations.

"Do you mean the staircase to the widow's walk?" Emily asked. "I found that. But it's on the third floor."

Roy clapped loudly then, as though suddenly delighted. "You never found it! The servants' staircase."

Emily shook her head. "But I've seen the schematics of the whole house. Your speakeasy was the last hidden place on there."

"Something's not hidden if it's on schematics!" Roy exclaimed.

"Show us," Daniel said. He seemed excited, like he had been when the bar had been discovered.

Roy led them into his study. "Didn't you wonder why there was a chimney breast against this wall?" He knocked it, and it let out a hollow sound. "All the other chimney breasts are on external walls. This one is internal."

"It didn't even cross my mind," Emily said.

"Well, it's behind here," Roy said. "If you wouldn't mind giving me a hand, Daniel."

Daniel readily obliged. They removed what Emily saw now was a fake wall, papered to be the same as the rest of the room. And there it was. A staircase. Plain, nothing particularly beautiful to look at, but it was its very existence that excited them.

"I can't believe it," Emily said, stepping inside. "Is this why you chose this room as your study?"

"Of course," Roy replied. "The stairs were a shortcut for the servants to get to the sleeping quarters without being seen by the people in the house. It just goes from here down into the basement, which is where the servants would have slept back in the day."

"And this is the only way in," Emily stated, realizing now why she hadn't found it. The basement still contained rooms unexplored to her, and her father's study was the room she'd messed with the least.

Roy nodded. "Surprise."

Emily laughed and shook her head. "So many secrets."

They headed out of the study and Roy went into his bedroom. Emily went to close the door behind him, but he reached out for her and gave her a kiss goodnight.

Emily stopped, stunned. Her father hadn't kissed her for so many years, even well before he'd walked out of her life.

"Good night, Dad," she said hurriedly.

She shut the door and scurried to her room. Once safely inside, Daniel immediately wrapped her up in a much needed hug.

"How are you holding up?" he asked softly, gently rocking her in his arms.

"I can't believe he's really here," she stammered. "I keep thinking this is a dream."

"What did you guys talk about?"

"Everything. I mean I know I'm still processing everything but it was cathartic. I feel like we can put all the hurt behind us now and start afresh."

"So those are happy tears making my shoulder wet?" Daniel joked.

Emily drew back and laughed at the dark patch on Daniel's shirt. "Oops, sorry," she said. She hadn't even realized she'd been crying.

Daniel kissed her lightly. "There's nothing to apologize about. I get that this is going to be tough. If you need to cry or laugh or shout or anything, I'm here. Okay?"

Emily nodded, so grateful to have such a beautiful human in her life. And now with her dad here, she felt like everything was really slotting into place. At last, after so many years living an unfulfilling life, she felt like she was now finally going to get to live the life she deserved.

Her wedding was only a week away. And now, for the first time, with everyone around her whom she loved, she felt truly ready for it.

Now it was time to get married.

CHAPTER TWO

The next morning Emily awoke earlier than usual, feeling elated. She skipped downstairs to make breakfast, cooking up a feast of eggs, toast, bacon, and pancakes, humming happily to herself the whole while. Daniel came down with Chantelle a little while later. Emily looked at the clock as time passed, becoming worried that her father hadn't yet made an appearance.

"Why don't you knock on his door?" Daniel suggested, clearly having picked up on the reasons behind her furtive glances.

"I don't want to disturb him," Emily replied.

"I'll do it," Chantelle said, leaping up from the breakfast bar.

Emily shook her head. "No, you eat. I'll go."

She wasn't sure what it was that was worrying her so much about disturbing her father. Perhaps it was the niggling feeling in the back of her mind that he wouldn't be there when she knocked, that it would all reveal itself to be a dream after all.

She approached his room cautiously, then cleared her throat, feeling silly. She knocked loudly.

"Dad, I made breakfast. Are you ready to come down?"

When there wasn't a reply, Emily felt her first jolt of panic. But she talked herself down from it. Roy might well be in the shower, unable to hear her.

She tried the handle of his door and found it unlocked. She opened it and peered into his room. His bed was empty, but there was no running water sound coming from the open en suite door, no sign of Roy at all.

Emily immediately gave up on trying to contain her fear. All at once it whooshed at her. Had she pushed him too far last night? Made him too uncomfortable to stay?

She rushed out of the room and into the corridor, then flew down the staircase into the kitchen. It was only the sight of Chantelle's bemused blinking from the breakfast bar that prevented her from screaming for Daniel. Instead, she skidded to a halt and managed to compose herself.

"Daniel, could you give me a hand quickly?" Emily said, trying to stop her face from cracking.

Daniel looked up and frowned. Evidently he could see right through her plastered-on smile. "What with?"

"Umm…" Emily floundered. "Heavy lifting."

"Lifting what?" Daniel pressed.

Emily blurted the first word that came into her mind. "Toilet rolls."

Chantelle giggled. "Heavy toilet rolls?"

"Daniel," Emily snapped. "Please. Just help me for a moment."

Daniel sighed and got up from the table. Emily grabbed his arm and pulled him out into the corridor.

"It's Dad," she whispered. "He's not in his room."

By the change in Daniel's expression, Emily knew it had finally sunk in why she was behaving so oddly.

"He won't have left," Daniel reassured her, rubbing her arms. "He's probably wandering the grounds."

"You don't know that," Emily replied. She was fully giving in to her panic now and was starting to tear up.

"I'll check the yard," Daniel said. "You check the house."

Emily nodded, glad to have been given direction. Her own mind had blanked out from fear.

Daniel hurried outside and Emily took the stairs, rushing two at a time. She checked each of the open guest rooms but to no avail. Through the windows in the landing she could see Daniel out in the yard, rushing about. So he hadn't had any luck either.

Then Emily hit on a brain wave. She ran to the end of the corridor and flung open the door to Roy's study.

The room was dark, the curtains drawn, but the desk lamp was on, creating a spotlight effect on the surface of the wood. Hunched behind it was the unmistakable silhouette of Roy Mitchell, bent over something, tinkering.

Emily let out a huge sigh and dropped her shoulder against the door frame, letting it support her weight as the tension left her body.

"Oh, good morning," Roy said innocently, looking up at the sound of her exhalation. "I was just fixing this." He held up a cuckoo clock, its back door hanging open. He closed it gently and the cuckoo sprang out the front. Smiling, he set it back down. "Good as new."

Emily's panic disappeared and was replaced just as swiftly with happiness. Seeing her father tinkering away was odd in its familiarity. It was like he'd always been there. The sight filled her with joy.

"Are you ready for some breakfast?" Emily asked.

Roy nodded and stood up. As they went downstairs together, Emily knocked on the window of the landing where she could spy Daniel rushing around the yard. He looked up at the noise and Emily flashed him a thumbs-up sign. She watched him sag with relief.

22

They went into the kitchen, where Chantelle was still eating her breakfast, oblivious to the goings-on.

"Looks like you put on a feast," Roy said, chuckling as he slid into the seat beside Chantelle.

"How did you sleep Papa Roy?" Chantelle asked. She had fallen asleep the night before in the process of cleaning her room and was only now seeing him again.

Roy poured himself a glass of juice. "Wonderfully, thank you, my dear. The bed was just as comfortable as the one I used to sleep in when this was my house."

As she heard his words, Emily had a sudden worry. The house still *was* his. She'd taken it on the assumption that he was missing presumed dead, but now that that was no longer the case, he legally had every right to take it back from her.

Daniel came in to rejoin the family breakfast.

"Early morning stroll?" Roy asked him as he took his seat.

Daniel caught Emily's eye knowingly. "Nothing like fresh air first thing in the morning," he said with a hint of sarcasm that Emily knew was for her benefit.

"Papa Roy was just telling me about when this was his house," Chantelle informed Daniel.

"Well, it actually still is," Emily explained. She looked up at her father, worried. "Do you want it back?"

Roy began to laugh then. "Goodness, no! I'm thrilled for you to have it, darling. It's not like I'm planning on moving back to Sunset Harbor."

Emily should have felt happy to hear confirmation her father wasn't planning on taking the house back from her, but instead it was sadness she felt at the confirmation that he was only here temporarily. She wasn't sure what she'd been thinking, whether she had even thought that far ahead at all, but it now felt so stark that he would be leaving her all over again.

She forked her grapefruit glumly and took a bitter bite.

"How long will you be staying with us?" Chantelle asked in her innocent childhood manner.

"Just until after the wedding," Roy explained in a soft voice that he seemed to save just for Chantelle, one that Emily remembered him using with her when she was that age. "That's why I'm here. To help prepare." He looked up at Emily. "Is there anything you'd like me to help with?"

Emily was still trying to wrap her head around the fact that Roy's appearance in her life was to be brief and fleeting, that no sooner had he returned than he would be leaving again. The last thing she could think of now were the things that needed organizing! And anyway, he was a bit late to the game. It was just over one week before the wedding, so pretty much most things had already been done.

"You could keep an eye on Chantelle when I'm rushed off my feet with things," Emily said. "If she doesn't mind?"

Chantelle grinned. "We can fix up Trevor's greenhouse!"

Roy looked interested. "Trevor's greenhouse?"

"Trevor Mann from next door," Emily began. Then she shut her mouth. Her grief over Trevor's death was still raw. She wasn't quite sure how to explain the situation. "We became friends recently and, well, he passed away. He left me his house in his will."

Roy's eyebrows rose. Emily could tell from the expression on his face that his own relationship with Trevor had been bad.

"Trevor Mann left you his house?" Roy asked, surprised.

Emily nodded. "I know. It was an unlikely friendship. I was there for him at the end."

"How did he die?" Roy asked, softly.

"Perhaps we shouldn't discuss this at the table," Daniel interrupted, looking over at Chantelle, who had gone quite pale.

Roy turned his full attention to Chantelle. He dropped his voice into his soothing, paternal one.

"I'd love to fix up the greenhouse with you," he said. "You can be the boss and tell me what needs doing."

Chantelle brightened instantly. She'd been desperate to check on the fruit trees ever since Trevor's passing, but Emily had always held back, not quite ready to open that wound.

"Can I show Papa Roy right now?" Chantelle asked, looking first from Daniel, then to Emily.

Daniel gestured to Emily, leaving the ball in her court. She'd spoken to him so many times about not being ready to set foot inside the house, he clearly thought it best for her to make the decision now rather than promise Chantelle something that they weren't able to keep.

"Sure, okay," Emily said.

She was a little reluctant to set foot inside the dead man's home, but with her father and loved ones by her side supporting her, perhaps it wouldn't be as painful as she anticipated.

*

24

Emily took a deep breath and turned the key in the lock of Trevor's front door. It swung open, letting out the stale air that had been cooped up inside for months. The corridor was in darkness and Emily shivered, feeling unnerved.

She went in first, leading the way. Behind her, Daniel held tightly onto Chantelle's hand, soothing the little girl.

As she walked along the corridor, Emily couldn't help but recall snippets of the conversations she'd shared with Trevor. Memories flooded back to her as she took in the sight of the table where they'd sat and shared tea, of the plastered up bit of ceiling from when a storm had crashed into the house. This place was filled with memories of Trevor. It was overwhelming to think of one day organizing this place.

"The greenhouse is just through here," Chantelle said.

Emily stood back and allowed the girl to take command. They all followed her out the back of the house and in through the glass door of the greenhouse.

Though Trevor had enjoyed sitting out here in his final weeks, the greenhouse was in a terrible state. Everyone glanced around, taking in the enormity of the amount of work that would need to be done in order to get this place restored to its former glory.

Chantelle pulled out her notepad and began taking notes. "I think we need a fountain," she said. "Benches so we can sit and read in the summer. A swing, too. A place where Daddy can grow his vegetables. And a flower garden."

"I know all about which plants grow in which climates," Roy told Chantelle. "I can help you pick the right types."

He was taking Chantelle very seriously, which delighted Emily to see. He was even carrying a matching notepad and pink feathered pen, which he used to write down supplies they needed.

"What color scheme were you thinking of?" Roy asked in a businesslike manner.

"Yellow and pink," Chantelle said. "Or rainbow."

"All excellent choices." He jotted down some notes in his pad. "We're going to need some new glass," he added. "To make sure this place is watertight and to keep it warm. Want to go on a trip to the hardware store?"

Chantelle nodded excitedly. "Then we can go to Raj's and get the seeds for the flowers."

"Tell me, do you have your own gardening tools? Gloves? Apron?"

Chantelle shook her head.

"Then we'll have to get all of that as well," Roy explained. "Every gardener needs their own outfit. You'd look quite splendid in green gingham."

Chantelle grinned and Emily found that she herself was smiling just as widely. Seeing her dad bonding with the child over the greenhouse was a moment she would treasure forever. She thanked Trevor silently for having given her such a generous gift that had allowed for such a beautiful moment to happen.

Daniel ruffled Chantelle's hair. "Come on. I'll drive you and Papa Roy to town."

They headed back out into Trevor's garden, then crossed the lawns in the direction of the driveway where Daniel's pickup truck was parked.

"Are you coming too, Emily?" Chantelle asked as they reached the car.

Emily pulled open the back door and helped her inside. "I can't," she explained. "I have guests coming. Amy and Jayne. You remember them."

Chantelle pulled a face. She hadn't been so fond of Emily's New York City friends last time they'd visited. Emily couldn't blame her. They were hardly cuddly and calm like Papa Roy was.

Emily shut the door and Daniel gunned the truck to life.

"Have fun!" she called out, waving at her family in the truck as it began crawling out of the driveway.

It might not look like the conventional picture of a family, but it was hers and that was what mattered to Emily.

Just as they turned the corner and out of sight, Emily saw Amy's car appear at the other end. She was struck with the sudden feeling that however crazy things had felt over the last day, the craziness was about to ramp up even more.

CHAPTER THREE

"Sorry we're late!" Amy cried as she got out of her car. "I really wanted to get the drive done in one day but there was a problem with one of our Japanese suppliers and it took forever to sort out."

"A PR nightmare," Jayne added, clambering out from the passenger side. "Compounded by the fact we had to stay in a disgusting roadside motel."

"I'm just glad you guys are here now," Emily replied, hugging them both in turn.

Amy opened up the trunk and started pulling out bags. She had brought a lot of luggage, Emily noted.

"What is all this stuff?" Emily asked, heaving a case from the back. It weighed a ton.

"Wedding supplies," Amy replied. "Swatches for color schemes. Fabrics. Fragrances. All sorts of things."

"But everything is organized," Emily protested.

Amy rolled her eyes. "You'll change your mind about things. Right down to the last second. What kind of friend would I be if I hadn't brought things to cover every eventuality?"

Emily laughed. She couldn't see herself changing her mind on anything but she trusted Amy. Plus her friend was always happier when she had a project, hence becoming a successful businesswoman while still a teenager.

"So where is hotcakes?" Jayne asked.

"You mean Daniel?" Emily replied, raising an eyebrow. "He's in town with Chantelle and my dad. They're buying some stuff to fix up the greenhouse."

"Your dad, huh," Jayne said, shaking her head with what Emily recognized from herself as disbelief. "When Ames told me I couldn't believe it. I really didn't see that one coming."

Amy shot her a daggered look.

"What?" Jayne said, defensively. "I just totally thought he was dead."

Just then Lois appeared to help them with their cases. She dragged two behind her along the driveway and up the porch steps.

"She's still here?" Jayne asked loudly out the corner of her mouth. "I thought you were firing her."

Emily shook her head. "Keep your voice down," she hissed.

They went inside the inn and Lois checked them in. "I can show you to your rooms and take some of your cases," she said.

Amy looked impressed. "She can do her job at last!" she whispered to Emily as Lois began lugging some of the cases upstairs.

Emily cringed. She loved her friends but they could be insensitive and rude sometimes.

"I need a shower," Jayne said. "Get some of that motel grime off my body!"

As they disappeared upstairs to settle in and freshen up, Emily heard the bell ring. She could already tell today was going to be a whirlwind. She trotted down the steps and answered the door.

A young woman with black curly hair and glasses stood there. She had dangly earrings and lots of beaded necklaces hanging over a paisley patterned scarf.

"Hey, I'm Bryony," she said confidently, holding out a hand covered in rings. "Serena's friend from Maine U. I'm here to do the marketing for the website." She grinned, showing off a gap between her teeth.

"Of course," Emily said. "Come in."

Bryony swirled inside, bringing the smell of incense with her. She had a laptop case slung over one shoulder.

"Okay if I set up in your reception room?" she asked, nodding toward the guests' lounge.

"Sure, of course. Whatever you need," Emily replied.

"Wi-Fi password," Bryony replied. "Oh, and a coffee would be great. I live off the stuff."

"You and me both," Emily replied.

She fetched some coffee for Bryony but didn't have much of a chance to talk to her further because the bell rang again. She answered the door.

This time it was a slim man in leather pants standing on her doorstep. Beneath his fedora he had long hair, and his eyes were covered by sunglasses. She knew some of Daniel's friends were supposed to be arriving today but this man didn't look like the kind she'd expect Daniel to be friends with.

"Can I help you?" Emily asked.

"I have a booking," the man said. He had a distinct swagger about him, a sort of confidence that oozed from him.

As Emily led him inside and went behind the reception desk, she heard whispering coming from one of the rooms. She looked behind her and saw Marnie, Vanessa, and Tracey peeping out from behind the kitchen door, giggling.

When Emily turned back she saw that the man had removed his sunglasses, and to her surprise, she was staring at a very familiar face. It was the famous singer Roman Westbrook.

"Mr. Westbrook?" Emily said, trying to maintain her composure but freaking out at the same time. To think that her little B&B could be host to someone so famous! She really had come far!

"You can call me Roman."

Emily felt a bolt of excitement shoot through her.

"You're booked into our cottage for two weeks," she noted, reading aloud from the computer screen. She saw that Serena had made the booking and wondered why on earth her friend hadn't shared the information of a famous singer with her. It was very unlikely that Serena wouldn't know who Roman Westbrook was. She must have kept it secret specifically to surprise them.

Emily turned around and found her fingers trembling as she unhooked the keys to the cottage. Behind the kitchen door, she caught sight of Marnie, Vanessa, and Tracey still watching, bug-eyed and giggly. Emily flashed them a surprised and excited grin.

Just then Lois appeared at the top of the stairs, having finished settling Amy and Jayne into their rooms. She stopped short on the staircase when she saw Roman Westbrook standing in the hallway and her eyes turned as wide as saucers.

Emily fought hard to keep her composure, turning to Roman and smiling with what she hoped was her professional hostess manner. "If you'd like to come with me, I'll get you settled in."

She led him along the corridor and back out the main door, turning to look behind to see whether Lois was still frozen to the spot on the staircase. Vanessa, Marnie, and Tracey had all emerged from the kitchen, tiptoeing as close as they dared behind her, giggling in a huddle like a bunch of school girls. Lois galloped down the stairs and joined them, whispering excitedly behind her hand.

Emily showed Roman along the pathway to the carriage house, her heart fluttering every time she allowed herself to think about just who she was walking beside. When she reached the door, she unlocked it, fumbling a little in her excitement, then gestured for Roman to enter.

"This will do nicely," Roman said, glancing around at the self-contained apartment with a satisfied nod.

Emily felt a thrill of excitement to know that her little inn was good enough for a pop star of Roman Westbrook's caliber! It was almost like she was floating along in a dream.

She showed him the bedroom and bathroom, as well as some of the utilities he had at his disposal, pinching herself the whole time, thinking, *Did I really just show Roman Westbrook a washer-dryer / oven / coffee machine? How is this my life?*

When the time came to hand over his key and their fingers brushed, Emily felt as wobbly as a teenager. It wasn't every day one made skin-to-skin contact with a famous pop star!

"I'll leave you to settle in," Emily said. "The big house is always open for guests so please feel free to come in anytime you want. We have a bar and lounge inside for guests."

Roman flashed her one of his famous smiles.

She twirled out of the carriage house, feeling light, as though walking on air, and hurried back to the inn to rejoice in the experience with her staff.

When she got back to the inn she found the four of them still giggling away.

Lois was beside the computer. "Serena booked him in," she announced. "I bet she didn't say a word because she wanted to surprise us."

"Well, that worked," Marnie laughed, joining Lois at her side. She pointed at the computer enthusiastically. "Oh my god. He's here for TWO WEEKS!"

"That means he'll be here for the wedding!" Lois squealed.

Everyone began to cry and whoop.

"I wonder why he's in town," Tracey said.

"It can't be a vacation," Marnie added. "He could vacation anywhere in the world. I doubt he'd want to come here."

"Perhaps he's recording his new album here?" Tracey guessed.

"In what recording studio?" Vanessa exclaimed.

"Maybe he's shooting a video!" Lois cried, growing even more excited. "And we'll all get to be extras!"

The bell rang yet again but the girls were so lost in their conversation they didn't seem to even hear; at least Emily assumed that was the case because none of them moved. She took it upon herself to get the door.

To the background sound of her gossiping female staff, she pulled open the door and saw three men standing on the step. Burly. Tattooed. Rough-looking, in faded jeans and patched up leather jackets. Emily wondered if they were part of Roman Westwood's entourage. Security guards or something. They certainly didn't look like they were here to soak up the quaint seaside vibes.

"Can I help you?" she asked.

"We're here for Daniel," one of them said. "Hear he's marrying some broad from New York City!"

They started laughing.

"We're his friends," one added. "His best men."

Emily felt her face drain of blood. These were Daniel's school friends? The ones she'd pushed for him to invite? The ones who were going to be in the wedding party?

She opened her mouth to tell them to come in but found her voice had completely failed her. All she managed was a shrill squeak and the weakest of smiles.

CHAPTER FOUR

Emily was still standing there gaping like a fish at the tattooed men who would soon be in her wedding party when Daniel's pickup truck trundled up the driveway.

"That must be the groom!" one of the tattooed men said, turning on the spot.

The pickup truck slowed to a stop and Daniel hopped out with a spring in his step that was unfamiliar to Emily. She watched, stunned, as the three men bowled down the porch steps and tackled Daniel.

They'd better not bruise his face, she thought, wincing at the rough-and-tumble of old friends reunited.

Finally, Daniel's face reemerged from the rabble of denim and leather. He was pink-cheeked, grinning widely. By now, Roy had opened up the passenger side door and was halfway out. To Emily's surprise, he was also smiling.

"Well, look, haven't you three grown up," Roy said, laughing.

"Is that Roy?" the first man said.

"I said this was the place!" the second yelled, smacking the third across the chest.

"It was decades ago," the third argued back. "How am I supposed to remember?"

"Because it was the best vacation we ever had!" the first exclaimed.

Roy emerged fully now and extended his hand. "Stuart?"

The man nodded. "Yes. And you remember Clyde and Evan?" He gestured first to the man with the scraggly ginger beard, then to the shorter, overweight man.

"How could I forget that weekend when Daniel invited you all over for fishing?" Roy replied.

"That was great," Evan added. "I don't think we've all been in the same place since that weekend, you know."

"So you're his best men, I presume?" Roy queried.

Stuart beamed widely. "Of course we are. It's only fitting that Daniel's oldest school friends should be in the wedding party."

"Even if it has been over a decade since we all got together," Evan added.

"Have you met my daughter Emily?" Roy said, gesturing to where Emily continued to watch on in disbelief. "I'd never have guessed Daniel would grow up to marry my little princess one day!"

Now it was the three friends' turn to look shocked. They glanced at Emily on the doorstep, mouths open. But rather than appear embarrassed by their mistake, Emily realized they were relishing it. They were clearly the types of men to enjoy embarrassing others. She inwardly cringed.

"*That's* the missus?" Clyde exclaimed. "Well, why didn't she say so?"

He laughed and ran up the porch steps toward Emily. When he reached her he swept her into a bear hug. Predictably, he smelled of stale sweat.

Emily tried to maintain her composure. But really she was panicking inside. She didn't want to judge Daniel too much on his choice of companionship, especially if they were old school friends—kindergarteners tend to pick their friends at random after all—but she just couldn't reconcile the four of them together. This was the closest she'd been to Daniel's bad-boy past. A glimpse of the boy he'd once been and could easily have become had he not left Maine for Tennessee when he did. She should be grateful that he'd chosen these three really, when the other option was Tennessee friends who knew Sheila.

Just then, Chantelle hopped down from the truck and gave a cursory glance in the direction of the three men. She wasn't fazed, however. She was used to random people coming to the inn and had certainly come across hillbilly types in her earlier years in Tennessee.

"Papa Roy, can we start on the greenhouse, please?" she asked.

"Of course," Roy said. Then, turning his attention to Stuart, Clyde, and Evan, he added, as polite as ever, "If you gentlemen will excuse me."

Roy and Chantelle busied themselves with unloading the pickup of all the items they'd purchased.

"Let me give you the tour," Daniel said to his friends.

He led them past Emily and into the B&B.

She watched them go, still stunned, still unable to reconcile Daniel with these three burly men. She turned to follow them inside, in time to see Amy and Jayne walking down the staircase.

Stuart whistled at the two women and Emily grimaced. Neither of her friends was the type to let that kind of thing fly. Not even Jayne, who usually loved male attention. Terrified it was all about to kick off, Emily rushed in to intervene in advance.

"Amy, Jayne," she called out. "Did you settle into your rooms okay?"

Amy flicked her narrowed eyes away from Stuart and to her friend. "Yes. Thanks, Em. But we have to get to work. There are tons of errands to run."

"Really?" Emily said with a groan. She felt like all she'd been doing for weeks was planning the wedding. Could there really be that much more to do? But on the other hand, leaving the inn was probably a good idea. The least amount of time spent with Daniel's friends the better. "Okay," she accepted. "Let's get out of here."

She rushed her friends out the door before Daniel had a chance to introduce his friends. Out the corner of her eye she caught sight of his expression. He seemed annoyed by her behavior, by her rudeness at not allowing everyone to become acquainted. But she couldn't help it. If he'd prepared her in some way maybe it would have been different. At the very least she could have told him to make sure they didn't catcall her friends, and warn her friends to expect some rube-like behavior. But just like always, Daniel had kept her in the dark about some of the more unsavory elements of his past. And once again, the blank spaces of his past niggled at her, making her doubt the very foundation their relationship stood upon.

*

Emily and her friends drove to the next town over in order to go to a perfume boutique that Amy had been wanting to visit for years.

"They make the fragrance specifically for you," Amy explained as she drove. "A bespoke scent for a unique lady."

"Sounds…" Emily paused. She'd wanted to say unnecessary but caught herself at the last second. Instead she finished with a meek and unconvincing, "…fun."

"Everyone's doing it these days," Jayne added from the back seat. "It would be simply uncouth not to."

Clearly excited by the trip, Amy parked and then steered Emily by the shoulders into the store, bouncing with every step.

The lady at the counter greeted them with a warm smile. Emily was grateful when Amy took the lead. She didn't much feel like interacting. Her mind was still stuck on Daniel's friends.

"Here," Amy said, shoving a smelling strip under Emily's nose. "What do you think? Blood orange."

Emily crinkled her nose. "I don't think that's very me."

"No, I suppose not," Amy said. She bent her head down and began looking through the other options of smells.

"You seem distracted," Jayne said to Emily.

"Sorry," Emily replied. "I'm just… thinking."

"Not about fragrances, I assume," Jayne asked. "Come on, Em. You know you can tell me anything."

Emily shook her head. "I don't want to say. I don't want to sound like a bitch."

Jayne gave her a look. "Honestly, this is *me* you're talking to. I'm the Queen Bitch. I doubt anything you could say would even come close to sounding bitchy to my ears."

Just then, Amy rushed over and grabbed Emily's arms. She dabbed some perfume onto her wrist.

"Smell!" she exclaimed with excitement.

Emily sniffed. The fragrance was fresh and floral. "That's much better," she said.

Amy grinned. "Okay. I've got it. I've got the perfect smell to complement this." She rushed away again and bowed heads with the girl behind the counter as they sifted excitedly through the samples.

"So?" Jayne pressed Emily. She clearly wasn't going to let her drop it.

Emily sighed loudly. "It's just those guys at the inn."

"The boars who looked like they hadn't showered in a week?"

"Yup, those ones," Emily replied. She bit her lip. "Well, they're Daniel's friends. His best men."

"Oh dear God!" Jayne exclaimed with a theatrical gasp. "They're going to be in the photos?"

Emily felt her cheeks burn. Jayne's horrified response was making her feel worse.

"It's just the way that he keeps these things about his past from me," Emily explained. "Like I would never have imagined in a million years that his best friends would be like that."

"Me neither," Jayne replied. "I thought he'd have some hunky lumberjack types."

Emily sank her head into her hands. "I wish I'd have let him ask his boss now," she replied glumly. "I'd prefer paint-stained hands over those three any day."

Amy came over with another scent stick, a look of concentration on her face. Without even speaking she grabbed Emily's arm and dabbed the new scent inside her wrist, on top of the first one. Amy sniffed. Frowned. Sniffed again. Then grinned.

"I think I've got it," she said.

Emily sniffed. "Yeah, that's nice," she replied in a lackluster voice.

"You don't like it?" Amy asked.

"It's not that," Jayne interrupted. "Emily met the groomsmen today."

Amy raised an eyebrow. "Oh? Daniel's elusive friends?"

Jayne grabbed Amy's arm. "You'll never guess. It was those three in the foyer!"

Amy's eyes widened. "The ones I almost unleashed all hell upon?"

"The very same."

Amy looked at Emily then. "Oh, babe. I'm sorry."

Emily cringed again. Daniel's friends were oafs, but she was revealing a very nasty side of both her and her friends' personalities. She knew they were being judgmental and petty. But she couldn't help it.

"Look," Amy said, taking charge of the situation as she was often wont to do. "Why don't we finish up here now we've found the scent and head back to the inn? We can have some drinks, get everyone's tongues loosened up a bit. Then we'll get to the bottom of it for you. Find out the deal. Who they are, what they do. Find out any juicy gossip."

"It's the juicy gossip I'm worried about," Emily replied glumly. "I just don't understand how Daniel can be who he is with this mysterious past and these strange friends. None of it matches up. There's like young Daniel who hated his home life and was flunking school and almost ran away, the one who was friends with those three. Then there's Tennessee Daniel, the one who fathered a kid and beat a guy to a bloody pulp. Neither of them are my Daniel. It just freaks me out."

Amy rubbed her shoulder. "You're just getting wedding jitters. It's fine. Everyone has pasts."

"But not everyone hides them like Daniel does."

"He's just embarrassed," Jayne said. "I would be if those were my friends!" She cackled.

Emily wanted to let her friends lift her spirits but it just wasn't helping. The idea of all of them sitting around a table conversing, not to mention with alcohol added to the mix, didn't seem that appealing to her. But it was going to have to happen sooner or later. May as well get it over with.

"Okay, fine," Emily said. "Let's just get it out of the way."

Amy paid for the fragrance, exchanging business cards with the girl behind the counter, and they left the store. Emily's friends linked arms with her, supporting her, like always, through every step of her journey.

"I don't know what I'd do without you guys," Emily said as they strolled together back to Amy's car.

"I do," Amy said with a mischievous twinkle in her eye. "You'd smell a whole lot worse!"

CHAPTER FIVE

It was an awkward mix of people, to say the least. The only relief Emily could feel as she looked at the strange array of faces scattered around the porch table was that her father and Chantelle weren't here, since they were too absorbed in their work in the greenhouse to participate.

Conversation was stilted. Even a pitcher of beer didn't seem to help.

"How did you all meet, then?" Amy asked, evidently trying to be as friendly as possible.

"I'm Daniel's oldest friend," Stuart said. "I met him at school, way back. Back when he was still called Dashiel!"

"The less said about that the better, thanks," Daniel replied. He'd changed his name from the one that matched his father's at a young age.

"I joined the gang in middle school," Evan added. "We picked Clyde up in high school."

"We got into mischief from that point onward," Clyde finished. "Then sort of went our separate ways."

"Daniel was the only one who left the state though," Stuart added. "Maybe to get away from us." He laughed.

Emily wondered. Maybe Daniel had wanted a fresh start away from his past when he left for Tennessee.

"There's nothing like a wedding to bring old friends back together," Clyde said.

"And it's great timing, Danny Boy," Stuart said, grabbing Daniel roughly around the neck. "I've only just gotten out on parole."

Emily took a huge swig of her drink. She felt Amy and Jayne shift uncomfortably beside her.

"What were you in for?" Jayne asked.

Amy and Emily shot her daggers. Jayne was clearly just trying to make conversation and, never one to think more than a millisecond before speaking, had asked the question that was on everyone's minds.

"Just a DUI," Stuart said, shrugging like it was absolutely nothing at all.

Emily started to feel very hot. She tugged at the collar of her shirt.

"Oh," Jayne said, exhaling her relief. "I was worried you were going to say murder or something."

Clyde and Evan laughed loudly. Emily kicked Jayne sharply under the table.

"He got off on that charge," Clyde informed Jayne.

Her eyes bulged in disbelief. "Really?"

Clyde and Evan laughed even more loudly this time.

"No!" Clyde exclaimed. "But you should have seen your face."

Jayne wasn't the only one not able to take the joke. Stuart himself looked furious.

"You're one to talk, Clyde," he said. "I'm not the only one sitting around this table who's been inside!"

Emily felt her whole body sag with deflation. These guys were coming across as completely unstable. So much for getting to the bottom of the mystery of these guys; the more they revealed the more she wished she didn't know.

"You guys must have some funny stories about Daniel," Amy said, trying to calm the situation.

Daniel went bright red. "Oh God no, let's not."

But it was too late. His friends' faces were immediately brightening.

"I'm glad you asked," Stuart said. "What would you ladies like to hear? The one where Daniel gets drunk for the first time ever and ends up ripping his pants climbing a chain-link fence or the one where he loses his virginity?"

"Neither," Emily said, shaking her head, feeling the panic begin to set in.

Daniel, too, was looking petrified at the prospect of those two particular stories being relayed.

Stuart nudged Emily. "Don't tell me you haven't told each other all your dirty secrets yet?"

Emily's embarrassment grew more and more. Maybe it was because her own past was so difficult and muddy that she hadn't forced Daniel to open up more about his own, but she was beginning to regret that now. What if both stories were so horrific they put her off marrying him completely?

"There was this girl, Astrid," Stuart began.

Daniel buried his face in his hands.

"Their eyes met across the room," Stuart continued. "It was love at first sight. She approached. Daniel couldn't believe his luck. Then she said the words that struck fire into his heart. 'Can I borrow your protractor?'"

"Wait," Emily said, frowning. "What?"

"It was in math class!" came Stuart's punch line. "Fifth grade."

Daniel had turned bright red.

Jayne looked confused. "I thought this was a story about when Daniel lost his virginity?"

"I'm getting to that bit," Stuart said. "So... fast forward, what, five years? Six years? Daniel's had this pathetic crush on Astrid for our entire lives and finally gets the guts up to ask her to the dance."

"The rest is history," Clyde said, winking. "How long did you stay together in the end? Four years?"

Daniel nodded tensely. "Four and a half thereabouts."

Emily felt a sensation like ice sweep through her. Daniel had never even mentioned the name Astrid. Now it turned out she'd been his first love? A girl he'd pined for, for years? She didn't want to compare herself to a teenage girl from the past but it sounded like she'd meant more to Daniel than your average first love. It sounded like his relationship with Astrid had been big and important. But he hadn't mentioned it at all.

"I'm guessing you two didn't keep in touch?" Stuart asked.

Daniel shook his head.

"Too bad," Stuart said. "She was great. I kind of thought you two would get back together at some point."

Emily's face must have gone pale because she felt a reassuring squeeze under the table coming from Amy's direction.

"Now what I want to know," Clyde said, "is what you ladies have planned for the bachelorette party?"

"There isn't one," Emily said. "Daniel and I decided against having gendered parties."

"Uh-oh," Clyde said, looking at Daniel. "Busted."

Emily frowned. "What?"

Daniel looked guilty. "I didn't get a chance to tell you," he said. "The guys decided to throw me a surprise bachelor party. We're going away for the weekend."

Emily couldn't even speak. All she could do was blink.

"Road trip," Clyde said. "Visiting all the finest strip joints Maine has to offer."

Beside Emily, she could see Amy balling her hands into fists of rage. Emily herself could feel all the blood draining from her face. In her peripheral vision she could see Daniel's worried expression.

Suddenly the three men burst into laughter.

"Oh, you should have seen your faces!" Evan cried.

"We're not really going to strip joints," Stuart laughed. "We're going hunting!" He grabbed Daniel around the neck again and pulled him into a rough sort of headlock-embrace. "We leave on Friday morning."

Emily had heard enough. She couldn't stand it anymore, sitting here listening to this, her thoughts becoming increasingly chaotic, her nerves increasingly frayed. She'd been trying all day not to freak out but she couldn't hold it in anymore. She stood, making the table wobble in her haste, and darted inside.

CHAPTER SIX

"Emily. Emily, wait!"

She drew to a halt in the corridor, hearing Daniel's pleading tone approaching from behind. He reached her and touched her arm with a tentative hand.

"I'm sorry," he said. "The stripper joke was one step too far. I'll have a word with them."

Emily led him into the living room, away from any prying ears, and closed the door. She faced him, finally, and saw the earnest expression in his eyes. Daniel's friends weren't a reflection on him, she knew that, but she also couldn't help her contradicting feelings, the ones telling her that in some way they were.

"They're jerks," she blurted out.

Daniel sighed. "It was a dumb joke. I can only apologize. But you know I never would do that, right?"

"It's more than just the joke, Daniel. It's everything. Their whole attitude stinks. How are you even comfortable having felons in the house with Chantelle?"

Daniel's expression began to change, to grow a little darker. "They're not dangerous."

Emily folded her arms. "Sure, as long as we keep them away from the hard liquor and hide all the car keys," she said sarcastically.

"What's gotten into you?" Daniel challenged. "I thought you'd be pleased to meet my friends. You know how much I struggle with compartmentalizing my life. Having you all together is stressful for me too."

"Oh, well I'm so sorry your childish oaf friends are making this difficult for you," Emily replied bluntly.

Daniel seemed to grow increasingly frustrated. He paced away, his arm folded, then back again, facing Emily down. "Sometimes I can't win with you. You asked me to invite my old friends and now they're here you're somehow angry with me?"

"I didn't know they'd be so horrible!" Emily wailed.

Daniel shook his head. "I get it. They're not smart or successful like your friends. But can I remind you that Amy and Jayne aren't always the easiest people for me to be around either?"

"Come off it, Daniel. Amy and Jayne aren't even in the same league as those ..." She struggled to find a suitable word, and regretted the one she eventually blurted. "...baboons!"

Daniel grew immediately infuriated. "That's so unfair. You haven't even given them a chance."

"And I don't want to." Emily could hear the petulance in her voice but she couldn't help herself.

"Tough," Daniel retorted. "You haven't got a choice. They're my friends, they're part of my life."

"Hardly," she scoffed. "It's not like you ever talk about them, or talk on the phone to them. Sounds like you've barely even seen each other in the last decade!"

"That's just life," Daniel huffed. "Things get in the way. Hence people making the effort for weddings."

He'd started to sound condescending. Emily felt riled.

"What kind of things?" she snapped. "Prison sentences?"

Daniel seemed to suddenly deflate. He sat down on the couch and let his head drop into his hands. Emily paused, watching him. She'd never seen Daniel look so defeated.

The fight went out of her immediately. She sat tentatively beside him, perching on the edge of the couch.

"I'm sorry," she said, suddenly filled with remorse. "I'm just freaking out. They weren't what I was expecting and it's reminded me how many things I still don't know about you. I just don't understand how they fit into your life."

Daniel shook his head, his hair tousling as he did. "I know they don't make a good first impression," he said quietly. "But they've helped me through some really tough times. I'm eternally grateful to them for that."

"What kind of things?" Emily asked.

The conversation had taken on a different tone entirely. Now Daniel was the sad one and Emily in the comforting role.

"After my dad left, there were days when my mom was just out of it. Stuart's family used to feed me. Sometimes they even let me shower at their house, join in special occasions with them. I mean, they weren't exactly saints but they were there for me during those times when my mom couldn't be and my dad didn't want to be. Clyde has had a hard life, like me, but even though he acts dumb he's actually super smart. If he hadn't helped me with my school work I would have flunked out of school, I'm certain. And then Evan helped me get a job at his parents' mechanics store. We learned to fix up bikes together. That's where my love for them came from. And it kept us out of trouble. It meant I had a skill I could fall back on, a passion I could occupy myself with. A reason not to give in to the temptations of liquor like all the adults around me had. I owe that guy a lot. I owe all of them a lot."

43

Emily touched his arm lightly. Daniel spoke so rarely of his parents' problems with addiction. She always felt closer to him when he did; it was something they had in common.

"So how come you all fell out of touch?" Emily asked softly, curious. If they'd been so bonded in their youth what had caused them to become such infrequent players in one another's lives?

Daniel looked guilty. "It was me. My fault. I took off."

"What do you mean?"

"Don't judge me, Emily," he said, looking at her sadly. "I'm a different person now. I don't do things the same way I used to. But I had to leave. I'd changed my name and gotten a taste of the freedom I needed from my family and my ties to them. So one day I took one of the bikes Evan and I had fixed up and I left."

"You stole from your best friend?"

Daniel nodded glumly. "And I didn't tell any of them what I was doing. When I finally got in touch with Stuart he was so angry, saying the police had been informed and everything. I got him to swear to secrecy, to just let the cops know I was safe, that I'd gone of my own accord. Anyway, when Clyde and Evan found out that Stuart knew I was safe and hadn't told them, it tore the group apart. And typical me, I just avoided it."

"When did you make up?"

"Well, I came back to Maine seven years ago and took up the carriage house to look after this place as best I could. Whenever I felt brave I would ride back to our hometown and look around for them. I bumped into Stuart, finally, a couple of years ago. We went for a drink and he filled me in on what I'd missed out on. Who was in prison and why, that sort of thing. He said he'd talk to the others for me, see if we could start patching things back together. So over the last few years, here and there, we've met up a few times in various combinations for a bike ride or fishing trip, that kind of thing. But never as a group. Never like this. So really this has brought us all back together. I'm really hoping the trip will help us heal."

Emily's fears were finally set at ease. She understood now how they had been such important parts of each other's lives, how they were all trying to find their feet with each other again.

"Won't a long weekend hunting be a bit of an intense environment to sort through your past experiences?" Emily asked gently. She still wasn't happy about the trip, even if she was relieved that no strippers would be involved.

"I guess we'll find out," he said, smiling sheepishly.

Emily squeezed his arm, then pulled him into an embrace. She felt closer to Daniel now that she understood what his past had been like, what he had been through with these guys, and what they had been through together. Perhaps, however unlikely it seemed at this moment, they might grow on her, too. Either that or they'd have a huge bust-up on the trip.

Emily couldn't help but secretly wish for the latter.

CHAPTER SEVEN

Being in Trevor's house was still difficult for Emily, but the next morning that's exactly where she found herself. She removed two glasses from the kitchen cupboard, remembering those times near the end of his life when she and Trevor would sit together drinking juice and ice tea. She went to the fridge, noticing the fingerprints still on it, his large ones, her smaller ones, and a tiny set belonging to Chantelle, then took out the pitcher of homemade lemonade she'd placed there. She poured two drinks, then placed them on the tray she'd used many times to carry bowls of soup and steaming cocoa to an ailing Trevor, and went out through the back door, into the greenhouse.

She could hear the laughter immediately, the chattering, the sounds of joy and excitement. As much as it warmed her heart to know her dad and Chantelle were bonding so much, Emily couldn't help the pang of jealousy she felt. She'd barely had any time to spend with her father since he'd got here. She wished she could be a part of it, but there was still so much to organize, so many different things to juggle, she just didn't have time. Life seemed to always intervene, to keep them apart.

"Who's thirsty?" she called, walking across the stone slabs that formed a path through the greenhouse.

Roy and Chantelle both turned around to look at her. They were mud-stained, both pink-cheeked from effort and laughter. Wisps of Chantelle's blond hair stuck to the sweat on her forehead.

"Thank you, sweetheart," Roy said.

Emily set the tray down on the picnic table. Chantelle and Roy both came over, discarded their mucky gloves, and took a drink. Emily looked around at the greenhouse.

"You've made some progress already," she said, admiring the way the cracked glass had been replaced and the old panels had been cleaned and buffed, and looking at the array of black sacks filled with twigs and weeds.

"Once we've finished with these tomato plants, we're going to fix the tables over at the far end," Chantelle said, wiping beads of lemonade off her top lip with her sleeve. "Then the trellis for the rosebush."

"Sounds like you have plenty to keep yourself occupied with," Emily said, smiling.

"What about you?" Roy asked. "I see your friends have been keeping you quite busy."

Emily nodded and consulted her watch. "Actually, that's a good point. Amy's dragging me to another outing. I'd better go."

As excited as she was to be visiting the dress shop for last-minute alterations and amendments, she was also a little frustrated that she had to leave so quickly. Sitting out in the greenhouse with a book and cup of coffee while Roy and Chantelle buzzed around her like bees would have been a wonderful, tranquil way to spend the morning, but alas it was not to be.

She kissed her father on the cheek and squeezed his hand, still reveling in his realness, in his very being.

"You keep an eye on her," she said, smiling toward Chantelle. Then she approached the child and ruffled her hair. "And you make sure Papa Roy doesn't slack. You have my permission to order him around."

Chantelle nodded triumphantly. "Oh, I know," she said. "I'm the boss."

Roy raised his amused eyebrows.

Emily laughed. "That's good to know."

*

They took Amy's car to the bridal store and were greeted by Maggie, the sweet woman who had been involved in all the dress preparations. Amy kissed her on both cheeks like they were old friends.

Jayne waltzed in behind them, dropping herself into a chair in the corner and busying herself immediately with her phone. She hadn't been showing that much enthusiasm about all the preparations but Emily didn't mind; it was Amy's domain after all.

"Here are those silk roses I was telling you about," Maggie said to Amy, leading her over to the counter. They huddled together with their heads bent over. Emily couldn't see at what from this view.

"They're just perfect," Amy gushed. "Could you make them in champagne pink?"

"Of course," Maggie replied. "That would look fantastic."

They giggled. Anyone could be forgiven for thinking that Amy was the bride-to-be in this situation.

"Have you guys been planning something behind my back?" Emily asked, frowning.

Maggie turned to face her, looking suddenly guilty. Amy turned too, but she was wearing a completely different expression, not guilt but mischief.

47

"Of course," she said with a crooked smile. "What kind of maid of honor would I be without making a few tweaks here and there?"

Emily folded her arms. "That's not fair," she said. "I should have been kept up to speed with everything."

Maggie was turning a deep red color. She'd clearly not been aware that Amy was working covertly and seemed ashamed to have had any part in it. From the corner, lounging in her chair, Jayne began clapping.

"You tell her, Em," she said with a laugh. "I've been wondering when Bridezilla would show up."

Emily frowned at her. "I'm not being a Bridezilla. I just thought all of this was organized. I thought we were just coming here to make final adjustments, not to add silk roses and change the color scheme."

"You'll love it," Amy insisted. "Honestly, Em. I just wanted it to be a surprise for you. Don't be mad."

Emily realized that her frustration was less about Amy not consulting her on changes, but more about the extra time that had been taken away from her. She could be with her father right now, bonding, healing some old wounds. Instead, she was going to be stuck in the dress shop for significantly longer than planned, just because Amy was flexing her perfectionist muscles.

She sighed deeply. "It's okay. I'm sorry."

"Babe," Amy said, "no apologies needed. This is your wedding, it has to be perfect. If you didn't lose your chill at least once a day I'd be concerned."

Realizing a catfight was not about to materialize, Jayne returned to her phone with a disappointed grunt. Maggie visibly relaxed.

Emily walked over to the counter and saw the silk roses that had gotten Amy and Maggie so excited. They really were beautiful, so small and intricate, almost imperceptibly made of fabric. Each one had a collection of glass beads and diamonds to look like dew drops.

"These are fantastic," Emily gasped. "How many will be on my dress?"

The mischievous twinkle returned to Amy's eye.

"Fifty," Maggie explained. "Which makes a total of two hundred diamonds."

Emily's mouth dropped open. "Amy," she stammered. "I can't afford this!"

A huge grin spread across Amy's face. "That's the great thing," she said. "You don't have to. The diamonds are loaned."

"Loaned?" Emily gasped. "Who would *loan* diamonds?"

"How about your old friend Anne Maroney?" Amy said triumphantly.

Anne Maroney was a diamond trader. She'd bought the expensive diamond that Emily had discovered in one of Roy's safes, the one that had saved her from bankruptcy. They'd kept in touch since. Anne had even been to stay at the inn with her family. Emily wouldn't call her a friend as such, but they were certainly on friendly terms. With such a generous gesture, perhaps Emily should reconsider Anne as a friend!

"She's really going to do that?" Emily said, surprised. "But what if something happens to one of them? What if one falls off and falls down a crack in the floorboards or something?"

"They won't fall off," Maggie assured her.

"And Anne's going to use pictures of the dress for her website," Amy added. "So everyone wins."

Emily could hardly believe this was real. Trust Amy to make some kind of business deal. She was going to be walking down the aisle in the most expensive, beautiful dress! She'd always thought of herself as a simple girl who took pleasure in the simpler things in life—friends, books, strolls on the beach—and so it surprised her to realize how excited she was about all those glittering diamonds.

"Shall we get the dress on?" Maggie said. "Then we can place some of these prototypes to get a feel for how it will look when it's finalized."

Emily nodded and went to the dressing room out the back with Maggie. She hadn't seen the dress for quite some time and it took her breath away to see it there now, hanging from the rack with all the other bespoke designs Maggie was working on. The lace was beautiful. She'd gone for a Bardot-style neckline, so it would fall straight across her chest, exposing her delicate collar bone and connect onto her arms, missing her shoulders but stretching down to her wrists. It was a very elegant style, and something that made her feel like royalty.

Maggie helped her into the dress and used pins to pull in the waist. She affixed some of the prototype roses into place, then smiled.

"Time for the big reveal."

She drew back the curtain and Emily stepped out into the bright daylight of the shop floor. She caught sight of herself in the floor-length mirror and gasped. The dress looked even better than she remembered, than she could ever have hoped. She didn't quite recognize herself. She looked so classy, so tasteful and elegant.

Jayne leaped up from her seat, mouth agape. "Give us a twirl, Em!" she said.

Emily spun gently on the spot, her dress floating out all around her. Amy began to clap.

"It's just stunning," she said, beaming.

Just then, they heard the approaching roar of a motorcycle engine. Jayne craned her head to see out the window and down the street.

"Uh-oh," she said. "Incoming."

Amy frowned and went over to the window. Emily couldn't move fast enough in the heavy dress to see what they were looking at.

"Is that Daniel?" Amy exclaimed, sounding immediately outraged. "Emily, get out the back! Hide!"

Maggie rushed forward in a flurry of activity, trying to help Emily down off the small platform she'd been on. Emily, desperate not to damage the delicate dress in any way, took a small, careful step down, using Maggie as support.

But she just wasn't fast enough. The sound of the motorcycle engine cut out and only a few seconds later, the bell over the door tinkled. Emily was dead center of the bridal store floor. She couldn't have been more exposed if she tried. She stopped still and glanced over her shoulder at Daniel as he waltzed in.

"Surprise," he grinned. "Roy said you were doing the final dress alterations and I thought it might be nice to do something together."

Amy huffed. "You're not supposed to see the dress before the wedding!"

Daniel rolled his eyes. "We're not planning on being quite so formal," he laughed. Then he walked in and kissed Emily lightly. "You look divine."

"Thanks," Emily blushed. "It's not quite done. There's going to be a waterfall of roses."

Then she caught sight of an outraged Amy behind her and snapped her lips shut.

Amy folded her arms. "Why aren't you angry?" she demanded. "He's not supposed to see what you look like until you appear at the end of the aisle!"

Emily shook her head. "I don't mind. It's going to be stressful enough standing up there in front of everyone without the added pressure of not quite recognizing the person walking toward you!"

"You're both crazy," Amy said. She sounded genuinely horrified that they'd be breaking the tradition. "Oh God, please tell me you're sleeping in separate rooms the night before?"

Emily shrugged. She hadn't really thought about it.

Jayne piped up for the first time. "You have to," she said. "It makes the reunion on the wedding night way more fun." She winked.

Everyone laughed.

"Good point," Daniel said, raising his eyebrows.

Emily blushed. "It's a bit weird that my friends are so invested in this," she said with a giggle. "But sure. We'll sleep in separate rooms."

Daniel grinned with excitement.

Amy seemed to get over her initial outburst. "We may as well do your tux alterations while you're here," she said to Daniel. "Is that okay, Maggie?"

"Of course," Maggie said.

She led Daniel out the back to try on his outfit, closing the heavy curtain behind them.

Once alone, Amy leaned in to Emily and whispered in a conspiratorial tone. "Have you spoken to Daniel any more about his friends' outfits? About them being in the photos?"

Emily spoke in the same hushed voice. "I figured if we just told the photographer to take one portrait of Daniel and all the groomsmen, then just one of all of us together, then leave them out of everything else official, he probably won't even notice."

Jayne grinned. "Sly, Em. I like it."

Emily chewed her lip. "I mean, he's not going to know, is he? We're not doing too many traditional things anyway, so he's not going to know how many photos they ought to be in or whether they've been left out. And he's hardly going to gaze adoringly through the photo album every night like I probably will for the next fifty years."

Amy laughed. "Excellent point."

"Your strategic scheming will save you from having to look at their ugly mugs and disgusting tattoos too often," Jayne said gleefully. "As long as Daniel gets his bro photo then I think you'll get away with it."

"I'm really glad that's resolved," Amy confirmed. "And that no one's feelings got hurt in the process."

They heard the sound of the curtain being drawn back then, and all swirled around guiltily, pressing their mouths shut. Luckily, Daniel seemed oblivious to their shame-faced expressions; either that or he just didn't get the chance to see them because they each visibly melted at the sight of him in his tux.

"Oh, lumberjack," Jayne cooed. "You scrub up so handsomely."

Amy whacked her. "No flirting with the groom."

Everyone laughed.

Still in her own wedding outfit, Emily sashayed over to Daniel, her dress swirling around her as she went, and laid an arm on his sleeve. She went up on her tiptoes and kissed his cheek.

"You look so gorgeous," she said.

They oriented themselves in front of the mirror, side by side, straight-backed and confident. The sight took Emily's breath away. She could hardly believe it was them, could hardly believe that after all the hardships they'd experienced they were really standing here preparing for their wedding. She swelled with love and happiness and felt like they were back on track again.

"I have a surprise for you," Daniel said, speaking to the reflection of Emily before him in the mirror.

"I don't know if I can take any more surprises," Emily confessed to the reflection of Daniel.

"You'll like it," he said. "But you're going to have to come with me."

"On the bike?" Emily said.

Daniel nodded. "Let's get back into our comfy clothes."

Emily took one last long look at them in the mirror, her smile so wide it hurt her cheeks, then they turned and headed behind the curtain to change.

Emily felt a sense of sorrow as she removed her wedding dress, but reminded herself it wouldn't be long before she got to wear it again, and that the next time it would be completely finished and transporting her down the aisle to begin the rest of her life with Daniel.

Back in their ordinary clothes, Emily and Daniel emerged back around the curtain and onto the shop floor. Amy and Jayne were at the counter with Maggie, Amy writing a check for the final alterations.

"Thanks for today," Emily said, kissing both of her friends. "It was awesome."

"Would've been more awesome without the intrusion," Amy replied, shooting mock daggers in Daniel's direction.

He grinned sheepishly, then took Emily's hand. "Ready for your surprise?" he asked.

She shrugged. "I guess so!"

Waving goodbye to Amy and Jayne, Daniel led Emily from the store.

"Whose bike is this?" Emily asked as Daniel handed her a helmet.

His own bike had been totaled in an accident and they didn't have the money to get him a new one just yet.

"This is Evan's," Daniel replied. "My friends all rode their bikes here."

Emily placed the helmet firmly on her head. *Of course they did,* she thought.

She clambered onto the back of the bike, feeling somewhat nervous because of what had happened last time Daniel had ridden one. But she also trusted him, and knew that the accident before had been caused by unchecked emotion rather than bad riding per se. Usually, Daniel was very safe and trustworthy. Evan must think so too if he was able to allow his friend to borrow his bike after everything they'd been through.

Daniel kicked the bike to life and she felt the thrumming of the engine beneath her. She encircled Daniel's waist, feeling suddenly young and carefree, just as excited as she had been the first time she and Daniel had ridden together. It felt like they were dating again!

Daniel accelerated away and they sped along the roads. Emily felt the sting of cold air on her hands and held on more tightly to Daniel, her stomach flipping as they careened over bumps in the road. It felt so exhilarating to be flying along together like this, and so completely different from how they had been just moments before, looking so formal, like royalty in their wedding garb. Now suddenly they were bikers with the smell of oil and engine fumes all around them. Emily loved both incarnations of them.

Daniel drove them all the way out of Sunset Harbor, following the paths that cut alongside the beautiful forests and hillsides, following the coast. Emily watched the twinkly ocean whiz past, a sight that brought her so much peace and tranquility.

The further they went, the more excited she grew for what surprise lay ahead. She wondered if it was a date. Perhaps he'd packed a picnic and they were going to eat it on the granite peaks of Acadia Park. But they kept on driving, riding right past it.

Emily continued guessing where Daniel could be taking her. Perhaps it was to the lobster restaurant in the next town over that Daniel always wanted to visit. But they passed that too, and kept on riding.

Finally, they turned off the main road and headed along a small street where only a collection of houses stood. Emily frowned, confused. There didn't seem to be any shops or restaurants around here for them to visit. This area seemed purely residential.

Daniel slowed the bike, then drew to halt. They were outside of a beautiful house, quaint but sprawling. It had red ivy climbing the side.

Emily pulled her helmet off. "Where are we?" she asked Daniel.

Just then, the door to the house opened and to Emily's surprise, she recognized the woman coming down the steps to greet them. Anne Maroney.

"What's going on?" she asked, confused, climbing from the bike.

Daniel just winked.

Anne reached them and took Emily by both the hands. "It's so wonderful to see you," she said. "Did Maggie get the diamond delivery okay?"

Emily nodded but felt more confused than ever. It felt like some scheming had been going on behind her back, between Anne and Amy, Daniel and Maggie. What on Earth did he have in store for her?

"It's very kind of you to loan all those diamonds," she said.

"It's very kind of you to model them," Anne replied.

Emily blushed. "I only just found out I was going to!" she exclaimed.

She followed Anne inside her home. It was a gorgeous property with honey-colored floorboards polished to perfection. An old grandfather clock stood in the hallway, its pendulum no longer swinging.

"My father would love this," Emily told her. "He fixes clocks for a living."

"He does?" Anne asked. "Perhaps he could fix mine? It's a family heirloom but I'm afraid I haven't kept it in a good condition."

"I'll send him over," Emily said, smiling. "Tinkering is his passion in life."

She smiled to herself, realizing just how normal it felt to now be speaking of her father like this, to be able to offer his services to a friend, to have him just *there.*

Anne took them into the living room.

"Would you like any drinks? Tea? Coffee? Or do you just want to skip to the grand reveal?"

Emily looked at Daniel, confused. "What grand reveal?" she asked, her eyes widening.

54

"I think we should just go for it," Daniel told Anne.

Anne nodded and went over to a cabinet. She pulled out a box and presented it to Daniel. "You should do the honors."

Daniel took it, and Emily could see the way his chest was rising and falling beneath his shirt, as though he were nervous about what he was about to show her. Then he turned and snapped open the lid of the box.

There, lying amidst black velvet, was the most beautiful diamond-encrusted necklace Emily had ever seen in her life. It was delicate, not too over the top, but intricate in its design.

"What's this?" she gasped, looking at Daniel. Then she looked at Anne. "Is this another loan for the wedding?"

But Anne just smiled. Emily looked back at Daniel.

"Not a loan," he said, shaking his head. "It's a gift. For you."

Emily just stared at the necklace. She couldn't speak. Her throat constricted with emotion. Of all the overblown romantic gestures Daniel had done, this was by far the most overblown!

"But why?" Emily gasped.

Daniel laughed. "I didn't realize I needed a why," he said. "Because I adore you. Because you deserve the world and more. Because I want to, in some small way, give you a token of my love."

"I have a ring for that," Emily stammered. She still couldn't quite believe that the necklace was hers, that Daniel had gone to all this effort for her, speaking to Anne, choosing the perfect gift.

"Don't you like it?" Daniel asked softly.

"I love it!" Emily exclaimed. "I just can't believe you did this!"

Daniel relaxed and took the necklace out of the case. He affixed it around her neck and Emily could feel that his fingers were shaking. He must have been so nervous about giving it to her, so anxious about her reaction. Emily had wanted to ask him how he'd been able to afford it, but decided not to. She didn't want to spoil such a perfect moment.

She walked over to the mirror above the mantel and touched the necklace with her fingertips. "It's so beautiful," she murmured. "Thank you. Thank you so much."

It had been the most perfect morning. She and Daniel thanked Anne and left—Emily assuring Anne she'd send her father over to fix the clock—and rode back the way they'd come. Emily hadn't realized there was even a chance she could feel happier than she had on the way out, and yet here she was, feeling more delighted than ever before in her life. Emily felt like nothing could bring her down.

But as they pulled into the driveway of the inn, that all changed. Because there, parked in the driveway, was a beat-up car that Emily recognized, one she'd hoped she'd never see again: Daniel's mom's car.

And there, on the porch steps waiting for them, sat Cassie.

CHAPTER EIGHT

Daniel killed the purring engine of his bike. Emily watched him cautiously as he leapt down and removed his crash helmet. He had gone deathly pale, his jaw rigid with fury, his eyes locked on his mother on the porch steps. Emily reached out and touched his arm lightly.

"Stay calm," she said gently.

But she could already tell Daniel wasn't listening, that he'd become single-minded, focused only on Cassie as though he had tunnel vision.

Emily watched as Cassie's expression turned into a sneer at the sight of Daniel pacing toward her. She stood and wobbled toward him on the unstable legs of someone inebriated.

Emily leaped down from the bike, hurriedly removing her own helmet, and followed Daniel, concern rippling through her at whatever drama was about to go down.

"Mom, you're drunk," Daniel said, reaching Cassie and grasping her elbow.

"I can't believe you're marrying this woman," Cassie slurred, flaying an arm in Emily's general direction.

Emily tried not to take offense but it felt like a slap in the face. She'd never done anything to Cassie to deserve her disdain. But then again, neither had Daniel really, and he was often on the receiving end of his mother's anger. In fact, Emily had never seen Cassie behave in any way other than angry and antagonistic. She ached for Daniel, for the hard upbringing he must have endured at the hands of this woman.

"I told you," Daniel said sternly. "If you sober up you can be part of my life. But until then, you need to leave me and my family the hell alone."

Cassie yanked her arm away from Daniel and suddenly lunged toward Emily.

"This is all your fault," she sneered, the stench of liquor on her breath. "You've poisoned him against me, haven't you?"

Daniel was there in a second, his arms keeping Cassie back from Emily. Emily took a trembling step backward.

"Leave her out of this," Daniel said in his mother's ear, his tone becoming sterner still.

"Why? Things were fine between us until she came along!" Cassie cried.

"That's not true, Mom, and you know it," Daniel refuted. "I'm the one who cut you out."

"Because she told you to!" Cassie accused.

Emily stood there, flabbergasted. No words formulated in her mind, she was too shocked to speak. It wasn't often an aggressive drunk person threatened her.

"You need to leave," Daniel said to Cassie, shoving her toward her car.

Cassie fought back. "No! I have to stop you marrying that snob. It will never work. You're from different worlds."

"You don't know anything about me," Emily stammered, finally finding her voice.

"I don't need to," Cassie barked. "I can see it in your clothes, in your arrogant face. I hear it in your voice. You think you're better than me. Before you came along, Daniel wanted to help me, to put me through rehab. But now he doesn't even bother with me."

"That's nothing to do with me," Emily said, feeling suddenly the need to defend herself. Daniel rarely spoke about his mom, and had never even told her that he'd attempted to help her with her addiction in the past, or recently, so she could hardly be blamed for him giving up.

"Two phone calls," Cassie continued, ranting angrily now. "In a year! From my own son. And one of them to tell me that he's marrying *you*!" She spat out the last word like it was an insult.

Daniel was still holding Cassie, trying to maneuver her toward her car. It wasn't the first time he'd had to wrestle her off the property. Emily hated to see the altercations between them, to see the anger and fury in Cassie's eyes. How could she be so mean to her only child? It was heartbreaking to see.

"As if I'd want to come to your pretentious wedding," Cassie continued rambling, her loud voice carrying across the grounds. "I don't recognize my son anymore. This isn't you. This big fancy house. Do you really think you fit in here? Look at this place!" She threw her arm out, then pointed at Daniel's pickup truck in the driveway. "That's you. Sticking out like a sore thumb. A pickup truck surrounded by fancy cars."

She wobbled through the driveway, weaving past Amy's Chrysler, Roman Westbrook's Lamborghini. Emily suddenly worried that she may damage them with her flailing. The last thing she needed was a bump in her insurance premiums or a lawsuit from a millionaire pop star.

"Mom, I'm going to ask you nicely," Daniel said through his teeth, "to get off this property before I call the police. If you ever turn up here drunk again, I will file a restraining order against you. Am I clear?"

Emily could tell Daniel was burying his emotions. He sounded so calm and composed but he was clearly anything but. Emily recognized the rehearsed behavior, the attempts not to infuriate the fire-breathing dragon that was a drunk and volatile parent, because she'd done the same as a child with her own mom. Only hers had been surrounded by the comforts of suburbia, of a nice house in a nice neighborhood, with the privilege of school counselors and support groups, of older, calmer relatives and long trips away to the coast. Daniel had had none of that. Since the age of five it had just been him and his mom in a rundown neighborhood, in a dumpy apartment, moving houses and schools numerous times. It pained Emily to even think of the struggles of his younger life.

Daniel's warning seemed to finally start to sink in with Cassie. Her rigid body seemed to loosen, to deflate. Her lips turned downward.

"Don't you dare," Daniel said. "Don't you dare cry. You have no right. I've given you a thousand chances. I've told you a million times that my door is open to you as soon as you dry out. But until then I can't have you in my life."

Cassie leaned against the top of her car and wiped her first tear away with an angry fist. "You don't understand how hard it is. It's not like I haven't tried. But I need your help."

Daniel shook his head. Pleading, begging Cassie clearly had more sway over him than angry, leering Cassie. Emily could see his resolve start to weaken.

"Rehab?" he said, his voice quieter. "What do you need? Money?"

Cassie bent her head into her arms and began to sob. "I've booked myself in."

"Mom," Daniel said, even softer now. He put a hand on her back. "If you need money to pay, you know I'll always help. Just tell me what facility you're going to and I'll send them a check."

Cassie peered out through her arms now. "That's the thing, son," she said. "I need to pay them myself. It's ones of their rules, something to do with taking responsibility, investing in yourself. Can you write the check out to me instead?"

Emily could see as plain as day what was happening. This was a tactic, one Cassie had used before, one that must have worked. She was trying it on. Seeing what she could get out of Daniel, what strategy she could use to get him on her side.

59

Emily wasn't going to stand for it. She strode toward Cassie's car, her hands clenched into fists. But she didn't know what to say, how to break it to Daniel that his mom was using him without breaking his spirit entirely.

"Daniel, we don't have the money," she said. "With the wedding and the attorney fees for Chantelle's adoption."

Daniel looked at her sharply, almost insulted, and Emily could tell he'd completely fallen for Cassie's routine. She couldn't blame him. His desire for his mom to get better was so powerful he'd fall for anything.

"This is important," he said. "We'll sell Trevor's house if we have to."

"I want to dry out," Cassie wailed. "If it's the only way I can have a relationship with my granddaughter."

Emily felt livid that Cassie would stoop so low as to bring Chantelle into this. She was pushing all of Daniel's most sensitive buttons, using any tactic she could.

"Then let's discuss it," Emily said, keeping her voice steady. "Daniel, please. We can't rush into anything."

Daniel seemed so angry. The heat was pulsing from him. The tendons in his arms stretched out against the car hood were taut. He let his head fall, his shaggy hair tumbling forward to obscure his features, giving Emily no way of reading him.

She looked at Cassie. The woman was grinning at her, her stained teeth showing through wrinkled lips.

"You're not going to be the one to drive a wedge through me and my son, are you?" she said coldly.

Emily wanted to scream with infuriation. Cassie was calculating. Manipulative. She'd clearly decided that Emily was the enemy, had latched onto her as the new thing to blame, probably as a way of staying the victim of circumstance and never having to take accountability for her actions.

"There's nothing more I would like," Emily replied, "than to have the mother of the groom at my wedding. To have my daughter have a warm and loving relationship with her grandmother. But you're not prepared to be that person, are you, Cassie? You're just here to get money out of your son so you can fund your lifestyle."

Daniel looked up at her, frowning. Emily hadn't wanted to make it so starkly clear what was happening, had wanted to protect him from any such pain, but it was impossible. She couldn't have him falling for Cassie's routine, parting with money to help her to only discover she'd run off with the cash.

It seemed to dawn on Daniel then. He looked crestfallen. Emily looked at him sympathetically, her heart aching at the sight of his expression.

"You need to go, Mom," he said. "I'm calling you a cab."

Cassie must have realized she'd been caught out because she dropped the act immediately. "See!" she screamed. "It's her! She's the problem! She's got you under her thumb, son! She's turned you against me!"

Daniel shook his head. "You turned me against you yourself," he said with a deep, resigned sigh.

Cassie looked from him to Emily, her face red with anger. "You won't be happy with her," she said nastily. "This marriage is doomed. You should have married Astrid when you had the chance. She was nice. She did everything she could to help me."

Emily felt like she'd been slapped in the face. Cassie had had a friendship with Daniel's ex? Why had she never been told any of this? She'd only just learned of Astrid's existence and now she was discovering the girl had tried to help Cassie.

For the first time Emily doubted herself. Maybe she really was the enemy, the wedge between Daniel and his mom? Maybe he'd tried harder to help when he was younger because he'd had a partner who supported him through it all, someone who was more on his level? Emily herself had brought her own judgments into Cassie's situation based on her experiences with Patricia. Had she poisoned Daniel against his mother? If Astrid had stuck around would Cassie have cleaned her act up? Emily felt a sudden insecurity for this girl she'd never known, this saintlike creature.

Cassie yanked open her car door. "Fine. I'm going. I can see I'm not wanted. That you don't want to help me."

"Mom, don't get in the car," Daniel said through his teeth. "You're in no fit state to drive. I'll get a cab."

But Cassie, ever petulant, slumped into the driver's seat of her car, leaving the door standing open. Emily felt like she was watching a sulky child trying to do everything she could to get her way, to get sympathy and attention.

Daniel leaned against the car, breathing raggedly.

"I'm not letting you drive like this," he said.

"You can't tell me what to do," Cassie said, spitefully, and Emily could see the glint in her eye to know she was getting a reaction from Daniel, that she was twisting him and manipulating his emotions.

"Please, Mom," he said. "I'm begging you. Don't drive like this. Something terrible could happen."

"I wouldn't have to if you weren't making me," she snapped back. "If something terrible happens it will be on your shoulders for not helping me when I asked."

"If you get into rehab then you can send me the bill," Daniel said, repeating his offer for the umpteenth time. "That option is always open to you and I will never turn my back on that. But that's as much contact as I want with you. Do you understand?"

Cassie looked up at him with an angry, pouting face, then reached out and slammed the car door. Daniel had no choice but to take a step back. His whole body seemed to be wilting from the helplessness he must be feeling, from the fact that at the end of the day he could never protect his mother from herself.

Cassie gunned the car to life. It spluttered and belched out a cloud of smoke. Emily heard the gears grind as Cassie threw it ungracefully into reverse. Weaving back and forth, she began to wonkily reverse away from them. Then she did a three-point turn, kicking up a spray of gravel.

There was a pause, the car now facing the other way, idling. Daniel seemed to perk up as if in anticipation, in that never failing hope that the message would get through to Cassie, that she would just do the right thing for once. But then the car revved and sped away, leaving Daniel standing in the driveway, looking broken, defeated, and dejected.

CHAPTER NINE

Emily could feel Daniel's heart racing as she wrapped her arms around him and led him back into the house. He was a trembling bag of nerves.

They sat together on the couch in the living room. Daniel looked stunned.

"I can't believe I almost fell for that," he said. "She was just going to take the money and run, wasn't she?"

Emily gripped his hand tightly and nodded sympathetically. "I think so," she said quietly. "I'm so sorry, Daniel."

Daniel continued to stare into the distance. He shook his head. "She first went to rehab when I was in high school," he said. "I had so much hope, you know?"

He looked at Emily then, and she could see the pain in his eyes. It was like looking into the eyes of the younger Daniel, watching his hopes dashed by his mother's failed attempts to get clean.

"I really thought," he continued, "that the only thing that had been holding Mom back from recovery was the fact that we couldn't afford rehab. I thought that was only something rich actors got to have. But Astrid did all the research and found a local place that was part charity funded."

Emily nodded, feeling somewhat dazed. It felt like all she ever heard about at the moment was Astrid. And while she always liked to hear stories of Daniel's past—he was usually so tight-lipped after all—hearing about Astrid and the significance of her role in his past stirred some strange latent emotions inside of her. How could she feel jealous of Daniel's teenage girlfriend when she was long forgotten and Emily herself was about to marry him? It was ridiculous, and she couldn't help but berate herself. She tried to keep her face neutral and alert so that Daniel could continue to open up without risking upsetting her. It seemed to be working as he kept on with his story.

"The charity was specifically there to help teens with alcoholic parents. We spoke to them and they agreed a certain sum that they could contribute. So we had to cobble together the rest of the money." He shook his head, looking more emotional than ever. "We worked all summer, me and Astrid. We gave up all our spare time so we could work and get the money together. I did night shifts for the extra pay, and sometimes my shift would start when Astrid's finished. We didn't get to see each other for days at a time and when we did, we were both exhausted."

"That sounds so hard," Emily said, noting how hypnotic and detached her voice sounded. The more she heard of Astrid, the more this girl sounded like a saint. She desperately wanted to know what had happened between them to break them up. But now was not the appropriate time to ask. Emily realized, sadly, that Astrid would remain a mystery to her for as long as Daniel felt the need not to speak of her. If his friends hadn't brought it up, he probably would never have even mentioned it.

Daniel continued. "Finally we got the money together and Mom went off to the center." He looked at Emily, his expression so mournful it broke her heart into a thousand pieces. "She lasted three weeks before taking off."

Emily let out a heavy sigh. "I'm so sorry."

"All that effort wasted. All those sacrifices. That's when my heart started to harden towards her. I'd always had the *what-if* of rehab in the back of my mind but it was gone now that she'd failed. She must have been ashamed because she stayed away for months. I lived at Astrid's during that time because I was young and completely alone. Not to mention reeling, emotionally fragile."

"Astrid's family took you in?" Emily asked gently, hoping that her question wasn't too probing, that it didn't reveal the pain she was feeling.

Daniel nodded. "Mom came back just before Thanksgiving. She didn't speak about it at all, put on a massive feast as though everything was fine and normal. I just looked at all this food wondering whether it was my money that was paying for it. Mine and Astrid's. If she'd just blown it all on some wild bender then saved up just enough to come home and attempt to patch things up." He shook his head bitterly. "I think that was also the beginning of the end for me and Astrid, if I'm really honest with myself. It put a huge strain on our relationship. I mean we were only kids really. That's not the sort of thing two high-schoolers should be dealing with."

Emily nodded, but she also knew from Daniel's friends' stories that he and Astrid had remained together for years, that the experience he'd just shared with her could not have been the thing that broke them up. There'd been something else.

Emily desperately wanted to know more, but just then, she heard the sound of thundering footsteps.

Both she and Daniel turned as the door swung open and Amy and Jayne burst inside.

"Thank God you're back," Amy said.

Emily frowned, her hands still clasping Daniel's in his lap. Amy seemed to realize she'd interrupted a moment but Jayne, ever oblivious, did not.

"Your appointment with the minister!" Jayne cried. "Come on, you need to go now!"

Emily felt a sudden wave of realization crash over her. She'd gotten so lost in the magic of the bike ride along the coast followed so swiftly by the crashing anguish of Cassie's appearance that she'd completely forgotten.

She looked at Daniel. An appointment with the minister felt like the last thing she could focus on right now. He hardly looked like he was in a fit state to do it either.

Amy, ever perceptive, said, "I'm pretty sure Em can just go on her own for this appointment. It's not like a walk-through or rehearsal for the wedding or anything. I think Father Duncan just has a couple of questions, that's all."

Emily squeezed Daniel's hand. "Would you like to stay here?" she asked, feeling a little like she was talking to a sick child, offering him the day off school.

The emotional toll it had taken on Daniel to speak of his mother's first failed rehab attempt was evident on his face. Emily wasn't sure if he'd want to revisit that moment again any time soon, to scratch open that particular wound. She couldn't blame him. She herself had locked away so many painful memories they'd resurfaced in terrifying, uncontrollable flashbacks. Thankfully, as she healed from her past, the flashbacks lessened in their frequency and power. She just hoped Daniel felt able to release some of the steam, to make sure his own troubles were shared to make sure they didn't fester in the same way Emily had let hers. It was hard to talk about painful memories but so necessary to avoid the kinds of problems Emily had faced.

"I should come," he said, sighing, looking more sorrowful than Emily had ever seen him. "It's important."

"If you're sure," Emily replied.

Daniel nodded and stood, his body seemingly filled with anguish.

Amy gave Emily a curious look. Emily shook her head gently to tell her friend that now wasn't the time to talk about it.

"We'll see you later," she said to her friends.

She took Daniel's hand and led him like a dazed hospital patient out of the house and down to her car. He was in no fit state to drive. She wasn't sure if he'd be in a fit state to see the priest, but he'd seemed convinced he ought to come and Emily felt that it wasn't up to her to decide what the best way for Daniel to handle his difficulties was. She just hoped that he would find someway to release his pain, to find peace with the situation, before it ate him up like Emily had allowed it to eat her up for all those years.

*

Emily always felt calm when she entered the local church. Sunset Harbor had an interfaith church, which was shared amongst the many different faiths in the area. Father Duncan, who was doing their wedding ceremony, met them at the door.

"Emily," he said, smiling, lightly taking her hand. Then he shook Daniel's. "Come and sit."

He led them out the main church and along the corridor into a small room. Rabbi Peter Shultz was inside, chatting happily to Reverend Wendy White. They smiled as Emily and Daniel entered.

"I love that you all share a church," Emily said as she sat.

Reverend White smile and nodded, her sleek gray bob swishing as she did. "Sharing resources and services is a key way for us to foster cooperation and collaboration, and ultimately peace. Our whole aim is to work towards acceptance and tolerance in the community. We all believe in a creator, after all." She gave a little shrug. "All religions share spirituality in common."

Father Duncan took the main seat, facing them all. "Have you worked out what faith you will raise the children with?" he asked.

Wow, Emily thought, *he's cutting right to the chase here!*

"We feel that interfaith is the most appropriate," she explained. "Since we have this church nearby and we both have different religions it seemed like the most sensible route to take."

Father Duncan watched her, exuding calmness. "Will you teach any traditions?"

Emily faltered and looked over at Daniel, remembering the way he'd had so much fun teaching Chantelle about the menorah. He seemed a million miles away.

"Yes, I suppose so," she told the priest. "Daniel wants to reconnect with his Jewish traditions."

Rabbi Schultz grinned. "That's excellent news," he said, addressing Daniel. "It's so important to give children all the knowledge they need to make their own spiritual decisions."

Daniel finally seemed to be coming back around. He nodded at Rabbi Shultz and a flicker of a polite smile appeared on his lips. He was still far from recovered from the ordeal of Cassie but at least he seemed to be more present.

"So you will raise them with Hanukkah?" Father Duncan asked. "As well as Christmas?"

Emily nodded. "Any opportunity for a party," she joked.

"And what about schooling?" Rabbit Shultz asked. "Chantelle is at a public school at the moment, is that correct?"

Emily nodded. "She goes to her local school. We haven't discussed a religious school."

She looked across at Daniel. He was looking contemplative. Emily had been pretty certain that they'd send any future kids they might have to the local public school like they had with Chantelle, even though they hadn't really discussed it at length. But now it seemed like Daniel was having other ideas. She began to wonder if his religious and cultural heritage was becoming more important to him. She wondered if the wedge his mother had driven between them was making him feel closer to his Jewish father.

"It's something to consider," Reverend White said. "They offer a first-class education."

Rabbi Schultz handed them some pamphlets. The top one, Emily noted, was for the private Jewish day school in the next town over, Kavod Elementary.

"This school is fantastic," he said. "They teach Judaic culture and some classes are taught in Hebrew."

"Thank you," Daniel said, taking the pamphlet and looking at it with interest. "We're certainly going to have to think about this."

Emily shuffled in her seat, a little uncomfortable with the way the conversation was going. Could they afford to send Chantelle to a private school? The drive would be very long for the child, and Emily knew it would fall on her shoulders to do the driving since Daniel was working long hours at Jack's now. And what of Chantelle's best friends, Bailey and Toby? Moving her to a new school would be so disruptive. She always thought that she and Daniel were on the same page about that sort of thing, but he seemed to be shifting his perspective. Emily felt the first hints of worry rippling inside of her.

"Shall we talk about the wedding itself?" Father Duncan suggested.

Emily nodded, relieved that the topic of conversation had changed.

"Were you thinking of having any particular religious texts read out at the wedding?" Father Duncan asked.

"I haven't thought about it, to be honest," Emily said. "Do you have any suggestions?"

"Of course," Father Duncan replied with a smile. "Corinthians 13:4-8 is the most beautiful passage for the occasion of marriage." He began quoting. "'Love is patient, love is kind. It does not envy, it does not boast, it is not proud. It does not dishonor others, it is not self-seeking, it is not easily angered, it keeps no record of wrongs. Love does not delight in evil but rejoices with the truth. It always protects, always trusts, always hopes, always perseveres. Love never fails.'"

Emily felt a swell of joy inside of her. "I love it," she gasped. She looked over at Daniel. "Can we have that passage read at the wedding?"

"Yes, it's beautiful," he replied. "I'd like something from the Old Testament too, though." He looked at Rabbi Shultz.

"Might I suggest Ruth 1:16-17," Rabbi Schultz said. "It is a very popular reading for interfaith weddings, for someone who is not Jewish marrying a Jewish spouse." He began his own recital. "'Ruth said: Entreat me not to leave thee, Or to return from following after thee: For whither thou goest, I will go, And where thou lodgest, I will lodge. Thy people shall be my people, And thy God my God. Where thou diest, will I die, And there will I be buried. The Lord do so to me, and more also, If ought but death part thee and me.'"

Daniel smiled in response. "My aunt and uncle had a reading at their wedding that always stuck with me. The one that begins, 'I am my beloved's and my beloved is mine'?"

"The Song of Solomon," Rabbi Schultz said. "A wonderful choice, also. 'Set me as a seal upon your heart and seal upon your arm; for love is strong as death, jealousy cruel as the grave.'" He produced another pamphlet and handed it to Daniel. "There are some wonderful options in here that are suitable for interfaith weddings. Please peruse it at your leisure and let me know if there's anything in there you would like me to read."

Daniel added the pamphlet to the other. "Thank you," he said, earnestly.

Emily fidgeted her hands, wishing she had her own pamphlets to hold onto. She felt suddenly very out of her depth. There wasn't much time to organize the wedding and now she had to work out whether she wanted these unfamiliar passages included in it.

"Have you thought of including any religious rituals?" Father Duncan asked then. "Bride and groom's family separated and seated either side? Father of the bride walking her down the aisle?"

"Oh yes," Emily said. "My father will be giving me away." She smiled for the first time since the conversation had begun. This she was certain of, and was overwhelmed by the knowledge that her father was here and able to do it.

"Cake cutting and feeding?" Reverend White added.

Emily nodded again, eagerly. These were all the traditional elements she found most enjoyable, and she certainly wanted them included.

Then she looked over at Daniel, wondering whether there were any traditions he remembered from his aunt and uncle's wedding that he might want to include.

"Do you have anything you'd like?" she asked him.

Daniel smiled then. "You know, it's traditional to have the bride sit on a throne to greet her guests."

Everyone laughed, Emily included. "That sounds pretty neat," she said.

"And would you like a chuppah?" Rabbi Shultz asked. "The canopy that symbolizes the home you will build together?"

Emily felt that it would be very fitting to have something symbolizing their home at their wedding, since it was the inn that brought them together in the first place.

"That sounds nice," she said, nodding.

"Yes," Daniel agreed, looking at Emily. "I'd also like to break a glass, if that's okay with you?"

"What does that symbolize?" Emily asked, curiously. "And do I get to break anything? That sounds fun."

"It would just be Daniel," Rabbi Shultz explained. "It's to remind us of the destruction of the Temple of Jerusalem, to make sure one is always mindful, even during one's most personal moment of rejoice, that Jerusalem is set above the highest joy."

Emily felt a little flutter of panic then. She wasn't sure if Daniel felt strongly about his religion and was worried if he did that he hadn't spoken yet to her about it. Not that she cared—she would admire him for it. Yet at the same time, it scared her. Was there a part of his life he wasn't telling her about? What if over time he decided to become very religious? Would they grow apart?

"It would just be for me," Daniel explained, softly. "You don't have to do it."

"Is it that important to you?" Emily asked quietly, feeling confused and a little overwhelmed.

"I'd like it included," he pressed. "We can't have the traditional plate breaking as neither of our mothers are coming, and I'd like something broken. It wouldn't feel right otherwise."

Emily couldn't understand where all this was coming from. Daniel had always been so easygoing about wedding preparations, about everything really. But now he seemed to be acquiring some fixed ideas of how things should be, and she felt a bit out of her depth since it was coming out of the blue for her.

"Sure," she said, a little dazed. "If it really means that much to you."

Perhaps seeing that she was looking lost, Reverend White addressed Emily then. "Will you be changing your name and title once married?" she asked. "We see lots of women now who keep their maiden name and adopt Ms. rather than Mrs."

Emily hadn't yet decided. She'd always thought she'd double barrel her surname once married but Mitchell Morey was such a mouthful. And she hadn't even given any consideration to whether she'd be a Ms. or a Mrs.!

"I don't know yet," she confessed.

"There's no hurry," Reverend White said kindly. "You can change your name, if you choose, whenever you want to. There's no timeframe here."

Though her words reassured Emily, she couldn't help but feel confused. There were so many things to consider, so many unknowns that would need to be resolved, especially when it came to children and how to raise them. What if Daniel felt a spiritual calling to return to Judaism fully, or she a pull to be closer to Christianity? Could such a thing tear them apart? Or with the support of the interfaith church would they be able to negotiate any such hurdles?

Emily didn't know the answer, but the seeds of doubt seemed to be germinating in her mind.

CHAPTER TEN

That night, as she climbed into bed, Emily wished that she and Daniel had time to speak about Cassie, but there just wasn't any. Plus the mood didn't seem right to focus on the heavy stuff. After a day of dresses and diamonds and meetings with church leaders, the last thing Emily felt able to do was broach the topic of Daniel's mother. Not to mention they were both exhausted and barely able to keep their eyes open long enough to hold a conversation. So instead, Emily reasoned that she and Daniel could speak tomorrow. They held one another and fell into a deep, long slumber.

They woke to the sound of Daniel's alarm. It was early, too early, and Emily frowned, confused that they'd be roused at that time.

"Did you set your alarm wrong?" she asked wearily.

"No, we're leaving early," Daniel said. "The boys don't want to hit any traffic."

It took a while for Emily to remember what Daniel was talking about, and when she did, she inwardly groaned. "Oh, the hunting trip," she said unenthusiastically.

Daniel must have picked up on her tone. He turned and kissed her forehead. "Yeah. I'm sorry. I know there's a lot going on right now. The timing kind of sucks."

Emily sat up and shrugged. "I guess that's the thing with weddings. You collect all these people together and they want to do things with you in return."

Daniel smiled. "Why don't you go back to sleep?"

Emily shook her head. "I'm awake now. May as well make my man a hearty breakfast before he leaves to live off the land for days."

Daniel laughed. They both dressed and headed downstairs to discover that Daniel's friends were already in the kitchen. And since it was too early for the breakfast shift to start—meaning neither Matthew nor Parker was available to cook—Evan had taken it upon himself to do so. The kitchen was a mess, a smashed egg on the counter, its white mixing with spilled coffee granules.

"Who wants bacon?" Evan said, turning and holding out a greasy pan.

Emily slumped into a chair with a sigh. She would have to clear all this mess up before her chefs arrived or they'd be mad at her!

"Coffee, Emily?" Clyde asked, holding out the glass pot.

Realizing they were making an effort for her, Emily nodded and allowed him to pour her a mug. When she took a sip of the too strong and very burned coffee she hid her grimace.

Daniel seemed in great spirits by the impromptu breakfast, however, and he grinned as he sat down beside his three friends, accepting the breakfast they'd cobbled together with enthusiasm. Emily felt very out of place sitting at the table with the four old friends and wondered if maybe it might have been better to go back to bed after all.

Just then, Chantelle appeared at the doorway, dressed in her pajamas.

"What are you doing up, sweetie?" Emily asked. "Were we too loud?" She cast a slightly cool gaze in the direction of Daniel's friends whose thunderous footsteps that morning had probably been heard by every guest in the inn.

Chantelle rubbed the sleep from her eyes. "No, I just smelled bacon."

Clyde burst out laughing. "Well, she's definitely your kid, Danny Boy!" he laughed. He jabbed a thumb in Daniel's direction. "He was the only Jewish kid I knew who ate pork."

Daniel blushed. "I was only part-time Jewish," he said meekly.

Emily knew Daniel hated reflecting on that part of his life, when his mom and dad were separated and pulling him in two different directions, in a tug or war between hometown, school, and religion. No wonder he'd been so reticent to bring that stuff up. But now, Emily viewed it through a slightly different lens, knowing that Astrid had been there all along. Was she Jewish too? Had they shared that? Or did she practice another faith, one that had moved Daniel away from the stricter rules of his own?

"We want Chantelle to make her own choices," Emily explained. "And when she's older."

Oblivious to everything, Chantelle grabbed a plate and accepted a piece of crisp bacon from Evan's pan.

Once breakfast was over, the guys began loading up the pickup truck with gear. Tents, guns, camping equipment. There was so much to take it looked like they were off for a year rather than a few days.

"I wish you didn't have to go, Daddy," Chantelle said as Daniel came up to the porch steps to say goodbye.

She looked very upset and Daniel hugged her tightly.

"It's just for a few days, sweetie," he told her reassuringly.

Chantelle nodded and held her chin up high in order to hide her upset. Emily looped an arm around her shoulder and held her tightly. Daniel leaned in and kissed Emily goodbye and then hurried down the porch steps, bouncing with excitement, before leaping into the truck.

Emily and Chantelle stood together on the porch step, watching Daniel wave as his friends whisked him away on an adventure.

Just then, they heard footsteps coming from behind. It was Amy and Jayne. They were both carrying two bulging tote bags each, one slung over each shoulder.

"What's going on?" Emily asked, confused.

"Can't say," Amy said, grinning. "We want to surprise you."

Emily wasn't much in the mood for surprises; she was feeling too glum now that Daniel was gone, now that she was facing several days to stew with her thoughts about Astrid.

"I don't know how much I want a surprise that involves four tote bags," she said unenthusiastically. "What's in them anyway?"

"Nuh-uh," Amy said, stepping away so Emily couldn't peek. "And trust me, you're going to love it. I'd never surprise you with something I didn't think you would absolutely adore."

Amy had a point, Emily reasoned. She did have impeccable taste and, at the very least, was more able to organize a fun event than Jayne was. But that still didn't stop the fact that she wasn't feeling much like doing anything right now. Especially if that meant leaving Chantelle for any period of time.

"Well, what do I have to do?" Emily asked, folding her arms.

"Just come with us," Amy said. "And a smile wouldn't hurt!"

Emily shook her head stubbornly and dug her heels in. "Not until you tell me where we're going."

Jayne, never one to hold onto secrets, suddenly blurted out, "To your bachelorette party!"

Amy frowned at her and rolled her eyes. Then she looked at Emily and said with lackluster, "Surprise."

Emily froze. Beside her, she felt Chantelle stiffen also. They'd just waved goodbye to Daniel and now Emily was also supposed to leave the child? It wasn't that she didn't trust Papa Roy to look after the girl, or that she thought the two wouldn't have fun together, but she didn't like the fact her friends were springing this on her in this manner. Chantelle had abandonment issues and was struggling enough as it was with Daniel being away.

"You want to go right now?" Emily stammered.

She could feel Chantelle's arms tightening around her waist.

Jayne nodded and reached forward to grab Emily's hand. Emily allowed her to, but without any enthusiasm.

"Come on, it will be great! We've booked a spa on the coast, it's supposed to have amazing views."

"Jayne!" Amy cried. "Can you shut your mouth for five seconds? It's supposed to be a surprise."

But Emily didn't care about where it was or what had been planned. All she cared about was Chantelle, about what suddenly leaving might do to the child.

"I can't go," Emily said, squeezing Chantelle to her protectively. "I'm sorry, but with Daniel leaving I need to be with Chantelle."

Amy seemed to suddenly relax. "Chantelle's coming too," she stated.

Emily raised her eyebrows. "She is?"

"Of course!" Amy said. "Is that why you looked so distressed by the idea? Because you thought we'd forgotten about Chantelle?"

"Well, yes," Emily confessed.

Amy shook her head. "Oh, babe, don't be so dumb. We're not about to leave out the most important person in the wedding party." She gave Chantelle a little pat on the shoulder. Then she grabbed Emily and hugged her. "I thought you were pissed at me for a second there."

Emily laughed, relaxing too. "I was just worried about Chantelle."

Amy took one of her tote bags off her shoulder and opened it up so Emily could see. Inside was a fluffy white dressing gown. A sparkly pink letter E had been embossed onto it.

"There's one for each of us," Amy explained.

"They're amazing!" Emily exclaimed.

Amy grinned in a know-it-all kind of way.

"Now that issue is resolved," she said, "what do you say? Spa outing? Four ladies, eight cucumber slices on our eyes, three champagnes, one sparkling apple." She winked at Chantelle.

Chantelle beamed. Emily looked down at her and smiled too. Perhaps this was just what Chantelle needed to get over missing Daniel.

"What do you think?" Emily asked. "Your first ever spa day?"

Chantelle grinned and jumped up and down excitedly. "Yay yay yay yay yay!"

Emily looked up at Amy and smirked. "I guess we're both in."

*

74

They took Amy's car since it was the biggest and fanciest of them all. Chantelle seemed to love it and Emily wondered if she'd spent her entire life in pickup trucks like Daniel's.

The drive along the coast was as stunningly beautiful as ever, and spring was well and truly in the air, making the tree leaves a vivid green and the blossom gloriously white. Down the cliff edge sparkling waves lapped against the sand.

The spa Amy had booked was just a few towns over. As they pulled up outside, everyone gasped. The building was incredible, an old converted mansion much like Emily's own house, but even grander. It had columns outside and stone steps rather than wooden porch steps.

"There's a pool," Amy explained as she parked. "And a sauna. We're getting facials, mani-pedis, and massages. They also do cupping here but I figured you wouldn't want to do that in case it leaves marks."

"You figured correctly," Emily laughed. "I don't want to walk down the aisle covered in red ovals."

"That would be one way of surprising Daniel," Jayne quipped, "since he spoiled it with the dress."

Everyone laughed and climbed out of the car. Emily took Chantelle's hand as they walked along the path to the grand old building. Chantelle seemed awestruck and clutched her tote bag tightly.

Once inside the grand foyer, Amy went up to the reception and checked them in.

"Changing rooms are this way," she said, leading the excited party through the corridors.

They reached the cozy changing rooms. They smelled of calming lavender and were filled with beautiful white flowers set in glass vases. Emily found the setting very inspirational, and wondered whether she could redesign some of the bathrooms in the inn to be as fresh and relaxing.

"I wonder how much it costs to have fresh flowers in here every day," she said, touching the petals.

"Are you thinking about work?" Amy said as she shrugged on her dressing gown. "Because that's strictly off limits."

Emily laughed. "Okay. I'll stop."

But she still eyed the reed diffusers and small bottles of moisturizing oils with curiosity. Those were the sorts of things that would make her inn more high class. She remembered Cynthia giving her similar advice when she was first getting the inn up and running. She simply hadn't had the money to follow it all back then.

Maybe it was worth considering a renovation now though, after the wedding was over and things were back to normal.

Just then, Chantelle came over in her dressing gown and flip-flops. Jayne had lent her a pair of her sunglasses. Emily burst out laughing as Chantelle posed.

"You look like a diva!" Emily exclaimed.

"Or a beauty queen," Jayne added, grinning.

Everyone giggled, in high spirits. They went out of the changing rooms and along the corridor to the heated pool area, their embellished pink letters glittering under the spotlights. The pool was set in a large glass conservatory-style room right up on the cliff edge, overlooking the ocean. The sight took Emily's breath away.

They found four lounge chairs and settled in, awaiting their drinks and nibbles.

The nail technician arrived first, a slight girl with shiny black hair lying poker straight against her white apron. She was wheeling a trolley filled with polishes of every conceivable color.

"I hear we have a bride-to-be today," she said. Then she grinned at Chantelle. "It must be you."

Chantelle dissolved into giggles, and it warmed Emily's heart to see her in such high spirits.

The nail technician showed Chantelle all the different colors she could have, all the styles with crystals and designs.

"She has school on Monday," Emily said. "So nothing that won't come off with remover, please."

Chantelle pouted. She'd clearly been a little swept away by all the options and felt dashed not to be able to have exactly what she wanted.

"Although," Emily said, "no one's going to be seeing your toes at school, are they, so you can have as many gems and jewels glued onto them as you want!"

Chantelle seemed thrilled by the prospect, as odd as it would be for her to be walking around with bejeweled toes. She slipped her flip-flops off and the technician got to work.

Another lady in the same crisp white uniform came over with a tray of champagne and canapés. She poured them each a glass.

"This is the sparkling juice," she said, handing it to Chantelle.

Chantelle took the drink in the champagne flute and took a sip. She looked like a spoiled princess in her lounger with her nails being polished and her drink. Emily laughed with amusement.

"Oh my God, these are divine," Jayne cried, holding up a half-eaten shrimp bite. "Em, please say you're having this sort of thing at the wedding."

"We decided against anything too fancy," Emily explained. "But there'll be freshly caught Maine fish, of course, since it is a Sunset Harbor specialty."

"Oh good," Jayne said, melting into her chair as she popped the rest of the shrimp into her mouth. "The fish here is to die for."

Emily laughed.

Just then, a male voice said, "Is anyone ready for a massage?"

Everyone turned to see the most gorgeous man imaginable standing in the spa's crisp white uniform. He had sparkling white teeth and a chiseled jaw. Emily made sure she kept her mouth from dropping open. Jayne, on the other hand, did not.

"Me," she said, leaping up, her eyes glittering. "I am. Me."

The man smiled courteously. "Of course, if you'd like to come with me."

Jayne followed him, turning around and mouthing, "OH MY GOD!" to her giggling friends.

Emily relaxed into her bachelorette party, taking her turn to have her facial, her manicure, her massage, lazing in the Jacuzzi and steaming in the sauna. Muscles she never even realized were tight seemed suddenly elasticized. She had never felt so relaxed in her life!

"Thanks so much for doing this," she said to Amy as they congregated in the changing room at the end of their session. "I had a blast."

"You're welcome," Amy said. "I'm proud of you for not stressing about the inn."

Emily laughed. It wasn't often that the inn left her mind but she hadn't even thought of it for hours.

"We should come back here sometime," she said. "Make it an annual thing. What do you say, Chantelle?"

Chantelle was positively glowing with health and vitality. She'd chosen lime green and pink stripes for her nails, a headache-inducing combination that she was thoroughly proud of, accentuating select toes with crystals. Her skin gleamed from the steam and the facial. She looked every inch the pampered princess.

But Emily noticed then that Chantelle was looking glum.

"What's up, sweetie?" she said.

"I just miss Daddy," Chantelle replied.

Emily hugged her. Chantelle was such a sweet child that even a day of pampering didn't compare to spending time with her good old dad. It warmed her heart to know that Chantelle and Daniel had bonded so much.

"I miss him too," Emily confessed. "But I bet he's having a blast out in the forest. We're all clean and sparkly and he'll be all dirty and covered in mud."

Chantelle laughed at the thought. "I like muddy," she confessed.

"More than saunas?" Jayne queried.

"Maybe," Chantelle said with a little shrug. "Me and Papa Roy get muddy in the greenhouse and that's loads of fun."

"Ew," Jayne said. "Greenhouses are full of creepy crawlies and bugs."

"I like bugs," Chantelle said, proudly.

Amy laughed then. "She really is Daniel's daughter, isn't she?" she said.

That was the second time Emily had heard such a statement. She wondered whether there was anything Chantelle had taken from her, anything she'd taught the child. She was supposed to be adopting Chantelle, supposed to be becoming her legal mother, but right now it felt like Chantelle was just her stepdaughter, someone upon whom she had no influence.

"Maybe next time Daddy can take you with him," Emily suggested. "Would you like that?"

Chantelle nodded but still seemed a little sad, still pining for her father. Emily wondered if she viewed Daniel as more than just a father, because he was the knight in shining armor who'd whisked her away from her sorrowful life and brought her into a world of comfort and safety. No wonder she wanted to be just like him and do everything he did. He was her hero.

They left the spa together and got into Amy's car.

"I feel like all my limbs are made of cotton candy," Jayne said, sinking into the passenger seat. "Kody's massage was the most amazing thing."

"Kody?" Emily laughed. "You're on a first-name basis with the masseuse?"

"Of course," Jayne said. "I got his number too."

Everyone squealed with delight.

"He looked about twenty," Amy exclaimed.

"Nineteen actually," Jayne said. "He's saving up to go to college."

Amy shook her head in mock distaste. Typical Jayne not to let a sixteen-year age gap dissuade her!

Amy started the car and drove them back along the coastal path. The light was starting to fade, giving Emily a different landscape to look out on, one of a sunset reflected in the ocean. It was as equally beautiful as the drive out had been. She sighed with contentment and rested her chin on her fist. There really was so much to be grateful for in life. Despite all the ups and downs, all the hardships and difficulties, she really did live a charmed existence.

They reached the inn and Amy pulled into the driveway, crawling along the gravel path to the parking lot. In the dimming light, the orange glow coming from the inn looked warm and inviting. Emily always loved this sight of the inn from the outside, knowing inside it was filled with happy guests and bustling staff.

She noticed something then, a small glowing red light.

"What's that?" she said, frowning through the windshield.

"Looks like the cherry of a cigarette," Jayne said.

Emily squinted and realized she was right. Someone was standing on Emily's porch smoking. She wondered if it was Roman Westbrook. They were certainly standing in the confident sort of pose of a megastar.

But as she climbed out of the car she noticed the figure was female, with a slim yet hourglass figure. She was wearing a tight white top underneath a denim jacket and tight jeans that showed her figure off to the max. Long brown hair trailed over her shoulders. Perhaps Roman Westbrook had brought a female companion back to the inn?

Emily walked along the path and saw the girl stub out her cigarette on the porch. She'd have to clean that up ASAP. She hated the place to look grubby and unhygienic.

"Good evening," she said, trotting up toward the woman. "Are you a guest?"

The girl shook her head. "I'm looking for someone. I think he might be in the carriage house but there was no one there when I knocked."

Emily nodded. She'd been right in her intuition that this was a suitor of Roman's. The girl, up close, was stunningly beautiful, with pillowy lips and almond-shaped eyes.

"Are you looking for Mr. Westbrook?" Emily asked.

But to Emily's surprise, the girl shook her head. "No, I'm looking for someone named Daniel. Daniel Morey. Do you know him?"

Emily frowned, taken aback by the sound of Daniel's name tumbling from this goddess of a woman's mouth.

"Yes, I do. But who are you?" Emily asked.

"I'm an old friend," the girl said. Then she shrugged. "More than an old friend, actually. We used to date. My name's Astrid. I'm the girl Daniel proposed to."

CHAPTER ELEVEN

Emily stood on the darkened porch, staring at Astrid, stunned. The figment of her most recent anxieties had manifested before her very eyes. Yet somehow she was even more beautiful than Emily had even imagined. And now she was not just Daniel's first love but someone he'd once been *engaged* to? Why hadn't he told her that he'd been engaged before, that she wasn't the first? That was surely the sort of thing his wife-to-be deserved to know!

Behind Emily she could hear Amy and Jayne trying to distract Chantelle. She quickly decided that if there was about to be a showdown Chantelle needed to be shielded from it.

"Honey, can you run along inside and ask Matthew to start on dinner?" she called down to the girl. "Jayne and Amy can help."

Chantelle nodded cheerily and skipped inside. Jayne and Amy followed, each of them flashing sympathetic glances at Emily as they passed.

Finally alone with Astrid, Emily turned to face her. Her beauty was astounding, almost enough to make her wince with jealousy.

"What are you doing here?" Emily finally said. "Why do you need to see Daniel?"

Astrid narrowed her eyes slightly. "So you know him? He lives here?"

Emily took hold of the wooden porch railings behind her for support. "I'm his fiancée," she finally managed to say.

A look of knowing appeared on Astrid's features. She looked suddenly guilty. "Oh. I didn't realize. I should go."

But Emily stepped to the side, blocking Astrid's way out. Something had ignited inside of her, the flames of paranoia. What had caused Astrid to turn up out of the blue like this? Had Daniel invited her? Or worse, what if he had arranged a secret rendezvous, a last hurrah with his first love? Emily's mind raced with thoughts she knew she shouldn't be having. She was supposed to trust Daniel, and yet at the first whiff of suspicion her mind leaped to infidelity.

"Did Daniel tell you to come here?" Emily asked, folding her arms sternly.

Astrid shook her head, her beautiful mane of silky hair swishing as she did. "It wasn't him. I just found out he was getting married and—"

"Found out?" Emily interrupted. She knew she was coming across as slightly menacing by the way Astrid swallowed. "Found out how?"

"Through a mutual friend," Astrid stammered.

"Which mutual friend? Let me guess. Stuart? Clyde? Evan?"

Astrid seemed to lose patience. "Look, it doesn't matter which one. The point is that I found out."

"And you came straight over here? Why? To confess your undying love for Daniel? To tell him he's the father of your secret child?"

Astrid looked more confused than ever. Emily knew she was probably coming across as somewhat unstable but she just couldn't help it. First Sheila turned up and wrecked things for the two of them for weeks and now Astrid?

"No, nothing like that," Astrid stammered. "I just wanted to see him."

"Why? What are you expecting to happen?" Emily continued, her voice tumbling out of her in a torrent of anger. "That Daniel would confess his love for you and run off and leave me? You're a bit late! You could have come here any time in the last fifteen years!"

"I didn't know where he was," Astrid protested. "I only know now because of Stu. He said he was blindsided when Daniel got in touch to say he was getting married. No one's spoken to him or heard from him for years. Last I knew he'd run off to Tennessee."

She shook her head bitterly and Emily noticed there were tears glittering in her eyes. The sight of Astrid's heartbreak cut Emily to the core.

"He left without saying goodbye?" Emily asked.

Astrid nodded and wiped a tear from her eye. "I just came for some closure."

Here was yet another person that Daniel had walked out on. His history of running off made Emily more than a little anxious, especially with her own experience with her father. Was she being completely crazy to think that Daniel had changed? Was she about to become the next victim of his lothario ways?

"But why did he do that?" Emily asked. What she really meant was how could he leave someone as gorgeous as Astrid? How could he treat her so badly after so many years together?

"For a lot of reasons," Astrid muttered in response. "Being young and foolish was probably top of the list. I'm hoping he's become more sensible over the last twenty years."

"I'm sure he has," Emily replied. But she felt horrible talking to Astrid about Daniel like this, like she had any kind of history with him. The Daniel that Astrid knew was still a mystery to Emily since he spoke so rarely of his past. But Astrid had known him four times longer than Emily had, even if he was a completely different person now from the one he'd been back then. They'd shared so much more than Emily and Daniel had. They were each other's firsts. That was the sort of bond that could never be erased.

"But why now?" Emily questioned. "Why so close to the wedding?"

She felt like she was standing on the edge of a precipice staring into the abyss, and that abyss was Astrid. Did the girl possess the power to ruin Emily's life and end her happiness?

"I didn't know it was close to the wedding," Astrid said. "Like I said, Stu just told me that the old gang was reuniting and I just got the sudden urge to be here with them all."

Emily couldn't trust her. She was certain Astrid was here to ruin her wedding, to steal Daniel back. The timing was too suspicious.

"Well, Daniel's not here," Emily replied. "None of them are. They went hunting."

Astrid pulled her arms about her middle and stared out over the lawns. She blinked her long lashes, making them wet with tears. "Look, I know you're the last person in the world who would do a favor for me, but if I leave my number can you just give it to Daniel? For when he gets back. Just to talk."

She rummaged in her jeans pocket and handed a small slip of card to Emily. In the yellow porch light Emily could just work out from the business card that Astrid was a Pilates instructor. *Typical,* she thought.

Emily took the card and shrugged. She at first had zero intention of passing it on to Daniel. In fact, part of her wanted to forget the whole thing had ever happened, erase Astrid's beautiful face from her mind entirely. But she wasn't Daniel. She didn't paper over the uncomfortable parts of her past, she didn't hide things from him. Even if in doing so it rekindled some old feelings of lost love he'd buried deep inside, she couldn't keep Astrid's visit a secret from him.

Emily watched as Astrid trotted down the porch steps and to her car. Her visit had brought up more questions than answers, and had stirred Emily's paranoia. She rushed inside and grabbed the phone off the reception desk.

Shaking, Emily dialed Daniel's number. Immediately it went to voicemail. He probably didn't have any cell phone service out in the forest. She slammed the phone down.

"Emily Jane?"

The voice coming from halfway above on the staircase was her father's. More than at any point in her life, Emily was so grateful to see him there. Her tears burst out of her. Roy hurried down the steps and swept her up in his arms. Emily buried her face into her father's shoulder and began to sob.

*

Emily sat curled up on the couch with her father rocking her gently. He'd lit the fire and poured them both a sherry and now the room felt cozy and comfortable. But inside, Emily was still reeling from her encounter with Astrid and from the fears it had stirred inside of her.

"Am I just a fool, Dad?" Emily said, clutching her tear-stained tissue in her fist. "Should I be packing my bags right now and getting out while I still can?"

Roy shook his head. "I don't think you're a fool at all. And I don't think you should walk away from this."

"But he's never straight with me!" Emily countered. "How am I supposed to have a happy marriage if I can't trust him?"

"Trust can take time to build," Roy said calmly. "The important thing is that you know Daniel and love him."

"But do I know him?" Emily cried. "I mean, really?"

The words brought on a fresh bout of crying.

"I think you know the answer to that in your heart," Roy said. "I don't think you would have said yes to marrying him if you didn't think you knew him. Understanding, patience, time, all those things can be worked on in due course."

Emily sniffed and dabbed at her tears. The impulsive part of her wanted to throw in the towel, but her dad was right. She knew Daniel in her heart, even if she didn't know everything about him.

"I just don't understand why he always has to lie about his past," Emily added.

"Not revealing the truth and lying are different things," Roy said softly. "Some white lies are told for protection."

Emily wondered whether he was perhaps speaking about himself and his own situation, attempting to explain the reasons behind some of his more covert and eccentric behaviors. Had Emily not been so consumed with thoughts of Daniel the comment might have irked her. Instead, she was just grateful that he was here to listen to her and support her. He'd been absent for all her breakups in the past, had never been there to soothe her numerous broken hearts.

"I'd prefer honesty," Emily said. "There's nothing in Daniel's past that could upset me more than the things my own mind conjures."

Roy chuckled kindly and rubbed Emily's shoulder. "There are always many sides to a story. Why don't you wait to hear his before conjuring anything up in that vivid imagination of yours?"

Emily whimpered out a laugh and rested her head against her father's chest. He wrapped his arms tightly around her. All the crying had exhausted her, and with the warm fire and the sherry starting to take effect she felt very sleepy in his arms. It felt safe, like being transported back in time, to a more simple era when she had been a little child, unburdened by life and memories.

"I have a story for you," Roy said, his voice rumbling through his chest into Emily's ear. "It's about when I first met Daniel."

"I think I know this one," she said, stifling a yawn. "He does tell me some things." She smiled sadly. "But I'd love to hear you tell it. What was he like at sixteen?"

Roy took a deep breath. "He was a scared little boy. Lost. Hurt. Angry. In desperate need of affection."

Emily felt her heart clenching at the thought. For all of Daniel's faults, she had to remember where it was he had come from and how far he had come. He could have turned out very, very differently.

"Did you ever have doubts about taking him in?" Emily asked.

Roy chuckled. "Not at all. He pretended to be tough but I could see through the act. It wasn't hard since he was shivering in the barn, trying to keep out of sight. Did he tell you that he stole some of my carrots that night? Ate them raw, straight out of the ground. They'd barely even grown longer than an inch. Must have been disgusting."

Emily found herself giggling in spite of herself, in spite of the sadness of the story.

"Did he tell you about what things were like at home?" Emily asked.

"Not at first," Roy explained. "I suspected it, though. There are very few teenagers who choose to run away from home, despite what we're led to believe. It takes a lot to drive a youngster away from their family, not just petty squabbles over allowances and being grounded too often." He sighed heavily. "I really wasn't sure how best to help him. He didn't want anything from me. His only request was that I not call the cops on him."

Emily listened sadly to Roy's story unravel. It was so painful to know that this was her Daniel he was talking about. If their paths had not crossed that night, how different might her own life have been?

"Of course I said he could stay as long as he needed," Roy continued. "I left him a thermos of soup and some tea."

Emily sat up then, surprised. Daniel had done the exact same thing for her the winter she'd first arrived here. Roy's kindness had never left him and he'd paid that forward to her, helping her when she most needed it, in the way someone had once done for him. It warmed her to think that his caring actions had been inspired by her own father.

"Then over time, with patience," Roy continued, "he opened up just a little bit. Enough for me to understand what was going on. I encouraged him not to drop out of school, but I never pushed him too hard. The most important thing to me was that he stayed safe and that he knew there was always a place for him, always a person who would be happy to see him, no matter how difficult he became."

Emily understood then the meaning of Roy's story. Daniel's past had been chaotic and confusing. But with love and kindness he would begin to open up, just like he had with her father that summer back when he was sixteen.

At last, Emily felt her bitterness over the Astrid situation dissipate. Daniel, the Daniel she knew at least, the one he'd become, was the kindest soul she'd ever met. She would get to spend the rest of her life with him, learning more about him as the months and years passed. She would not like everything about him but she would give him the patience and care he deserved. And she would always, always love him.

CHAPTER TWELVE

Emily was lying in bed the next morning when she heard the sound of tires crunching on gravel. She hauled herself up and rushed to the window. Daniel's pickup truck was coming up the drive toward the house.

Despite the long, reassuring conversation she'd had with her father the night before, she still felt a mixture of apprehension and sadness at the thought of seeing Daniel again. She would be looking at him, once more, through that old lens of distrust, of hurt at his failure to give her the full picture. She hated that part of her, the paranoid part, but it was because of Daniel's actions that she still possessed it. If he was more open about his past, even the things he knew would upset her like Astrid and Sheila, she would be far more able to work through such difficult emotions. But Daniel always kept her in the dark. And though she knew his aim was to protect her, she wished he could understand that these things always had a way of coming out, and that it was the way in which they did that hurt so much. She was sick of shadows from his past turning up on her doorstep, dragging his skeletons with them.

She wrapped herself in a long woolen cardigan and headed out her bedroom and down the stairs. By the time she reached the front door, Daniel and his friends had gotten out of the truck and had begun to unload their gear.

When he saw her approaching, Daniel grinned and opened his arms wide. But Emily hesitated, not wanting to initiate the conversation that she knew she and Daniel had to have.

A line of confusion appeared between his eyebrows. "Aren't you happy to see me?" he asked.

"Of course," she replied. She allowed herself to fold into his embrace, but she didn't hug him back.

"Daniel killed an elk," Stuart informed her.

"Did he now?"

Daniel released Emily and studied her face. Her concern must have been showing plain as day because right away he narrowed his eyes.

"You're mad about something."

Emily looked over at Stu, Evan, and Clyde with exasperation. She didn't really want the three of them overhearing this.

"What have I done?" Daniel pressed.

"Nothing." Emily sighed. "I tried calling you, you know."

"I had next to no reception in the forest," Daniel explained. "And then my phone died. Is that why you're mad?"

Emily shook her head. "No. I'm not mad."

"You are," Daniel said. "I know you well enough to know what face you pull when you're angry at me and this is it exactly."

His friends began to chuckle.

"Can we go inside?" Emily suggested.

She motioned for the door but Daniel reached out and grabbed her hand, holding her back.

"Emily, come on, let's not do this," Daniel said. "Whatever is wrong you need to tell me."

Realizing there was no more delaying the inevitable, Emily relented. She rubbed the creases on her forehead.

"You had a visitor," she began.

"An unwelcome one?" Daniel asked.

Emily folded her arms defensively across her stomach. "Only because I didn't know she was once your fiancée."

Daniel's friends stopped unloading the truck and looked at each other, their expressions both shocked and surprised.

Daniel froze too. "Astrid was here?"

"Yup," Emily said. "Lithe-limbed Astrid was on my porch."

Daniel looked like he'd seen a ghost. Emily wished she could read his expression. Was it disappointment that he hadn't been here to see her? Surprise that Astrid still cared, after all these years, enough to track him down a few days before his wedding?

"But how did she find out where I live?"

Emily flicked her cool eyes over Daniel's shoulders.

"That would be my fault," Stuart confessed.

Daniel turned and glared at him. For the first time, Emily thought she detected a hint of remorse in Stuart's eyes and realized that he hadn't gone intentionally out of his way to rock her and Daniel's relationship just days before their wedding. That was a comfort to her, at the very least.

"You told her where to find me?" Daniel accused Stuart. "But why?"

"It was a slip of the tongue," Stuart explained.

"I thought you said you weren't in touch with her anymore," Daniel continued.

"Just on social media, that's all. I posted some pictures and maybe accidentally tagged the inn in them. You know how it is." Stuart grabbed Daniel's tent and bag, heaving them up. "Look, dude, I'm sorry, okay? I'll carry this in for you. Give you two a chance to talk."

He scurried away, tail between his legs. The other two followed behind, their arms laden with the rest of the gear, their expressions strained.

As soon as they were gone, Emily looked sadly at Daniel. "Why didn't you tell me you were engaged before?" she said, her voice dripping with hurt.

Daniel rubbed his forehead with his palm and sighed deeply. "Please, can we not start with this again?"

"With what?"

"With this whole jealous streak you have!" Daniel shot back. "I have a past just like you. I've had serious relationships just like you have. I don't grill you about Ben every five minutes."

"Because you know he exists!" Emily shot back. She was suddenly incensed. Instead of feeling sorry for herself over yet another one of Daniel's failed communications, she suddenly felt furious with his attitude.

"You know Astrid exists," Daniel shot back.

"I do now. But only because your friends brought her up. And you would never have told me you proposed to her of your own volition. That's what I'm upset about, Daniel. The secrets. The hiding."

"I proposed to her. Yeah. Big deal," Daniel replied. "I was young. I thought I was in love. I thought I'd found The One. That's what kids do when they fall in love for the first time, isn't it? Any relationship that lasts longer than a month seems like a big deal."

"Don't try and downplay this," Emily fired back at him. "You wanted to marry her. You were going to commit to her forever!"

Daniel returned her glare. It seemed to Emily as though he'd lost all patience with this particular topic of conversation. His complete lack of empathy was making Emily feel even worse.

"What do you want me to tell you, huh?" he said. "I was bowled over by her beauty. That's what I thought love was about, finding a hot girl."

"Yeah, I noticed how attractive she is," Emily replied. "Thanks for hammering that particular point home."

Daniel sighed with exasperation. "I can already tell there's nothing I can say to calm you down."

Emily could feel herself growing more and more incensed. The two had fought before but this time felt different, worse. Usually Daniel seemed upset to know his actions had hurt her and would attempt to make it up to her. But this time it felt like he'd had enough of it, enough of her. The thought made her panic.

"How about you don't keep secrets from me in the first place?" she cried. "First Sheila, now Astrid! Daniel, how many more women are there I need to be watching out for?"

She hadn't wanted to lash out, but Daniel's attitude was causing her to panic.

"Watching out for?" Daniel scoffed. "What does that even mean? They're not wild animals. They don't bite."

"It's the lying I can't stand."

"I'm not lying!" Daniel shouted back. "I don't like thinking about the past, you know that. I hate dwelling on things. And to tell you the truth, I'm embarrassed about getting engaged at such a young age. It was a mistake. It was a relief when she broke it off with me."

Emily bit down on her trembling lip. So Astrid was the one who ended things, not Daniel? It wasn't even his decision. Somehow that made it even worse.

"How do I know you won't be saying that about me one day?" she stammered. "That I was a mistake. That you didn't realize what love was supposed to be like."

"How can you think that?" Daniel asked, exasperated.

"Because that's what you do, right? Make mistakes with women. Astrid. Sheila. Then you walk away without telling them where you're going."

Daniel looked stung by the comment. "Astrid broke up with me," he said firmly. "She had no right to know where I was. I didn't owe her an explanation about leaving Maine. We fell out of touch. That's just what happens."

Emily folded her arms. "I don't know if I can believe you. Because with Sheila you broke up with her, walked out without telling her where you were going. And you walked out on your friends, too. Do you notice a pattern here, because I certainly do. Why should I expect it to have been any different with Astrid?" Her voice lowered to a mumble. "Why should I expect it to be any different with me?"

Daniel gave Emily a withering look. "Because people can change. I know I have. We all make mistakes and we all deserve a chance to make up for it. I thought you of all people knew that."

"What does that mean?"

"Your dad, Emily. You've forgiven him. He hurt you in the worst way and you've let him back in. You're giving him a chance to change."

Emily felt the tightness in her chest loosen. Daniel's words were getting through to her. All she'd needed from him was reassurance but instead he'd acted defensively. She tried to look at it from his perspective, to feel like he was always being reminded of his past mistakes, having them dragged up and being judged for them. It must be exasperating for him.

Her anger faded. Instead, she now felt guilty. Ashamed.

"It doesn't have to be like this," she explained. "If you were just more honest with me I wouldn't have to fill in the blanks."

"I know," he said, relenting finally. His body sagged against the hood of his car. "But bringing that stuff up is hard for me. I'd prefer those things to stay in the past."

"It never does," Emily reminded him softly. "And if I'm going to find things out, I'd prefer to hear them from you. Not your friends. Not your exes turning up on my porch steps."

Daniel nodded. He looked up at her with hopeful eyes. Finally, he looked like Daniel again, like her Daniel. "So am I forgiven?"

Emily nodded. "If I am."

Daniel shook his head. "You don't need to apologize. It's not hard to see why those gaps in my history upset you. What with everything that happened with your dad."

Emily knew he was trying to be diplomatic. And while it was true that she often projected her fears over what happened with Roy into her current relationship, she didn't want to keep using that an excuse. At some point she needed to take responsibility for the jealous streak that kept rearing its head. It wasn't fair to him for her to keep dragging up painful parts of his past and using it against him.

"I shouldn't take that out on you," Emily said, sadly. "Not like that, anyway."

Daniel opened his arms for her, and this time she fell into them. They squeezed each other tightly.

"It's okay," he said. "I just hope one day you'll learn to trust me."

"I will," she said, "as long as you don't lose patience with me."

The Daniel she needed was back. His calmness and understanding were what made everything okay. She didn't always feel like she deserved his patience so when he gave it to her it felt almost therapeutic.

"Can we start this again?" Daniel said then. "Do it properly?"

Emily moved out of his embrace and frowned. "Huh?"

"Imagine I've just arrived back from the trip." He smiled. "And you're not mad at me."

"Uh... okay," Emily said. "Welcome home."

"I'm so glad to see you, babe," Daniel said. Then he grabbed her hand tightly. "I have a surprise for you."

Emily was shocked. "You do? It's not a dead elk, is it?"

Daniel laughed. "Nope. Something else. Something I was working on for a while and trying to find the right time to give it to you. I missed you so much while I was away I decided the time to show it to you was the second I got back."

"Oh," Emily said, stunned. She felt like she didn't deserve a surprise after the way she'd greeted Daniel on his return. "I'm not sure if now's a good time, though. I don't know if I deserve it."

Daniel rolled his eyes affectionately. "Of course you do! Come on. Don't beat yourself up. That fight is over. Let me show you this. Please." He smiled encouragingly.

Emily could help it. She smiled in return and felt a spark of excitement inside of her. "Okay!"

Daniel, immediately animated, tugged her by the hand. "This way!"

*

Daniel drove Emily in his pickup truck all the way into town and down the cul-de-sac where Jack Cooper's woodwork shop was located. Emily wondered what kind of surprise Daniel could have in store for her that would be in the woodshop. It must be something handcrafted.

They parked and Daniel strolled up to the steel shutters, rapping his knuckles against them. Emily got out and shut the passenger side door, then joined Daniel at his side as the shutters rattled open. The sound of spinning blades and radio music grew louder. The air was dusty with the fine particles of sawn wood, the smell of which Emily loved.

As the cloudiness dispersed, Emily could make out the figure of Jack Cooper standing before her, wearing dark blue coveralls and a white mask over his mouth. He pulled back the mask.

"Daniel, how's it going?" he asked. He shook his employee's hand. Then to Emily he added, "Emily, nice to see you. What are you doing here?"

"You tell me," Emily replied, laughing. "Daniel has some kind of surprise for me."

"Ohhh," Jack said, casting a knowing expression in Daniel's direction. "The top-secret wedding gift Daniel's been working on. It's taken him weeks. Glad I'm going to get to see the big reveal!"

Emily nodded, realizing she was a bag of nerves. Daniel liked to surprise her with romantic dates and wonderful gifts like the diamond necklace, but this was the first thing he'd actually crafted for her, the first time he'd physically created a gift for her. She was excited for the reveal, but also overwhelmed by the whole thing. Just moments ago she'd been accusing Daniel of all hosts of things and now he was going to surprise her with some thoughtful, romantic, handcrafted gift. She couldn't help but feel like she just didn't deserve it.

Daniel took her by the hand and led her through the dusty workshop, past a series of intimidating large saws and cutting machines. Some of the goods they were working on stood dotted around the place—a bed frame, a large banquet-sized dining table, and, to Emily's delight, a giant chess set. She marveled at the talent the men and women who worked here possessed, proud that Daniel was amongst them.

Finally, Daniel stopped in a shadowy corner where a grubby white dust sheet covered up a bulky object, rectangular and hip height. Seeing it made Emily shiver with a mixture of excitement and nerves.

Daniel smiled at her. "Just to warn you, there is no hidden message with this gift. No persuasion intended."

Emily frowned. "Intriguing."

"So don't freak out," Daniel added.

"You do realize," Emily said with a chuckle, "that telling someone not to freak out is the thing that makes them freak out."

Daniel laughed and Emily heard the hint of nerves in it. She wondered what on earth could be beneath the sheet that would require qualification from Daniel and cause him such anxiety.

He took the corner of the sheet and pulled it back in one large flourish. Fine particles of dust flew up into the air, clouding Emily's vision. But as they cleared, revealing the handcrafted item, Emily gasped and found tears springing into her eyes.

Standing before her was a beautiful wooden crib, a baby's rocking bassinet. It was painted a glossy white color.

"No pressure or anything," Daniel quickly said. "It's just for the future. When we're ready. Do you like it?"

Emily turned to him, her breath stuck in her lungs with surprise. She couldn't speak, and hoped only that the glittering tears in her eyes communicated to Daniel what her voice was failing to.

"I love it," she finally gasped.

She turned back to it, touching the wood with her fingers, and gave it a little push. It rocked smoothly back and forth.

"I still need to get a mattress for it," Daniel said beside her. "And I was thinking of stenciling on some designs at a later date."

Emily was speechless. Typical of Daniel to express what he wanted not through words but through action, through something solid, physical. He had never sat her down and said he wanted children with her, they'd never discussed it fully, and Emily had always wondered. But here was the physical proof that he wanted the same things she did, their own child, their own family. How stupid she had been to ever doubt that.

She turned and threw her arms around his neck. "Daniel, I can't believe you did this for me. For us. It's amazing."

Daniel blushed and accepted the torrent of kisses Emily bestowed on him. Then Emily realized that Jack had wandered over, clearly intrigue to see what it was that Daniel had created to cause such a reaction.

"Oh my," he said, his eyes widening. "Emily, are you—"

"No!" Emily quickly interrupted. "But I hope to be one day." She smiled.

Jack raised his eyebrows. "As long as you wait until the honeymoon," he quipped.

Emily and Daniel laughed.

Jack walked away, giving them their privacy once again. Daniel turned to Emily.

"Speaking of honeymoons," he began, "I have another surprise for you."

Emily's eyes widened. There was no way Daniel could top the bassinet and all it signified.

Daniel cleared his throat. "I've booked our honeymoon."

"You have?" Emily exclaimed. There'd been so many things to organize at such short notice the honeymoon had fallen by the wayside. Emily wasn't even certain whether she'd want one since leaving Chantelle was so difficult. She'd just assumed they'd leave it for a year or two before thinking about what to do. "Well, what is it? Where are we going?" She could hardly contain her excitement.

"I'm keeping it a secret."

"That's not fair! At least tell me *when* we're going."

"The day after the wedding."

"Are you kidding?" she cried, grabbing Daniel's hands with excitement. "Right away?"

He nodded. "For two weeks. Is that okay?"

Emily couldn't contain her excitement and gratitude anymore. She leaped into Daniel's arms. Laughing, he spun her round in a circle before setting her down on her feet and kissing her deeply.

93

When they moved apart from the kiss, however, Emily was struck by sudden worry.

"What about Chantelle?" she said. "Two weeks is a really long time for us to be away from her."

"I was worried about that too," Daniel confessed. "Which is why I asked Roy whether he would be okay to stay on a little longer to be with her."

"You did?" Emily said, surprised. "What did he say?"

"He said he'd love to."

Emily smiled, grateful her father was back in her life and willing to step up for her when she needed him. But she still wanted to speak to Chantelle about it, to hear it from the horse's mouth that she would be okay with them gone for so long.

As they headed home, Emily felt overwhelmed with love. All her suspicions were for nothing. Daniel had been working so hard on the crib to surprise her with, and at the same time he'd been secretly planning their honeymoon. She felt so guilty for ever doubting him. When exactly was she going to accept that she could trust him?

CHAPTER THIRTEEN

Easter

As the family congregated in the kitchen for Easter breakfast, they decided the weather was nice enough to eat outside. They carried plates, bowls, jugs of juice and milk, and mugs of coffee out to the table on the porch.

"Hey, look!" Chantelle exclaimed as they got outside.

Emily saw she was pointing at something in the distance. Chantelle placed her items on the table and rushed over to the base of one of the trees. She picked something up and returned, holding it out to them, beaming. It was an egg. Someone had placed it in the long grass growing beneath the tree.

"An Easter egg?" Daniel said, looking over at Emily. "Did you put that there?"

Emily shook her head. "It wasn't me." Then she looked in turn at Roy. "Did you do this, Dad?"

He nodded, smiling shyly. "There are twenty hidden around the grounds," he explained to Chantelle. Then he held out a small wicker basket for her. "You can put them in here."

"Thank you, Papa Roy!" Chantelle exclaimed, clutching the cute basket by the handle before pelting off on her hunt.

Emily was thrilled and delighted that her father had gone to so much effort for Chantelle. It always made her so happy to see Chantelle in high spirits but this time there was the added bonus of her father being the instigator.

"You didn't have to go to all this effort," Daniel said, clapping Roy on the shoulder with gratitude.

Roy blushed and brushed away the comment in his slightly self-conscious way.

"I'm just glad I have someone to spoil," he said.

They all watched and snapped pictures of Chantelle as she raced around the yard at lightning speed, her basket swinging as she went. In typical Chantelle fashion, she threw herself into the activity, reaching beneath prickly hedges, kneeling in the muddy grass in order to peer into the flower patches, and shaking the branches of trees in order to quickly dislodge any eggs that may have been hidden. By the time she'd collected all twenty eggs, she looked an utter mess!

"Now that you've found them all," Roy said as Chantelle placed the basket upon the picnic table, "we can paint them."

He led the family around the back of the house where he'd set out some pots of dyes to dip the eggs in, as well as some paints and brushes so they could add designs. Emily was amazed by the effort he'd put into making this occasion special for Chantelle. And it was very typical of him to keep it secret!

Chantelle dipped each of the eggs carefully, turning them an array of pinks, blues, oranges and greens, then set them out to dry.

"While they're drying, I thought you might like to try some of this," Roy said, producing a large Tupperware box and unclipping the lid. Inside sat a beautiful cake with white frosting and chocolate eggs all around the edges.

"Did you make it, Papa Roy?" Chantelle asked, her eyes widening.

Roy nodded. "With some help from Parker," he added.

Emily grinned, and reminded herself to thank the young chef the moment she saw him next.

Roy cut them each a slice of cake, placing them on napkins he'd also brought along with him, then poured them each a glass of cloudy apple juice.

"This is fantastic, Roy," Daniel said, wiping the crumbs from his stubble. "The picnic, the painting, the egg hunt. Truly."

Roy looked pleased with himself in his shy and dignified manner.

With the eggs now dry, everyone got to work painting them with squiggly lines and polka dots, targets and funny faces. Emily couldn't remember the last time she'd felt so happy and carefree. It reminded her of the Easters of her past which had often been joyous affairs.

"Are we going to do fun stuff like this every day when Emily and Daddy are on their honeymoon?" Chantelle asked Roy.

"If you want to," Roy said, chuckling.

"I was meaning to speak to you two about that," Emily said. She looked at Chantelle. "If you're worried about us being away you can say so. We can change our plans if you need us to."

Chantelle looked perplexed. "Why would I be worried?" she said, innocently, as though she'd quite forgotten she'd ever had a meltdown because of her abandonment issues. "Me and Papa Roy will have so much fun. We're going to work on the greenhouse mostly."

"Okay," Emily said, "but Papa Roy has to leave before we come back. Which means there'll be a whole weekend when Serena will be in charge of looking after you."

"That will be fine too," Chantelle said, rolling her eyes as if Emily was making a fuss over nothing. "Serena can bring Owen over for singing lessons. I'll get Parker to make my favorite spaghetti dinner. Yvonne will probably let Bailey come over for a sleepover."

Emily laughed at the way Chantelle was acting, like a mini organized Amy!

"I believe," Roy said, looking up from his painting, "that Chantelle thinks there will be nothing to worry about at all."

Emily looked at Daniel. "I guess we're all good then for this mystery honeymoon!"

Daniel grinned to himself.

"Emily, I was wondering," Roy said, pausing once again midway through his painting, "if you wouldn't mind accompanying me on a trip this afternoon."

Emily frowned inquisitively and placed her paintbrush down. "Oh? That sounds intriguing."

Roy smiled. "I just haven't spent much time with you and I wanted to get you something. A gift."

"I'm not going to say no to a present, am I?" Emily laughed.

Two decades had passed without her receiving gifts or cards on her birthdays, or Christmases and Thanksgivings. She wanted her father to have the opportunity to make up for it.

They packed up their breakfast items and painting supplies. Waving goodbye to Daniel and Chantelle, Emily and Roy got into her car. Then they headed into town.

"You do know most things for the wedding are organized now," Emily explained as she drove through the streets.

"Oh yes," Roy said. "You don't have to accept my gifts if you don't want them."

Emily looked across at him in the passenger seats and raised an eyebrow. "Gifts? Plural?"

Roy chuckled and pressed a finger to his lips.

He instructed her to park the car in a lot. They got out, and he gestured for her to walk down the sidewalk, his hand lightly touching her back to guide her.

"This is very intriguing," Emily said, smiling.

She allowed Roy to direct her towards a glass-fronted store. He pulled the door open and a bell tinkled overhead.

Emily looked around and saw that the shop was filled with unique gift items made of copper and wood, haberdashery, and other random trinkets. It seemed very much like the sort of store her father would like. She wondered what they were doing there.

Roy walked up to the counter and greeted the man who stood behind it. "We spoke on the phone earlier," he explained. "Roy Mitchell. I'm here to collect the favors for my daughter's wedding."

"Oh, Dad," Emily said, rushing forward and taking him by the arm. "I don't want you spending money on favors. There are so many guests. Amy was going to give everyone a scented candle from her business."

"I thought as much," Roy said. "But I was hoping you might allow me to add a little something extra as well. Since I'm not paying for the wedding I'd like to contribute in some small way."

Emily chewed her lip in consternation. Of all the things he could contribute, wedding favors could be one of the more costly! But she wanted to honor him, as the father of the bride.

The man behind the counter disappeared into a storeroom out the back and came back with a bulging garbage sack. Emily frowned, puzzled, growing curious.

Roy grinned as the man placed the bag on the counter and opened it up. Peering inside, he explained, "Just perfect! How much do I owe you?"

"Please, no charge," the man replied. "I'm happy for you to take them off my hands."

"Really?" Roy said, grinning even more widely. He shook hands with the clerk. "Thank you kindly!"

He heaved the sack off the counter and began leading Emily out of the store. She looked over at the store clerk. He gave Emily an expression she read to be sympathetic. Her curiosity turned to concern.

"What's in there, Dad?" Emily asked.

As he pulled the door open and went out into the street, Roy was grinning broadly. Emily couldn't help but feel like he'd misjudged his attempts to help out with the wedding.

"They won't be much to look at just yet," he said finally, setting the bag down on the ground.

He pulled open the top. A salty seaweed smell wafted out. Emily looked inside at what appeared to be shards of wood.

"I don't understand," she told her father.

"Like I said," he replied, "not much to look at just yet. But this wood is from one of the old boats down at the harbor. I'm going to whittle a keepsake for each of the guests, a plaque of sorts, with the name of the inn burnished into it."

Emily gasped. It was the perfect way for her dad to contribute, to use his talents as a tinkerer, to repurpose something old and turn it into something new, using material that came from the harbor and represented them so well.

"That will be so much work," she said. "How will you find the time?"

"I've been making these sorts of things for years," Roy replied. "I can get them done quicker than you'd expect. So, what do you say? Can I make some wedding favors?"

Emily threw her arms around his neck. "Yes!" she cried. "Thank you!"

*

Not wanting their outing to end yet, Emily and Roy decided to get lunch out. Emily drove them to a cute Mexican tapas place she'd been wanting to try, thankful that most businesses in this tourist town were open on Easter, and they each ordered several dishes so they could share and sample a bit of everything.

"It's nice," Roy said as he took a mouthful of bite-sized taco. "But not the same as real authentic Mexican tapas."

"You've been to Mexico?" Emily asked, curiously.

"Ah yes," Roy said, smiling coyly. "I suppose you wouldn't know about some of my more interesting excursions. I did a lot of traveling before I settled."

Emily shifted in her seat, a little uncomfortable that he was bringing up the past, touching on those difficult years during which they'd been separated. On the other hand, she was curious to know more about what he'd been up to for all those years.

"Where else did you go?" she asked, leaning on her elbow. "I'm not that well traveled at all."

"I've seen almost every country in Europe now, most of South America. I've been to Australia, New Zealand, Papua New Guinea."

Emily's eyes widened. She couldn't quite picture the humble watchmaker and antiques collector in all those exciting locations. She thought about Daniel's surprise honeymoon plans and wondered whether any of those exotic locations could be where they were heading.

"I spent a brief time in Bali but I had an encounter with a giant python and got the first flight out of there."

Emily gasped. "What kind of encounter?"

"I was on a hike," Roy said. He placed a bite-sized piece of tapas into his mouth and swallowed it with a grin. "It slithered across the toes of my boots."

Emily squealed, exhilarated by the story. Roy chuckled.

"So what about you?" Roy asked. "Any adventures abroad?"

"Not really," Emily replied. "I became a bit of a homebody. I didn't leave New York City that often. In fact, I hadn't left it for at least two years before I came here. I didn't have the confidence."

Roy looked a little uncomfortable that she'd brought that up. Emily knew it would be slightly touchy to remind Roy that his actions had caused her such great anxiety. But she also knew that honesty was necessary for them to fully heal.

"Do you blame me for that?" Roy asked, his voice strained.

"Yes," Emily confessed. "And Mom. And my boyfriend at the time. No one seemed to bolster me or tell me I could achieve things. It was easier not to try."

Roy looked sadly down at his plate. "I'm so sorry for my role in that. I wish I could have been there to tell you how amazing you are. I'm so proud of you, Emily. Of the woman you've become. In spite of me."

Emily felt herself choking up. "It's not in spite of you, Dad," she said. "It's because of you. Everything good about me has come from you. I mean, look at the inn. I would never have found myself if it hadn't been for that place."

"You know, I always intended for you to have it," Roy explained. "I rather foolishly thought that you'd return sooner, as soon as you'd left your mother's home, to be honest."

"You mean right after college?" Emily asked, surprised.

He nodded. It shocked her to think that Roy had wanted her to move out so young. It also hurt to think about how different things could have turned out if she'd been brave enough to leave when she'd been twenty-one, rather than returning back to her mother's home after college to have the woman erode her confidence more and more with each day that passed. She would have found Roy's clues so much sooner. Perhaps she'd have even seen him on one of his covert trips to the inn. Plus, she would have met Daniel so much younger. They'd probably be already married with their own family.

But what was the point of lamenting a past that never existed? If things had gone the way her dad had planned, Chantelle would never have been a part of her life. Maybe the hardships had been necessary to mold her into the person she now was, a person she was finally proud of, who was finally making her way in the world and finding her strength.

Emily reached out and patted Roy's hand. "Dad, I think the way things worked out in the end is okay. I'm all right with it."

He looked into her eyes and smiled. It seemed as if he had finally accepted that she'd forgiven him. And Emily, realizing it to be true, felt closer to her father at that moment in time than she ever had before. There was no point on dwelling on the past or holding onto guilt, not when they had the rest of their lives to look forward to together.

*

Emily felt happier than ever on the drive home. The lunch had been cathartic. She now felt that having her father back was better than she'd even imagined it could be. Everything felt so right.

But as she turned into the driveway and headed toward the house, Emily noticed a car in the lot that was painfully familiar to her. She swallowed the lump in her throat at the discovery of the unwelcome visitor who had arrived while they'd been out, the last person she wanted to see, the only person who could ruin the tranquility she and her father had finally found.

Roy squinted through the windshield. "Is that who I think it is?" he said.

Emily squeezed the steering wheel and gritted her teeth. "Yup. It's her." Then she turned a pained glance toward her father, wishing desperately she didn't have to confirm the reunion they'd both been expecting and dreading. "It's Mom."

CHAPTER FOURTEEN

Emily's stomach clenched with terror and dread as she looked upon the scene before her, of her mother and father, together in the same space for the first time in dozens of years.

"So it's true," Patricia growled, her gaze fixed on Roy. "You really did have the audacity to come back."

"It was time to make amends," Roy replied in a quiet, considered voice. "To Emily Jane. To you. I'm truly sorry for the hurt I caused you over the years."

Patricia barked out a laugh. "If you really were sorry you'd have gotten in touch with me to let me know you were back, instead of running here to score points with our daughter. To get her on your side first."

"Making amends with Emily Jane before her wedding was my priority," Roy tried to explain. "I thought you and I would have a chance to speak at a later date."

But Patricia interrupted him. "I can't hear this," she stammered. "It's always excuses with you. Excuse after excuse after excuse. You have no idea what it was like for me, for the both of us, not knowing where you were!"

Roy stood there, taking the brunt of Patricia's words, accepting his punishment. Emily felt for her father. Despite the damage his past decisions had caused, she had accepted that he wasn't in his right mind back then. She didn't feel like he should have to apologize for the rest of his life for it. And she didn't want her mom dragging her into her side of the argument.

"Dad and I have made our peace," Emily said firmly. "Leave me out of this."

"What did you think would happen?" Patricia demanded, turning to her daughter. "That after all these years everyone could play happy families? That I would just be able to forgive him?"

"I've forgiven him," Emily pressed. "So why not?"

"He deserted you!" Patricia exclaimed. "He walked out on us both!"

Emily faltered. She didn't want to be reminded of those painful years. It felt like her mom was rubbing it in her face. All Emily wanted was to heal and move on. Patricia, on the other hand, seemed determined to stay in the past, bitter and angry.

"I'm ready to move forward," Emily said. "I'm not going to cling onto the past anymore, or dwell on those miseries."

"You have a short memory, my dear." Patricia sneered at Emily. "And you're quick to forgive. He tore our family apart because he couldn't cope with his guilt at letting Charlotte die."

"That wasn't his fault," Emily cried.

"He was drunk!" Patricia yelled back. "He was supposed to be supervising her but he fell into another one of his drunken stupors!"

"That wasn't what happened and you know it," Emily snapped. "You're twisting the truth and I won't take it anymore. I've heard his side of the story now, Mom. You don't have a monopoly on that anymore. No one is to blame. Not him, not me, not you. It was an accident. Finding someone to blame won't bring Charlotte back to life."

Patricia's face was red with anger. She looked more furious than Emily had ever seen her. She flicked her gaze to Roy.

"Lucky for you our daughter's naive," she said. Then to Emily, she added, "Don't come crawling to me when he hurts you again, when he ups and leaves and breaks your heart. Because he will."

Emily shook her head, disgusted with her mother's words. Just because Roy had rejected Patricia didn't mean he was going to reject Emily as well. He had fallen out of love with her mother but she knew that he had never stopped loving her, that he never would.

She felt Roy's hand squeezing her arm and looked into his reassuring eyes.

"I won't ever leave you," he assured her firmly, in his quiet, dignified manner. "I'm not disappearing like that again. I promise."

"I know," Emily said with a nod.

She wasn't about to let her mom ruin the peace she had finally found with her dad. There wasn't a single thing in the world Patricia could say to her to break the bond she'd finally managed to forge with him.

Patricia looked at them both, an expression of distaste on her face. She scoffed, clearly disgusted by the sight before her, of father and daughter reunited, everything forgiven and forgotten.

"I've had enough of this," she bellowed. "You two deserve each other. I'm wiping my hands clean of you both."

Then she turned and stormed to her car. She sped off, kicking up gravel in her haste to get away.

As soon as she was gone, Emily felt tears coming. Her eyes welled up.

"Let's get you inside," Roy said to Emily, drawing an arm around her shoulder.

Together, they went inside.

Patricia's appearance had rattled Emily more than she'd thought possible. Sitting on the couch in the living room, Emily quickly found herself weeping bitter tears of frustration and hurt. Her father attempted to console her by pouring them each a brandy.

"She holds worse grudges than anyone I know," Emily said as he set the drink on the coffee table before her. "Did I tell you how furious she was with me when I left New York City to come here? I've been here over a year and she still isn't over it!"

Roy seated himself opposite Emily. "I'm not surprised she would be angry about that. She hated this place. And I understand why. I bought it as a way to begin disengaging from her, to get my space, my own assets. She knew it was the beginning of a betrayal before even I did."

Emily frowned at her father. "How can you stand up for her? After everything she just said?"

Roy took a long sip of his brandy. "I'm not standing up for her," he explained gently. "I'm just old enough and wise enough now to have empathy for her, to see things from her point of view. I hurt her deeply. I broke her trust. I wasn't the man I promised I would be at the altar."

"Is that an excuse?"

He shook his head. "Not an excuse. But an explanation."

He stood and came and joined her on the couch, wrapping his arms reassuringly around her. Emily snuggled into him. Her father had such a calming presence, such a gentle voice, she couldn't help but be soothed by his words. She wished more than ever that he'd been there during those difficult years with her mom.

"I put your mother through a lot before you and Charlotte were born as well," Roy added. "I wasn't a patient man in my past. I wanted everything too quickly, children, a house. She was a wild party animal when I met her, and thanks to me, your mom had to grow up too soon."

Emily considered his words. Her mother had never really taken to parenthood. She wasn't cuddly or affectionate, never had been, but was instead the sort of mother who paraded her children around like prizes. She couldn't imagine her mom being persuaded into anything, not marriage, nor children.

"You shouldn't blame yourself for the way she turned out," Emily told her father.

Her tears still fell softly down her cheeks and Roy wiped them away with his thumbs.

"I was never the right man for her," he explained. "I never treated her with the respect she deserved, as a wife and a mother. So I do blame myself for that. And I should."

Emily wanted to refute it but saw little point. Roy seemed to have become a glutton for punishment, filled with guilt and shame over his past actions.

Just then, Daniel came in carrying a tray of tea. He set it down on the coffee table and gave Emily a caring glance.

"I heard about your mom," he said, softly. "Do you want to talk?"

Roy picked up a tea and stood. "I'll give you some time," he said.

He left and Emily transferred herself to Daniel's side, taking his consolation instead.

"Promise me we won't make my parents' mistakes," Emily said.

Daniel shook his head. "We won't. I won't ever walk out on you like that."

She held onto him tightly, feeling closer to him than ever.

"I suppose we can safely conclude that my mom isn't going to come around and decide to come to the wedding," Emily said, glumly. In spite of everything, she still wished that Patricia was the cuddly mom she desperately craved.

"No," Daniel agreed. "But maybe this will cheer you up."

"Oh?"

"My aunt Eugenia got in touch earlier. She said she's going to come to the wedding."

Emily looked at him and frowned. "You have an aunt? Which side?"

"She's my mom's half sister. She's much older. And way nicer."

Emily laughed, pleased to learn that Aunt Eugenia wasn't like Cassie. She didn't think she could cope with a third unstable female in her life.

"We haven't been in touch for quite a while," Daniel explained. "She and my mom were never that close. But she used to live locally so I would escape there sometimes when things were too much at home. She was always really nice to me, even when I was acting out. She had a lot of patience."

"She moved away?"

"Sadly, yes," Daniel explained. "And Mom being Mom took it as an insult and refused to pass on any of her contact details. I tracked her down thanks to social media."

"Well, that's great," Emily said, smiling. She was a little apprehensive about meeting a member of Daniel's family. They hadn't exactly proven themselves to be affable so far, but she had only met his mom, and she was as crazy as they came.

"You'll really like her," Daniel added, as though picking up on Emily's nerves. "I promise you. She's the kindest most patient woman in the world. Nothing like my mom, or yours."

For the first time since hearing the news, Emily started to feel excited about meeting this long-lost aunt. After the display she'd just witnessed from her own mom, the thought of a new friendly female mother figure appearing in her life seemed very appealing. Perhaps Aunt Eugenia could fill that gap in her life.

CHAPTER FIFTEEN

Emily kissed Daniel softly on the lips and shut the pickup truck door behind him. She waved as Evan turned on the engine and drove Daniel away, with Stu and Clyde accompanying them. It was the day before the wedding and Daniel, as promised, was going to stay away. George had agreed to put up the four friends.

Emily herself had some last-minute errands to run, so she left Chantelle in Roy's care and the inn in the care of her capable staff, then headed into town with Amy and Jayne. Both were in full frantic mode trying to get the final things sorted for the wedding, ears latched to their cells phones, talking at a million miles a second.

If this is what they're like at work, I'm glad I turned down that job offer! Emily thought from the back seat of Amy's car.

Amy parked outside Raj's garden center, and the three friends piled inside to see how the bouquets and table arrangements were looking. Emily hadn't even finished hugging Raj hello when Amy began listing demands.

"Em, would you prefer this arrangement with a dusty pink flower rather than baby pink?" she said, peering at one of the table arrangements. "I thought the pink would be a bit more muted. This is more garish than I wanted. And the white is more ivory than eggshell, you know. It's just a bit off."

"We can change it," Raj said accommodatingly.

Emily shook her head. "Raj, as far as I'm concerned, pink is pink. White is white. Amy's just a perfectionist."

Amy was still frowning. "Babe, are you sure? This is your wedding. You deserve everything to be perfect."

"Everything *is* perfect," Emily assured her. "Having the flowers arranged by one of my dearest friends is my idea of perfect." She smiled at Raj.

"Fine," Amy said, narrowing her eyes slightly suspiciously. She looked at Raj. "What time will you be over to set up?"

"Seven a.m. sharp," he replied with a nod of the head, conjuring up the image of a soldier answering his drill sergeant. Emily got the distinct impression that Amy had asked him that question more than once over the telephone.

With everything in place regarding the flowers, they piled back into the car and drove to Maggie's bridal store to collect all the dresses. For the first time, Emily got to see the finished dress with all the champagne-colored, diamond-encrusted roses flowing down the train. The sight took her breath away.

"It's incredible," she gasped.

"We should do a final fitting to make sure we don't need to do any last-minute adjustments," Maggie said.

Emily agreed and with Maggie and Amy's help began to change into her dress.

"Are you excited?" Maggie asked as she began lacing up the bustier at the back.

Emily sucked in, feeling the tug as her waist was cinched in. "Right now I'm just nervous."

In the background she could hear Jayne on her cell phone talking to all the various people who needed to deliver things tomorrow, double checking—in some cases triple checking—that everything was going to run smoothly. *You don't run a successful business without being a little bit demanding*, Emily thought.

Luckily, there were no adjustments needed to the dress, so they packed it back away and left.

On the way out, the friends bumped into two men who were on their way in. One was George, the other was a man Emily had not met before.

"George, what are you doing here?" Emily said, hugging him.

"Is that George as in Daniel's friend who he's staying with?" Amy demanded. "Daniel isn't waiting in your car, is he?" She looked about her, trying to conceal Emily in case Daniel was around to spy on them.

George laughed and shook his head. "I'm just here to collect the tuxes," he explained with a grin. "And taking my brother out to lunch. Emily, have you met Harry before?"

Emily shook her head. Jayne barged her way forward, her eyes gleaming with excitement.

"We haven't met either. I'm Jayne. One of the bridesmaids." She held her hand out like royalty for both men to shake. They did, with slightly bemused expressions on their faces.

Emily quickly introduced them to Amy, and they all parted ways to complete their various tasks.

Once they'd gone, Jayne whispered to Emily. "They were so gorgeous! That's the kind of friend I was expecting Daniel to have. Why didn't he pick them as best men instead of those ugly guys?"

"I suppose George has a good body from his work," Emily confessed. "And Harry had a nice face. Boyish."

"He reminded me a bit of Fraser," Jayne said then, referring to Amy's ex fiancé. "But less rich looking, you know, not quite as boringly *perfect*. What did you think, Amy?"

Emily and Jayne turned to face Amy, who had been very quiet. They discovered their friend had turned somewhat pink.

"I guess he has the same kind of tall, dark, smiley thing going on," she mumbled, averting her gaze.

Jayne laughed. "Oh my God, Amy just admitted to finding a Sunset Harbor man attractive!"

Emily couldn't stop herself from mocking Amy too. "I thought you hated this town," she teased. "And said the people here were dull."

"So? I can be flexible in my opinions," Amy replied defensively. "And I never bashed it as much as Jayne did."

It was clear to Emily that Amy was feeling rattled. It wasn't often her friend lost her cool like this.

"Oh, I hate the *town*," Jayne quipped. "But I've never had a problem with the hunks here. They're certainly attractive enough for a fling. And you know dull isn't a turn-off as far as I'm concerned. Hey, Em, make sure you put in a good word with George about me. Maybe you could set Amy up with Harry as well and we can double date!"

Amy went a deeper shade of pink. Emily never saw her like this. In fact, Amy's no-nonsense approach to dating had only been interrupted by Fraser and that had ended disastrously. Maybe it was time for Emily to play matchmaker? After all the work Amy had put into the wedding, finding her a new boyfriend was the least she could do. She felt a twinkle of mischievousness inside her, realizing with delight that she now had a new project, to make Amy fall in love and move to Maine!

CHAPTER SIXTEEN

Back at the inn that afternoon, things were frantic, bustling with activity as everything started coming together for the big day tomorrow. Lois was on shift on the main desk, greeting the guests who began to check in.

A woman Emily didn't recognize came into the foyer.

"I'm here for the wedding," she explained to Lois with a large, affable smile.

She looked to be in her sixties, a little on the chubby side. She had a big, wide smile and bubbly personality.

"Aunt Eugenia?" Emily asked.

The woman turned to her. "Yes. Are you Emily? Oh my, you are a beauty!"

She reached out and hugged Emily tightly against her, then pressed a kiss on each of Emily's cheeks. Emily wondered how Aunt Eugenia and Daniel's own mother could be related; they appeared to be complete polar opposites.

"Thank you," Emily laughed, struggling to catch her breath since she was so firmly crushed against Aunt Eugenia. "I'm really pleased to meet you. Can I show you to your room?"

"Yes, yes, lead the way. Daniel's told me all about your stunning inn!"

Emily took her bags and led Aunt Eugenia up the stairs.

"I'm so glad Daniel's settling down," Aunt Eugenia gushed as they went. "He's had such a hard life. I was worried he might go off the deep end at one point. But he said that he'd been given a second chance from some gentleman in town who encouraged him back to high school."

Emily smiled to herself proudly. "That was my father," she explained.

"Oh!" Aunt Eugenia gasped. "I must shake that man's hand when I meet him."

Emily showed Aunt Eugenia into her room.

"Well, look at this place." The woman gasped again. "It's even nicer than I imagined it would be."

"I hope you'll be comfortable here," Emily said.

Aunt Eugenia bounced onto the bed exuberantly. "I will be quite comfortable, thank you, my dear!"

Emily laughed. "Well, once you've settled yourself, please feel free to come down to the lounge to mingle. I'm probably going to be running around doing my hostess duties but hopefully we'll get a chance to catch up. If not, there'll be a dinner at six."

"Sounds marvelous," Aunt Eugenia said.

Emily left Aunt Eugenia to settle in and headed to the kitchen to find Parker and make sure the dinner he was preparing for all the guests was going according to plan. He seemed excited by his dish.

"It's paella," he said, beaming. "Fresh shrimp."

"You'd better not give my guests food poisoning," Emily warned him jokingly.

"You can trust me," Parker said with mock affront.

Emily laughed and went out into the corridor. More guests had arrived, distant cousins and old friends from New York City. She was so happy to have them all here. She hadn't realized quite how much she had changed when she'd swapped her city life for the one in Sunset Harbor. The only thing missing was Daniel, and she couldn't help but wish Amy hadn't enforced the rules of them not seeing each other the day before the wedding.

As the evening wore on, Emily decided to take a walk around the grounds in an attempt to calm her fluttering nerves. She wondered what Daniel was up to and hoped his friends weren't getting him drunk. It was the sort of prank she could imagine them wanting to play, but George was sensible and hopefully could keep them in check.

As she rounded the corner by Daniel's rosebushes, she noticed a figure in the distance. It was Roman Westbrook. With all the wedding preparations Emily had almost entirely forgotten that a famous pop star was staying at her humble inn! She hoped her staff had been taking good care of him.

"Mr. Westbrook," she said when she was close enough. "I hope everything is okay with your stay here?"

"It is," he said with a smile. "I'm having a relaxing time. The people in this town are very respectful."

"Yes, they are," she agreed, thinking fondly of her own arrival in Sunset Harbor, of the community she'd found here.

"It's a very tranquil place to work on new music," Roman said.

"Oh, is that why you're here?" she asked. She, along with every other woman in the inn, had been curious as to what his purpose was for being in a sleepy town like Sunset Harbor. It would make sense that he'd be here for inspiration. She herself found the tranquility good for creative contemplation.

"Amongst other things," Roman replied with a wink.

Emily wasn't about to pry and find out what those other things might be.

"And you're getting married tomorrow, is that right?" Roman asked.

"What gave it away?" Emily quipped.

The B&B had been a hive of activity ever since Roman had checked in.

"I'm sorry that things haven't been as peaceful as usual here," she added.

Roman shook his head. "Not at all. I've enjoyed watching everything come together. It looks set to be a beautiful ceremony."

"Thank you, I hope it will be."

Just then, Tracey came out into the yard. When she saw Emily talking to Roman she became visibly star-struck. It was a funny sight to behold, considering Tracey carried herself with such calm and grace usually.

"Emily, I was wondering if you and the girls would like to have a yoga class to help you relax for tomorrow?"

"That's a great idea," Emily said.

"Is this women only?" Roman asked. "Or can anyone join in?"

Tracey's eyes widened. "You want… to come?"

Roman nodded eagerly. "I'm a huge fan of yoga and meditation."

"Well, of course! Please do!" Tracey beamed.

They all went inside to where Tracey had set up some mats in the ballroom. All the wedding decorations were in place and it looked beautiful, transformed into a grotto of delight. Amy and Jayne were already in tadasana pose, with their eyes closed, and didn't notice Emily enter with Roman. She wondered what would happen when they both opened their eyes and realized they were exercising with a celebrity!

She settled herself in and Tracey began the class, asking everyone to sit. Emily turned around and raised her eyebrows at Amy and Jayne, whose mouths dropped open when they realized who exactly it was sitting at the front on the fuchsia yoga mat.

As they worked through the poses, Emily felt herself feeling calmer and calmer, more at peace than ever. It had been a very good idea to have the yoga lesson. But they were midway through a sun salutation when Emily found herself become distracted by a strange flash of light coming through the stained glass window. Her first thought was lightning, though it seemed unusual. But when it happened again she realized it was the flash of a bulb. Someone was taking photos through the window!

Emily realized that it must be a journalist or paparazzi type trying to get photos of Roman. She looked around her and saw that luckily everyone else was upside down with their eyes closed. She quickly tiptoed out of the ballroom, then rushed through the corridors and out the front.

Rushing round the corner of the outside of the inn, Emily saw a man dressed in black stretching a large camera above his head through the crack in the open ballroom window.

"Hey!" she hissed. "What are you doing? You're disrespecting my guest's right to privacy. And standing on my rosebush!"

"Are you the owner?" the photographer asked, craning his head to look at her while continuing taking photos.

"Yes," Emily snapped. She stomped toward him and yanked his arm down. "And I'll call the police if you don't stop."

The paparazzi man didn't seem even slightly fazed by her threat. "Look, lady, we all have jobs to do. We're all trying to make money. How about you scratch my back and I'll scratch yours." He took out a notepad and pen. "We pay good cash for an exclusive scoop, you know. So what's the deal with Roman being here? Any signs of him having an affair with a local? What about visiting a secret love child in the area?"

He poised with the pen above the paper, his eyebrows raised expectantly. Emily snatched the book away.

"No scoop," she said. "Mr. Westbrook is my guest and is entitled to his privacy just like everyone else."

The journalist rolled his eyes. "How very admirable you are. But I'll credit your inn in the piece. Put it on the map. What's Mr. Westbrook's privacy worth to you, when advertising the fact he once stayed here will bring fan pilgrimages for years to come?"

Emily glared at him. "I wasn't kidding when I said I'd call the police. I'm sure they'd be very interested in seizing those photos you've illegally taken while trespassing on my property."

The man's expression changed then. "Oh I see, we're going to threaten each other, are we? Fine. I tried going about this the nice way but if you're not going to play ball then I can change tactics. How about you let me leave with my photos and a quote for my article and I *won't* trash your inn in my next piece."

"No deal," Emily barked. "Get lost!"

"Your funeral," the pap said with a shrug. He started to back away, looking as arrogant as ever. "I'll be sure to send you a copy of my critique once it's published. Maybe a hundred copies just in case you lose one."

Emily didn't care about his threats. She watched him, hands on hips, until he'd finally retreated off the property. Then she went back into the ballroom, her nerves on edge, feeling like she needed a relaxing yoga session more than ever.

When she got back, she found Tracey, Amy, Jayne, and Roman sitting on their mats, drinking tea.

"You finished the class?" Emily asked.

"There was an altercation outside," Jayne said. "It was a bit distracting."

Emily blushed. "Oh. You heard that?"

Roman looked up at her from his place on the mat. "I heard it all."

He got up, walked over to her, and, to Emily's shock, gave her a hug.

"No one has ever stood up for me like that," he said, and she could hear in his voice how surprised by it he was, and how much it meant to him. "Even when he threatened to defame your inn and destroy your business, you didn't give me away. I can't tell you how much I admire that, and what that means to me."

He seemed genuinely touched, and Emily blushed again.

"It was my honor to do so," she said. "Your privacy is sacred to me."

Tracey made her a calming cup of chamomile tea and she sat down to join them.

"So how long have you been practicing yoga, Roman?" Tracey asked.

"Since I was a teenager," Roman replied. "I had some difficulties after the death of my mom. Yoga helped calm my mind."

Emily felt a pang of sadness for Roman. She hadn't thought of him much beyond being a rich and famous star. It hadn't occurred to her that he would have faced hardships in his life.

"How old were you when she died?" Emily asked. "If you don't mind my asking."

"Not at all," he said. "It's all in the public realm anyway. Everything about me is. You could google it if you wanted to."

"I wouldn't," Emily said, shaking her head.

Roman looked surprised and somewhat touched. "I was fifteen."

"That's how old Em was when her dad disappeared," Jayne said.

Everyone looked at her for her bluntness and lack of tact in the delicate situation.

"That must have been tough," Roman said to Emily, sounding genuinely concerned.

"It was," Emily replied, feeling herself open up to him and the rest of them in this supportive, calm environment. "It was a while after my sister died. He'd never grieved properly and he just snapped one day, walked out never to be seen again. I didn't know whether he was alive or dead. For twenty years. But he's back in my life now. He'll be walking me down the aisle." She smiled, realizing how far she had come from those old, suffocating emotions that had weighed her down for years.

"That's remarkable," Roman said. "Have you ever thought of writing a memoir? My ex-girlfriend does autobiographies and memoirs. I could give you her number."

Emily was surprised by the offer. "I've got quite a bit on my plate at the moment with the inn to run and the wedding and the adoption."

"Adoption?" Roman asked curiously. He took a sip of his tea, his eyes still on Emily. She felt as if he was genuinely interested in her and her life here. He wasn't what she'd expected him to be at all.

"Yes, Chantelle, the little girl you've seen running about the place." She grinned. "She's Daniel's daughter and I'm trying to officially adopt her."

"Remarkable," Roman said, impressed. "You're like the antithesis of the evil stepmother. And I should know. I had seven of them."

Emily's eyes widened. Beside her Jayne gasped.

"Seven stepmoms?" she cried.

Roman chuckled and nodded. "My dad was a Hollywood film producer way back when. He had a penchant for twenty-year-old actresses, my mom included. Dad left a string of broken hearts behind him. We're close again now but for years we were estranged. When your dad's new wife is younger than you it puts something of a strain on the relationship."

"I think *you* should write the memoir!" Amy said. "Your life's been fascinating."

Roman shrugged. "I would. But my ex started writing one before we broke up. Turns out I accidentally sold the rights to my story to her. Crazy, huh?"

He didn't seem in the least bit concerned about this reality. Emily found herself becoming increasingly comfortable in Roman's company. He was far more down to earth than she'd ever expected, especially for the kid of a Hollywood lothario and one of his string of actress wives. How Roman had his head screwed on so well was beyond Emily.

Emily was thrilled to feel like they'd made a genuine connection that afternoon. By the time they left the ballroom, she wondered if she might just be able to count Roman Westbrook amongst her friends.

*

Later that evening, Emily was sitting at her vanity mirror removing the day's makeup when she heard a soft knock on the door. She turned as the door opened and Chantelle walked in. The little girl was dressed in white pajamas.

"I'm too excited to sleep," she said. "Can I come in here?"

"Of course," Emily said, gesturing to the girl. "But I need my beauty sleep so we can't chat too much. Here, want a face mask?"

Chantelle grinned and rushed over, leaping onto the bed. Emily applied the face mask to her soft skin.

"When you and Daddy are married," Chantelle began as Emily's fingers worked the sticky white goo into her skin, "will you have a baby?"

Emily thought of the crib that Daniel had made for her and wondered. She certainly wanted a family with him one day, but there was still so much going on that now didn't seem like the right time.

"Would you like a brother or sister?" Emily asked.

Chantelle nodded with excitement. "Mommy's having a new baby so I think you should have one too. So is Toby's mommy. It's only fair."

Emily laughed at the child's logic. She wondered whether Chantelle felt sad about the sibling of Sheila's she might never get to know.

"Well, first I need to make you my proper daughter, don't I," Emily explained. "Then maybe we can think about getting you a brother or sister."

"*Sister*," Chantelle explained firmly. "I don't want a brother."

Emily laughed. "You do know that you don't get to choose."

"If it's a brother then you'll have to have another baby," Chantelle told Emily.

"What if that's a boy too?"

"You'll just have to keep having babies until it's a sister!" Chantelle told her, giggling.

Emily liked the idea of having a whole brood of babies with Daniel. But she wondered at her age whether such a dream could ever be a reality. She'd left it late to start a family as it was. She hoped Chantelle's dream could come true, because it was her dream, too.

But hardly had she had the thought, when her stomached suddenly dropped. She could hardly believe it: tomorrow was her wedding day.

CHAPTER SEVENTEEN

Sun streamed in through the window, waking Emily. Beside her in bed, Chantelle was snoring softly. Emily suddenly remembered what day it was and leaped out of bed. It was the day of her wedding!

Her movements woke Chantelle and the little girl sat up, rubbing her eyes sleepily. Then she too must have realized what day it was because she burst into the widest grin Emily had ever seen on her face.

She squealed. "Wedding day!"

Emily nodded, feeling her stomach fluttering with excitement and nerves. She suddenly felt lost, like she couldn't put her thoughts in a row or work out what to do first. Dress? Hair? Makeup? What was first on the agenda?

There was a knock at the door and Emily turned as it opened. In bustled Amy and Jayne, both wearing their hen party fluffy white dressing gowns. Jayne was carrying a tray with coffee, juice, fruit, toast, and hard-boiled eggs on it.

"Morning!" she exclaimed, setting the tray down. "Who's hungry?"

Chantelle licked her lips and took a piece of toast. Emily felt queasy at the thought of breakfast.

"I don't think I can eat anything," she murmured.

"You have to," Amy said, already in fussy hen mode. "At least a banana. We can't have you fainting during the ceremony."

Emily relented and took a banana.

Amy checked her watch. "Okay, we have the hair stylist coming in fifty minutes. The makeup artist half an hour after. Then we'll get you in the dress. Serena, Yvonne, Cynthia, Karen, and Suzanna will be over in about an hour to get into their bridesmaids dresses. I've spoken to Daniel, he is awake and not hung over."

"Good," Emily said, exhaling. She sunk onto the edge of the bed and took a bite of her banana. The morning had only just begun and already she felt exhausted.

"Babe," Jayne said. "Just relax. We've got everything covered. You could literally fall asleep now and wake up transformed."

Emily laughed. "That does sound appealing."

Just then there was another knock. The door opened and in walked Roy.

"I wanted to catch you before all the chaos began," he said. "Is now a good time?"

"Of course," Emily said.

"We need to wash our faces and brush our teeth," Amy said, realizing it would be best to give them a bit of time. She held her hand out to Chantelle. The little girl took it and stood. Then she nudged Jayne. Jayne caught on to what was happening and put her toast down. They hurried out of the room.

Emily put down her half-eaten banana. "What's up?" she asked her father.

"I have something for you," he said. "A gift."

"Another gift?" Emily said, surprised. Her father had already handcrafted all the wedding favors, was taking care of Chantelle while they went on their honeymoon, and done up the greenhouse. There was nothing else he could do for her.

Roy sat on the bed beside Emily and handed her a small box wrapped in floral paper. Emily opened up the paper and saw inside an ornate wooden box. It looked hand-whittled, which Emily suspected her father had done himself.

The box was latched shut with a small bronze hinge. She opened it up and inside saw a gorgeous golden locket lying on a bed of black velvet.

"Dad? What is this?" she gasped, staring at the beautiful necklace.

"I made it," Roy said. "I've been working on it all your life."

Emily stared at him, shocked, feeling tears well in her eyes. "You have?"

Roy nodded. He picked the locket up and held it out to her so she could more clearly see the carved patterns, bits that had been cut away to show beneath the intricate workings of a clock. There was a small dial on the top, like the stopwatch from Alice in Wonderland.

"It looks like a dial to wind it," Roy explained. "But it's actually a secret button."

He pressed it with his thumb and the entire front part of the necklace pinged open. Emily's eyes widened with surprise. Now opened, she could see the cogs ticking away. So the locket was also a working clock! It seemed very apt for her father.

"Now, if you twist this little dial here," Roy added, reaching in and fiddling with a barely visible knob, "then you can open up the secret compartment."

Emily giggled, delighted by the intricacies of her father's gift. The small compartment opened, sliding out like a shallow drawer from the side of the locket. Emily saw that there was a picture inside.

"Charlotte," she stammered, recognizing her sister's face immediately, though the picture itself was unfamiliar to her, faded into sepia hues. "Dad, this is so amazing," Emily said, looking at her father through vision blurred with tears.

"There's a message on the back as well," he explained, flipping the locket over.

Emily read the inscription, recognizing her father's handwriting, knowing he had etched this himself.

My beloved daughter, who holds my whole heart.

Emily allowed the tears to fall in earnest. She threw her arms around her father's neck and held him tightly.

"I'm going to wear this today," she said. "And for the rest of my life."

Roy seemed touched. He helped her affix it around her neck. Emily realized she no longer felt sick with nerves. Now she just felt excited.

"I'd best get my suit on," Roy said.

He left the room. A moment later, Jayne, Amy, and Chantelle filed back in. They were all now dressed, Chantelle with beautiful flowers in her hair and a small wicker basket filled with flower petals.

"You look so adorable!" Emily cried. "You still have a while before the ceremony though. Don't get messy! Or lose those flowers!"

"I won't," Chantelle said. "I'm going to go and practice. Bailey will be here soon so we should practice together."

She hurried off, leaving Emily with her friends.

"You guys look great," Emily said.

The hairdresser arrived and worked Emily's hair into a beautiful updo. Then the makeup artist started working on them all, going from one bridesmaid to the next.

Once her hair and makeup were done, Emily was helped into her dress.

"It's time!" she squealed, more excited than ever.

*

Emily stomach swirled as she stood outside the door to the ballroom, her beautiful bouquet clutched in her hands. Anticipation had made her throat dry.

From the other side of the door, she could hear the sounds of happy chattering. Just a few feet away Daniel would be standing in his tux, waiting for her to enter. The thought of seeing him made

Emily feel weak at the knees. She was grateful for Amy forcing them to spend time apart. It really did make it feel more special.

Just then the sound of piano music cut through the hubbub, causing everyone to fall silent. Debussy's "Clair de Lune."

"Ready, flower girls?" Amy said, looking down at Chantelle and Bailey, who were clutching their baskets filled with petals. They both grinned and walked into the ballroom.

Emily's nerves grew and grew now that the wedding had officially begun. Amy gave Emily a thumbs-up.

"You're doing good," she said.

"I am now," Emily replied through her tensed jaw. "But once you guys go I might faint. Or puke."

Amy rubbed her arm. "You won't do either, babe. You'll do amazing. And that's what the father of the bride is for; to keep you on your feet when you think you might faint!"

Emily looked at Roy beside her. The emotion of having him there was almost too much to bear. Not wanting to become too overwhelmed, she averted her eyes, drawing her attention back to the bridesmaids.

The flower girls' song ended and Owen began playing Chopin's "Nocturne."

Jayne winked. "You'll be fine."

One by one, Emily's friends filed into the ballroom. As they went, they each touched her arm reassuringly or squeezed her hand. Suzanna looked absolutely glowing, her small baby bump on display. Yvonne had managed to tame her ginger hair into a gorgeous updo. There were already tears in Karen's eyes as she wished Emily luck as she passed. Serena, ever the beauty, exuded youth and elegance as she took up the rear.

Then they were gone, leaving Emily and her father standing there. Roy offered her his arm.

"Are you ready?" he asked softly.

Emily looped her arm through his and nodded. "I'm so glad you're here, Dad," she managed to say, though her voice cracked with emotion.

"So am I," he replied. Then with the kindest of smiles, he added, "You look beautiful, my darling."

Emily couldn't find the words to thank him. She just nodded and squeezed her lips together to stop herself from crying. Then her hand flew up to the necklace that her father had given her, touching it as if to reassure herself, knowing that Charlotte was contained safely inside.

"She'll be watching," Roy said with a kind smile. "And she'll be so proud of you."

Emily nodded. Finally she found her voice. "Thank you, Daddy."

Just then the first chords of the wedding march rang out. Emily's heart leapt in her chest. This what it. She was getting married!

Roy squeezed her arm close into him. Then the doors to the ballroom were opened from the inside and Emily got her first glimpse of the ballroom fully decked out. The flower displays were phenomenal, almost double the size of what she'd ordered. They cascaded down the walls, filling the ballroom with a fresh, floral smell. Emily gasped, surprised, knowing that Amy had either twisted Raj's arm or the two had schemed behind her back.

Light streamed in through the stained glass windows, turning the aisle into a glowing rainbow. Emily began the slow ascent through the rows of people, taking in the sight of their friendly faces, their beautiful smiles, their congratulatory expressions. It warmed her heart to be surrounded by such wonderful people. She was thrilled to have them here to witness her special day. It didn't matter to her that Cassie wasn't there, or Patricia, because she had her father and she had her friends. And most of all, she had Daniel.

He stood at the front of the hall facing her beneath the traditional Jewish canopy that represented their home, the inn where they had found each other and themselves in turn. Even from here, she could see the tears rolling down his cheeks. Daniel wasn't much of a crier and it stunned her to see him so openly emotional. She felt choked up in response. But there was a grin on her face that she could feel widening with every step she gained. Daniel, on seeing it, grinned back.

Then finally she was pulling up beside him. Roy offered her hand to Daniel and he took it, gently but firmly. Then Roy kissed Emily on the cheek and moved to the side to take his place. As he went, Emily noticed him wiping his tears away and was overwhelmed by the beauty of the moment.

"You look stunning," Daniel whispered to Emily.

"So do you," she whispered back.

Father Duncan began the ceremony.

"Friends. Family. Thank you for being here on this important day, to witness and celebrate the union between Daniel Morey and Emily Jane Mitchell. It is a human need to love and be loved in return. Indeed, it is the most joyous experience we as humans can ever have. To find one's soul mate is to become complete, for it is once our souls are joined in the union of marriage that we find our strength, courage, and patience. Marriage allows you to expand as individuals and to build as a unit, to create together, to support one another through the trials and tribulations of life."

Emily could feel herself trembling. Daniel, beside her, seemed just as nervous, just as touched by the emotion of the moment. From behind, Emily heard the sound of at least three different people sobbing.

"Marriage is a legal act," Father Duncan said. "It is also a spiritual one. Both Emily and Daniel have chosen their favorite religious passages for you all to hear today, words that define their love for one another, a love that has been blessed by God. If we could please have the first reader."

Emily looked at Daniel, frowning. They hadn't asked people to read the speeches, had they? She'd thought Father Duncan was doing it. But Daniel had a mischievous twinkle in his eye, and she realized this was something he'd planned behind her back. She looked behind to see who was emerging to read the passage and realized to her surprise that it was Chantelle.

Emily gasped with delight. Their sweet, initially shy daughter had grown so confident that she was able to read in front of all these people!

Chantelle stood beside Father Duncan and unfolded her paper. She cleared her throat and began to read Daniel's chosen passage, the Song of Solomon.

"Set me as a seal upon your heart,

as a seal upon your arm;

for love is strong as death,

passion fierce as the grave."

It was the cutest thing Emily had ever seen, and everyone around the hall beamed with delight as Chantelle spoke the words so beautifully and poignantly.

"Many waters cannot quench love,

neither can floods drown it.

If one offered for love

all the wealth of one's house,

it would be utterly scorned."

Chantelle finished and folded up her paper. Everyone applauded the child for her bravery and the flourish with which she'd spoken the words.

As she returned to her seat, Emily looked around, wondering who on earth would be reading the next passage. When she saw that it was Roy standing, her throat constricted with emotion. It was too much; her tears began to flow in earnest.

Standing beside Father Duncan, Roy began to read Emily's chosen passage from Ruth. As his deep voice rumbled through the church, Emily could hear more and more people crying behind her. She couldn't take her eyes off of her father. This moment was too beautiful. Too perfect.

When he was finished, he returned to his place. Emily was destroyed. She wiped her tears away and fanned her face, the people behind her giving little chuckles.

Father Duncan continued the service.

"Marriage is more than signatures on a contract. Marriage is about love. Love that is not momentary, not fleeting, but that lasts for eternity. Love that never dies." He turned to look at Daniel. "Please take Emily's hand."

Daniel did as instructed. Emily felt that he was trembling. She looked into his eyes, unable to take her own off him during this amazing moment.

"Daniel, if you could repeat after me," Father Duncan said. "I do solemnly declare…"

"I do solemnly declare…" His voice cracked.

"That I, Daniel Morey, do take this woman, Emily Jane Mitchell…"

"That I, Daniel Morey, do take this woman, Emily Jane Mitchell…"

"To love and to hold…"

"To love and to hold…"

"In sickness and in health…"

"In sickness and in health…"

"'Til death do us part…"

"'Til death do us part."

Daniel slipped Emily's ring halfway onto her finger.

"Daniel Morey, will you take Emily Jane Mitchell to be your lawfully wedded wife?"

"I will."

Daniel pushed the ring all the way onto Emily's finger. Her heart leapt into her throat. She'd never felt happier in all her life.

Father Duncan addressed Emily next. She repeated the vows, finding her voice strong and stable rather than nervous and trembling as she'd expected, because she realized this was exactly what she was supposed to be doing. She had no doubt, not even an ounce.

"Emily Jane Mitchell, will you take Daniel Morey to be your lawfully wedded husband?" Father Duncan asked.

"I will," Emily said, feeling her grin stretch across her face.

She slid Daniel's ring all the way onto his finger.

"Which leaves just one thing for me to do," Father Duncan said with a kind smile. "I now pronounce you husband and wife. You may kiss the bride."

Daniel gently took Emily's face in his hands. She rose onto her tiptoes. He kissed her deeply, sumptuously, lingeringly. It was the most beautiful kiss they had ever shared.

From behind them came the roar of applause. Emily laughed, pulling back from Daniel and facing all their friends and family.

"We did it!" she cried at Daniel, clutching his hand in hers.

"One more thing," Daniel said.

Chantelle rushed out then with a glass champagne flute and placed it in front of Daniel. He raised his foot and smashed it. Emily laughed, delighted and pleased they'd included it in the ceremony, seeing how much it meant to Daniel.

Then they walked down the aisle to the rapturous sounds of applause, hand in hand, both beaming from ear to ear, ready to begin their lives as husband and wife.

CHAPTER EIGHTEEN

"Cocktails!" Amy exclaimed.

She ushered everyone out of the ballroom and into the speakeasy where Alec was on duty behind the bar.

Emily went to get a drink when Amy swirled up to her.

"Not you, I'm afraid," she said. "It's time for your photo shoot."

Emily set the drink down and went out into the garden with Daniel to take their wedding portraits. It was a gorgeous spring day as they posed in several locations in the garden and the outbuildings, on the porch and swing. Emily could see her guests through the window in the speakeasy, drinking merrily, some watching the photo shoot. Emily felt like a rock star.

Once the couples pictures were done, Amy directed the group shots, sending out combinations of people, taking a cocktail glass out of Aunt Eugenia's hand. They posed for several shots with Chantelle, then added Roy to the group, then Aunt Eugenia as the closest thing to family Daniel had present.

Then there were photos with all the bridesmaids in a row, looking sexy in their slinky dresses, then hugging Emily supportively. Then the photographer went up to one of the guest rooms to take a photo out the window of the whole wedding party. Next, she took pictures of Emily lying in the arms of Daniel and his groomsmen, something she took to without dismay. Finally, it was time for the photographer to snap just the three best men—which would be them lifting Daniel into the air on a chair, which Emily thought was very apt—so she took the opportunity to scurry inside and grab that drink.

But she'd hardly made it into the speakeasy when she heard Amy's bellowing cry of, "Cake!"

Alec gave her an amused look as she picked up her heavy dress with a sigh and headed back to the ballroom.

Throngs of people filed in through the inn for the cake. Now it was more than just the guests who'd been at the ceremony; the evening reception guests were starting to arrive. Amongst them Emily spotted Bertha and Birk, Rico, the Bradshaws, Anne Maroney. Even Gus was there! Emily was delighted to see them all, greeting as many as she possibly could, promising to catch up with them later.

Back in the ballroom, Emily saw that a table had been set up with tons of gifts piled onto it. Emily couldn't believe how many presents there were, and felt overwhelmed by the generosity of her friends and family.

She went over to the table where the cake had been placed. Daniel joined her by her side. She held the knife, and he wrapped his hands around hers.

Together, they made their first cut in the cake. Cameras flashed all around them.

Emily took a small piece and held it up for Daniel to eat. But as he opened his mouth, she shoved the cake into his face, making frosting squirt all over his face. Everyone cheered.

Daniel laughed, wiping away the cream and crumbs. When Emily wasn't looking he grabbed another and smeared it all over her face. Emily squealed but everyone else laughed and clapped.

"My makeup!" she exclaimed as she wiped away the muck with a cloth.

"You look gorgeous," Daniel assured her.

Amy nodded in agreement. "I made sure the makeup artists used the strongest waterproof, weatherproof stuff available on the market. I knew there would be tears and cake smearing on the cards!"

"You're the best," Emily said. "You know that, right?"

"I know," Amy grinned. "Now, time for the first dance!"

Everyone crowded around in a big circle as Emily and Daniel took to the center of the room. They'd chosen "At Last" by Etta James for their first dance.

The lights dimmed except for a spotlight that shone on them and the refracted light from the stained glass windows.

"Would the young maiden be so kind as to accompany me in a dance?" Daniel said to Emily.

She laughed and wrapped her arms around him, feeling closer than ever. His heart beat to the same rhythm as hers. It was a beautiful moment.

Then the music changed and other couples began to seep onto the dance floor. Emily felt a tap on her shoulder. She turned and saw her father.

"May I take this dance?" Roy asked Daniel.

"Of course," Daniel said, offering Emily's hand to Roy.

Daniel went over to Aunt Eugenia, dragging her laughing onto the dance floor to be his new partner.

Emily clutched onto her father, feeling protected and loved more than any other point in her life.

"I'm married," she squealed excitedly. "And you were there to give me away. It's like a dream come true."

Roy clutched her tightly. "It was the proudest moment of my life. And I'll always be there for you, from this day forward. I love you more than anything in the world."

"I love you too," Emily choked.

They danced together silently for the rest of the song. When they broke apart, Emily saw that a table of champagne flutes had been set up. It was time for Roy's speech. He went over and picked up a glass, tinkling it with a fork to get everyone's attention. The room fell silent.

"Good evening, ladies and gentlemen," Roy began. "Old friends and new friends alike. For those who haven't yet met me, I'm Roy, Emily Jane's father. You might be able to tell, since I'm the one she inherited her beauty from."

Everyone laughed. Roy continued.

"May I start by saying what a fantastic day it has been. Truly. So thank you, Amy, for arranging so much of the day and making sure it ran smoothly."

Everyone clapped and Amy took a little curtsey.

"Now, onto the mushy stuff," Roy said. "No father wants to accept that their little girl has grown up or to give her away. But I couldn't think of a better man to be marrying my beautiful daughter. Daniel is such an asset to our family. He makes Emily Jane smile in a way I've never witnessed before. In his presence, she glows even brighter than the star that she is. His daughter, Chantelle, brings joy to every moment of every day. I'm thrilled to know they are now officially family. So if you could now raise a glass to Daniel, Emily Jane, and Chantelle!"

Everyone cheered and took a sip. Emily gestured for Roy to join her and as he did, she hugged him tightly. Chantelle pushed through the crowd as well and hugged her Papa Roy tightly. It was a beautiful moment, all of them together, united as a true family. Emily realized then there was just one thing missing to make it official and legal; Chantelle's full adoption. Things had been a bit quiet recently since their attorney had served the paperwork to Sheila. The ball was in her court. Emily just prayed that she'd see sense and sign Chantelle's parental rights over to her. Once that was done they would truly be a real family and Emily would feel complete at last.

*

The night wore on. There were so many guests people were spilling into the lounge, the dining room, and out onto the porch.

Alec continued serving his expertly created cocktails in the speakeasy. Owen resumed playing live music, this time accompanied by a full jazz band, with Serena perching on one of the couches nearby watching him with a loving expression.

Just then, Emily saw Stu, Evan, and Clyde approaching her. She tensed. They hadn't done anything to embarrass her so far and had seemed on their best behavior. But maybe that was all about to change!

They surrounded Emily. She looked up and gulped.

"What's going on?" she said, her voice a squeak.

It was Stu who spoke. He looked a little shy.

"We wanted to thank you," he said.

Emily frowned. That wasn't what she'd been expecting to hear. "Thank me? What for?"

"For making Danny Boy happy," he said. "I've never seen him like this."

"You've brought us all back together as well," Evan added. "I know we can be a bit rowdy so it means a lot that you accepted us."

Emily felt guilty thinking about just how much she'd *not* accepted them and all the judgments she'd made about them.

"So we got you something," Clyde said. "As a token of our appreciation."

"Oh!" Emily said, surprised.

Clyde handed her a gift and she took it, feeling a little stunned and also nervous about what sort of gift these three would deem appropriate for her. It was probably something crass, like lingerie.

"You didn't have to do this," she said.

They all looked at her eagerly and Emily realized they were expecting her to open the gift right now in front of them. She'd have to feign gratitude.

She unwrapped the gift slowly. But to her great surprise (and relief) the gift wasn't crass lingerie. It was a leather-bound book, an antique.

"*Alice in Wonderland?*" she gasped, looking at the gold-embossed letters on the cover.

"Dan said you liked to read," Stu said, shrugging. "And that you're into antique things."

"I am," Emily gasped, stunned by the gesture.

"We found it on eBay," Clyde added. "It's illustrated."

None of the three men seemed to even realize how thoughtful the gift they'd gotten her truly was. She jumped up and hugged Stu, then Evan, then Clyde. They looked shocked by her outpouring of emotion.

129

"This is just so touching, guys," she gushed.

Emily accepted then that she'd have to adjust her opinion on the three of them. They were soft at heart after all, their exteriors merely macho acts.

Just then, Emily got an even greater surprise when someone sauntered into the living room whom she hadn't formally invited. Roman Westbrook!

Everyone who didn't know the famous star was staying at the inn looked stunned as he waltzed in and kissed Emily on the cheeks.

"Congrats on the wedding," he said. "Mind if I sing a song?"

"Are you kidding!?" Emily exclaimed.

She could hardly believe it. People would pay millions to have Roman sing a song at their wedding.

She watched as Roman went over to the band, their expressions utterly star-struck, and took the microphone. Emily was impressed by the way Owen managed to keep his cool despite the surreality of the fact he'd found himself unexpectedly accompanying a famous singer.

Everyone was so excited and invigorated by Roman's appearance that they began dancing enthusiastically. The mood was jubilant and it made Emily so happy to see such joy and fun taking place in her Inn.

The main singer of the jazz band took the opportunity of a break in the set to approach Emily.

"I've been usurped," he joked.

"I'm sorry!" Emily replied. "I didn't know that was going to happen."

"No need to apologize," the singer laughed. "It's not every day you get bumped because of a famous singer. How did you make friends with him?"

Emily widened her eyes. "I don't know if friend is the right word. He's a guest at the inn at the moment. I never in a million years expected him to turn up! I mean we had a yoga class together which was fun but you'd think he'd have better things to do with his time!"

The singer laughed. "So I was wondering how you'd feel about this becoming a regular thing? The speakeasy is fantastic so the venue fits perfectly with the music we play."

Emily's heart jumped. She was amazed at how her inn was transforming. To have a professional jazz band perform here would be beyond her wildest dreams.

"That would be amazing," Emily replied. "When would you want to play?"

"How about every weekend throughout the summer? It would be great for us to get exposure for more weddings."

Emily was thrilled. "I'd love that!" she exclaimed.

Roman Westbrook finished his song and everyone erupted into cheers. He offered the microphone back to the jazz band's singer, who went back up on the stage and resumed his singing.

Roman approached Emily. "Those guys are fantastic," he said.

Emily reddened.

"I can't thank you enough," she said. "You've helped make this the greatest day of my life."

He smiled, reached in, and hugged her.

"It is I who has to thank you," he said. "Besides, after all, what are friends for?"

He turned and walked away, and Emily felt her heart swell with joy and appreciation at his use of the word friend. And she realized in that moment that he was right: as crazy as it sounded, they were friends now. *Real* friends.

And she had a feeling they would be friends for life.

*

It wasn't until the early hours of the morning that Daniel and Emily retired to bed. They both flopped down, exhausted but equally elated with how the day had gone. Everything felt perfect.

Daniel stroked Emily's face lightly, the simple silver band on his finger glinting in the dim dawn light.

"We're not going to get hardly any sleep, are we?" Emily laughed. "We're leaving for the honeymoon at eight, right?"

Daniel looked at the clock. It was 4 a.m.

"If I have my way, you won't be getting any sleep between now and then," he said with a sultry growl.

Emily giggled. "When do I get to find out where we're going?"

Daniel just smiled. "In four hours."

Emily rolled her eyes. "Fine."

The Daniel leaned in and kissed her, deeply and passionately.

"I love you, wife," he said.

"I love you too, husband," Emily replied.

Then Daniel slowly began to unlace Emily's bodice. She shivered with pleasure and delight, feeling more connected to Daniel than ever before, excited for the next four hours, and for the rest of their lives together.

CHAPTER NINETEEN

Emily woke the next morning after nearly no sleep at all. But her tiredness could not dampen her spirits. She was riding the high of being a married woman! It was like waking from one marvelous dream straight into another one.

As she lay in bed, her mind replayed some of the best moments of the wedding; her dad's speech, Chantelle's reading, Roman singing with the jazz band, her first dance with Daniel. In her mind's eye she could still see the light from the stained glass windows, Raj's cascading flowers, the glittering diamonds on her dress. She could smell the bespoke perfume Amy had created for her, taste Alec's sugary mojitos on her lips. Her head buzzed with memories, every one of her senses brought alive by the beautiful flashbacks.

The bustling coming from downstairs made her sit up. She could hear the sounds of clinking chinaware that told her breakfast was being prepared. The smell of coffee seeped under the door.

Emily remembered that today she was going on her surprise honeymoon. She sprung out of bed, waking Daniel in her excitement.

"What's the time?" he murmured.

"Seven," Emily replied. "How long do I have to pack? Come to think of it, what do I need to pack?"

Daniel just smiled knowingly. "Don't worry about that, it's all taken care of."

"Taken care of? How?"

"Amy, of course."

Emily laughed and shook her head. "Amy knows where I'm going?" she asked. "And she packed for me?"

Daniel nodded. "It's all part of the stress-free wedding package you ordered, remember?"

Emily laughed again. "When did you find the time for all this scheming?" she joked.

She took a quick shower and dried her hair in front of the vanity mirror.

"What's the weather going to be like?" she asked Daniel, who was now up and dressing himself for the day.

"Not telling."

"But I need to know what to wear while traveling. If we're going on a long flight I'd like to know so I can dress comfortably.

And if it's going to be colder than here when we land I'll need a sweater. If warmer then I can bring a strappy top to change into."

Daniel just looked at her, his finger pressed to his lip. Realizing he was going to keep mum, Emily dressed simply in jeans and a white shirt.

"Well? How's this?" she asked.

"Fine," Daniel replied.

"Fine isn't very reassuring," Emily said. "Do I need to put on sunscreen? What about shoes? Is this a sneakers kind of trip or sandals?"

Daniel just kept quiet and Emily accepted that he wasn't going to let her in on the secret.

"Fine," she said with a sigh. "But if it turns out that I'm completely inappropriately dressed I will be spending my first day as your wife in a very bad mood."

"I'll take the risk," Daniel said with a laugh.

As they went downstairs together, Emily smelled the strong odor of cleaning products. To her surprise, the inn was completely clean, spick and span and shining.

"When did Marnie and Vanessa find the time to do this?" she said, amazed.

The inn had been in a state when she went to bed. Both Marnie and Vanessa were inebriated and dancing on the couch together, singing cheesy eighties songs very loudly. Emily had gone to bed expecting to wake up to a complete mess.

Just then, Amy swirled out of the kitchen. "I brought in cleaning contractors," she explained the second she saw Emily's confused expression. "Their company is called the Magic Elves because they send a whole army of cleaners in the middle of the night and get everything cleaned within one hour. Isn't that just darling? You should use them again."

Emily's eyes were wide with surprise. Amy was like superwoman sometimes.

"When did you find the time to organize that?" she asked, amazed.

"Babe, I've trained myself to live off no more than five hours' sleep a night," Amy explained nonchalantly. "That extra couple of hours is essential for getting life admin done. Now, do you want some coffee?"

Emily just nodded, somewhat dazed by the fact that Amy was running at a hundred percent so early in the morning when she herself felt rather fuzzy-headed and more than a little worse for wear.

In the dining room, Emily was surprised to find a whole buffet of food set out. Parker and Matthew were there, waiting.

"What's all this?" she gasped.

"You'll need fuel for the day ahead," Parker explained.

He made up a plate of food and handed it to her. Matthew poured her coffee.

"This is crazy," Emily said, taking their offering.

Amy whisked her toward the ballroom. As she ducked inside, Emily was greeted by the sounds of clapping and cheering. All of her guests were awake and waiting for her! An array of cute tables had been set out in the style of a Parisian cafe. Yet more amazing floral arrangements adorned the tables and walls.

Emily felt delighted that Amy had arranged yet another surprise for her. The wedding really had been so special and it didn't look like the fun was over just yet.

"This is so fantastic!" she cried, hugging Amy tightly.

Emily sat at the head table with Daniel, Roy, Aunt Eugenia, and Chantelle and they began to eat their breakfast.

"I'm not sure if I got the chance to tell you how beautiful you looked last night, Emily," Aunt Eugenia said.

"You did." Emily smiled. "About fifty times."

"That must have been after the second cocktail," Aunt Eugenia chuckled. "You can't blame me for having forgotten."

"Second, third, or maybe fourth," Roy quipped.

Everyone laughed merrily.

"That bartender of yours is fantastic," Aunt Eugenia continued. "If I was thirty years younger I'd try to get his phone number."

"Actually…" Emily said. "You did try to."

Everyone's laughter turned into roars and exclamations. Aunt Eugenia shook from laughing so hard.

"Oh my!" she gasped, her face pink.

The wedding photographer came over and took some snaps of them sharing their happy moment, before heading off to get more of the other guests for their collection. Emily felt so happy that Amy had arranged such an awesome first morning for her.

Once the food was consumed, Amy stood.

"Okay, everyone," she announced. "Let's escort the happy couple to their honeymoon."

Emily saw then that this had all been planned meticulously, and perhaps even rehearsed without her knowing, because within seconds everyone was swarming around her. They herded her through the inn and out onto the porch steps where she discovered her packed suitcases waiting for her.

The whole thing was so delightful, Emily couldn't help but grin from ear to ear.

She looked around, expecting to see a cab waiting to whisk her and Daniel away. When she realized there was none she was struck by a sudden fear.

"Oh God, please don't tell me you've got a helicopter," Emily said to Amy, feeling immediately daunted.

Amy laughed and shook her head. "No! Nothing quite as lavish as that."

Emily let out a breath of relief. "Good. I don't think I could take a surprise like that. So…" She looked around. "Now what?"

"You have to walk with us," Amy explained.

Giving in to her bemusement, Emily walked along with the huge crowd of wedding guests, down the drive and across the street. Yvonne pulled her luggage along for her. Chantelle beamed with excitement, hopping and skipping, clutching Emily's hand and grinning.

They filed down the small path that led to the beach and strolled across the sand, heading for the harbor. With every step, Emily grew more excited.

They walked all the way to the yacht club, where a banner proclaiming "JUST MARRIED" flapped in the breeze. And, covered in ribbons, was a beautiful, sparkling yacht.

It dawned on Emily what was happening.

"This isn't for us, is it?" she gasped, looking at Daniel.

He wiggled his eyebrows and grinned. "Courtesy of Roy's old friend Gus."

Emily looked over at the two men standing side by side looking mischievous, Gus in his crisp white suit and cane, Roy looking scruffier in brown corduroy. They didn't look like they'd be friends, but Roy was so affable he seemed able to get on with anybody and it didn't surprise Emily to learn that they were.

"Where are we going?" Emily asked Daniel, her voice little more than an excited whisper.

"Martha's Vineyard," he said.

"Are you kidding?" Emily squealed.

The island was an infamous vacation spot for artists and politicians. She'd never thought in a million years she'd be honeymooning in such a luxurious place.

Daniel shook his head. This wasn't a joke.

"But how?" Emily said under her breath. "We can't afford this."

Daniel winked then. "A friend of yours managed to pull a few strings."

"Which friend?" Emily said, glancing around at the crowd of people.

Then she realized who it was that Daniel was referring to. Roman Westbrook! She spotted him standing next to Aunt Eugenia with his usual swagger, hands in pockets, but she hadn't even noticed him before. Emily couldn't believe how well he'd integrated into her group of friends and family. It really felt like he was part of the gang now, just another old friend she'd invited to the wedding.

"We'll be spending a few nights at a hotel in Edgartown," Daniel explained. "Right on the harbor. Then some on the yacht."

"Don't worry, it's heated," Gus interjected. "This is my most luxurious boat. You'll be very comfortable during the chilly evenings."

"I just don't know what to say," Emily gushed. "This is amazing. A fairytale. A dream come true."

"You'd better get on board then!" Gus exclaimed.

Overjoyed, Emily took it in turns to say goodbye and thank you to each of her friends. She even hugged Stu, Clyde, and Evan, whom she'd actually come to like over the few days they'd been guests at the inn. When it was time to say goodbye to Aunt Eugenia, she gave her the biggest, warmest hug. Emily was so happy to have met the woman and was looking forward to the future when she would get to know her better.

Then she hugged Amy and Jayne.

"It's been so great having you here," she told them. "I can't believe you'll be back in New York City by the time I get home. It won't be the same without you."

"We'll miss you, Em!" they said in unison.

Then Roy came over and Emily realized with a shock like electricity that the same would be true for him, that when she came back to the inn he wouldn't be there anymore.

"Which house will you be in," she asked him, taking his hands, "if I need to get in touch? Greece or Cornwall?"

"I haven't decided yet," he said. "But I will make sure you can get in touch with me. I might even invest in one of those devices you young people carry, the ones that can connect to the World Wide Web."

Despite her upset, Emily laughed. "You mean a cell phone?" she teased, wiping away her tears.

Joking aside, Roy placed both his hands on her shoulders and looked deeply into her eyes.

"We will see each other soon," he assured her. "I want you, Daniel, and Chantelle to come and vacation with me. Would you do that?"

Emily nodded, and felt a trickle of tears fall from her eyes. "Of course! I'd love to, Dad. I want to be part of your life as much as possible."

Roy pulled her into an embrace. "You will be, my darling. There'll be no more distance between us, ever. I promise you."

He released her and stepped back, allowing Chantelle to squeeze forward. She had Mogsy and Rain on leashes and the dogs leapt up at Emily to say goodbye, licking her hands. Then Emily looked at Chantelle with tender love.

"You'll be okay, sweetie," she said. "Me and Daddy will be home before you know it."

"I'll miss you," Chantelle said.

Daniel came over and swept Chantelle up into his arms, squeezing her tightly. "We'll call you every day."

"Twice," Chantelle corrected. "Once to say good morning, and once to say goodnight."

Daniel nodded in agreement. "Twice a day."

Then he set her back on her feet.

He took Emily's hand and together they boarded the yacht. Leaving Emily on the deck to wave goodbye to their friends and family, he went off to the cabin to start the boat up.

The engine thrummed and the boat began to slowly drift away from the jetty. Looking back at the harbor, Emily saw the whole group of her friends and family. She felt overwhelmed with love and appreciation. How lucky she was to have these people in her life. She blew kisses and waved, a smile stretching widely on her face.

Wind streamed through her hair as they pulled further and further away from the harbor. Just then, a banner unfurled from the back of the boat. Emily squealed with delight as she read the words CONGRATULATIONS MR. AND MRS. MOREY. Seeing it in print made her finally realize what name she wanted, what person she wanted to be. Daniel's wife. Mrs. Morey.

CHAPTER TWENTY

The ocean was calm, the sky clear. On the deck of the yacht, Emily lay on the sun lounger, her bare arms exposed, soaking up as much vitamin D as she could on the not-especially warm day. She felt completely at peace as the boat cut through the waves. Everything was so quiet out here, so tranquil.

At around midday, Edgartown's harbor appeared on the horizon and Emily went to the cabin to see Daniel.

"Well, hello, captain," she said. She kissed him. "Have we reached our final destination?"

"We have indeed," Daniel confirmed. He looked out the window at the approaching harbor. "And it looks like we've got the place to ourselves."

Emily saw then that the dock was almost completely devoid of boats. They must be arriving out of season. On one hand that meant their chances of spotting a celebrity had drastically diminished, but on the other hand it meant that they would have more solitude, quiet, and privacy for just the two of them.

Daniel maneuvered the yacht into the harbor. It was a very beautiful location and they moored up right beside the large, fancy-looking hotel that they would be staying in.

"I hope we have one of the rooms with a balcony overlooking the ocean," Emily said, gazing up at the hotel.

Daniel carried their luggage off of the boat and they walked the short distance from the harbor to the hotel. Once inside, Emily was floored. The foyer alone was like a palace. There was a large, sweeping wooden staircase that split in two different directions at the top, with a lush red carpet running up the middle. A large chandelier hung from the ceiling.

The lady behind the desk smiled at them warmly. "May I help?"

"We have a reservation," Emily said. "Mr. and Mrs. Morey."

Introducing herself by her new name for the first time made Emily feel tingly all over. She loved the feel of it coming from her mouth.

The woman tapped into her computer. "Mr. Westbrook's guests?" she said, a twinkle in her eye. She checked them in and handed them a key. "You're in our bridal suite."

Emily looked at Daniel. "The suite?" she stammered.

In her own inn, the bridal suite was far more expensive than any of the other rooms. In a place like this, though, somewhere so exquisitely luxurious, surely it would be absurdly expensive. She took a guess at $1,000 a night. It felt far too excessive. Emily was so used to spending money on practical things that to be so spoiled so thoroughly made her a little uncomfortable. Roman had been absurdly generous considering they didn't know each other that well. Thanks to him and Gus—and Daniel for orchestrating the whole thing—this really was going to be a once in a lifetime experience, a vacation she would cherish for the rest of her life.

Daniel and Emily were shown to the suite. It was phenomenal. Not only was it large enough for a separate bedroom, living room, and restroom, but the decor was exquisite. The walls were a crisp white, and a large gray stone fireplace was set in one wall. The beech-colored polished wooden floorboards were accentuated with rugs, fluffy and charcoal-colored. In the living room there were armchairs made of tan leather, and a large bookcase stocked with novels and guides to the local area. Emily counted four floor-to-ceiling windows letting in bright, beautiful light. In the bedroom there was an enormous white four-poster, with beautiful white muslin curtains around it that blew in the breeze coming through the large French windows.

Emily went out onto the balcony and saw that they had the view she wanted, of the harbor and the gorgeous twinkling ocean stretching on for miles and miles.

"Shall we go check out the town?" Daniel asked.

Emily agreed and they left the hotel hand in hand, to stroll along the sidewalk into town. There was hardly anyone around. But the place was stunning. The buildings were gorgeous. There were shrubs and trees everywhere, and spring flowers in bloom, surrounding them with bright, bold colors. At this time of year, many of the shops were closed. It reminded Emily of Sunset Harbor in the winter, when all the tourists were gone and only the stores that the locals needed stayed open. But there was a patisserie selling pastries, cakes, and freshly baked loaves, a coffee shop (something that was essential for Emily!), and a cute store selling handmade items like woolen scarves and bespoke jewelry pieces. Emily bought several things for Chantelle, including a cute sparkly headband and a figurine of a cat.

After an hour of gently strolling around Edgartown, Daniel yawned deeply.

"Want to head back for a nap?" Emily asked.

It had been a very long few days and neither had had anywhere near enough sleep. Plus they were here to relax and what better place to do it than in their gorgeous, luscious apartment at the hotel!

*

Once they got back to the hotel, Emily and Daniel both immediately fell asleep. After a very long nap they woke to discover that it was nighttime.

"We'd better wish Chantelle goodnight," Emily said, seeing that the time was fast approaching her bedtime. "We promised, after all."

Daniel used the hotel phone to call the inn. Serena answered.

"You just missed her," Serena said when he asked after Chantelle. "She and Papa Roy fell asleep on the couch watching TV. I put her to bed."

"What about Papa Roy?" Daniel joked.

Serena laughed. "He's old enough to put himself to bed."

Daniel looked over at Emily. "Chantelle's already asleep," he told her.

"Oh, I hope she won't be mad at us," Emily replied. "Tell Serena we'll call first thing in the morning."

Daniel relayed the message and ended the call with Serena. He placed the phone back on the receiver and looked at Emily. "I'm starving. We should eat."

"Will there be any restaurants open in town?" Emily asked.

"Good point," Daniel said. He checked the map of local amenities that had been left in their room for them. "There are a few but they all close before nine during the spring season." He put the folded map down and grinned at her. "I guess we're having room service!"

Emily took the news with good humor, though it wasn't quite what she'd had in mind for her first honeymoon dinner. As Daniel called reception and ordered, she tried not to think about how ridiculously overpriced it would be to get room service in a hotel like this.

When they heard the knock on the door, Daniel leapt up and opened it. A waiter wheeled in a tray with a silver dish on it, just like the types in fancy restaurants. When he removed the lid, Emily saw it had been hiding a huge cheesy pizza. From the shelf beneath the trolley he produced a bottle of cola and a basket of fries.

As soon as the waiter left, Emily started laughing.

"What is this?" she said to Daniel, hands on hips. "Another one of your surprises?"

Daniel nodded. "I thought it would be nice to have a relaxing first night eating pizza, watching a movie. Take some time to chill."

After the hectic wedding and their lives in general, Emily could certainly get behind some chill time.

"Okay, but we're not going to make a habit of this," she warned Daniel. "Greasy pizza in bed is hardly sexy."

"The bed part is," Daniel said, winking.

They snuggled up together under the duvet, eating pizza, drinking soda, and watching a comedy movie. Emily felt like a teenager, giddy with love.

Once the pizza was all gone and the credits of the movie were rolling, Daniel held his hand out for Emily.

"Come with me," he said.

Emily took his hand, a thrill of excitement running through her as Daniel led her into the bathroom. She was surprised to see it covered in rose petals. When she turned around to exclaim her shock to Daniel, he had disappeared. He reemerged a moment later, holding a bucket of ice with a bottle of champagne inside, and two champagne flutes.

Emily squealed with delight. "Okay, this is definitely a step up from pizza in bed!"

Daniel ran a bath for them, filling it with so many bubbles it was practically overflowing. There were warm jets inside, making it halfway between a bath and a Jacuzzi.

They sunk into the steaming water together, and Daniel popped the cork of the champagne bottle. Then he poured them both a glass.

"To my beautiful wife," he said, clinking his glass against hers.

Emily smiled and took a sip. The champagne tasted amazing. It was clearly a very expensive bottle.

They lounged together in the bath, letting the warm water soak their muscles and the champagne relax them even more. Emily reflected on the wonderful whirlwind of life, of the changes that had led her to this place. Despite the hardships she'd faced, she wouldn't change a single one of them now, knowing they had brought her to this perfect place and this perfect moment.

Once their bath was over, Daniel wrapped Emily up in a towel. He brushed her hair and then carried her to the bed, laying her out against the crisp white sheets.

Emily looked up at him, overwhelmed with love. She reached out and wrapped her arms around her neck, pulling him closer to her so that their bodies could merge.

CHAPTER TWENTY ONE

The next morning they ate a continental breakfast in the hotel's dining room. Emily's head felt a little sore from all the late nights and she sipped her black coffee slowly, rubbing her temples.

"I thought we could do an island tour today," Daniel said, pouring himself a glass of freshly squeezed orange juice.

"Do you mean like a coastal tour in the yacht?" she asked.

Daniel laughed. "Not quite."

"Well, what do you mean?" Emily asked.

"You'll see."

They finished eating and Daniel led Emily outside to where a moped was parked in the lot.

"I rented this," he said, patting the handlebars.

Emily gasped with excitement. She loved riding on the back of a bike with Daniel. The thought of doing so brought back many happy memories of when they were first dating.

"Come on," Daniel said, handing her a helmet.

She hopped onto the bike and Daniel kicked it to life. They whizzed out of the lot and onto the open roads. With her arms clasped around Daniel's waist, Emily marveled at the breath-taking scenery.

Their first stop was a quaint fishing village filled with boutiques and Victorian townhouses.

"Looks like they're having a farmer's market," Emily called to Daniel.

He rode them to where the stalls were set up. Emily went straight to the fresh seafood stall.

"Would you like to sample anything?" the gentleman manning the stall asked her.

"What would you recommend?" she asked.

He gestured to the fried clams. Emily put one in her mouth.

"That's amazing!" she gushed, feeling like her whole body was melting with joy. "Daniel, you have to try this."

Daniel sampled some of the local fried clams and let out an exclamation of pleasure.

"If you like that," the market stall owner said, "may I suggest you try this? Smoked bluefish."

Emily's eyes widened greedily as she took a forkful of the dish. It was just as exquisite as the first.

"Are you folks on your honeymoon?" the market man said, noticing Emily's wedding ring.

Emily's mouth was still full so she nodded.

"In which case, you ought to treat yourself to a bottle of our finest Chilean wine."

Daniel gave Emily a look and shrugged. It certainly seemed like a good idea. They bought the wine, as well as several more bottles the man recommended to them. Then they got back onto the moped and headed off to the next village.

Here, it was filled with quaint pastel-colored Carpenter Gothic–style cottages. Emily thought it looked like a place from a storybook.

Daniel slowed the bike and he and Emily jumped off.

"There's a gallery here," he said. "If you want to take in a bit of culture?"

"Of course I do!" Emily exclaimed.

They checked out all the beautiful paintings inside the gallery. Emily made a note of some of the artists so she could purchase prints for the inn once she was home.

Next door to the gallery they were surprised to discover an alpaca farm. Much to Daniel's amusement, Emily was quite taken by them and cooed. She leaned over the fence and stroked the fuzzy little creatures' heads while Daniel snapped a photo. So overcome with love was Emily she even treated herself by purchasing a luxury alpaca blanket!

Then Daniel rode the moped to the colorful clay cliffs of Aquinnah. They hiked along the cliffs, taking in the dramatic view, then went down the scenic trail, taking in the sight of wild heather, passing the brick lighthouse and rows of wooden beach huts until they reached the beaches of gorgeous red sand, pebbles, and clay. They sat on one of the huge boulders overlooking the sea. Sunset came, turning the sky a beautiful red color. The air was cold but they wrapped themselves up in their new blanket.

Daniel opened a bottle of wine and they drank together, watching the sun setting on another wonderful day spent as husband and wife.

*

Under a bright full moon and sky full of stars, Daniel drove them back toward Edgartown. On the outskirts of town, he drew to a halt outside of a lighthouse. Emily realized with surprise that it was a restaurant. It looked very high end.

"You booked this?" Emily asked Daniel.

He nodded.

"But I'm not dressed for a fancy meal," she protested.

"That doesn't matter," he said. "This is just for us."

Emily was surprised to see that Daniel had booked the whole place just for the two of them. There were three waiters in smart outfits waiting to cater to their every need. Emily couldn't believe it when she read the custom menu and saw that each dish was one of her favorites, an eclectic mix of seafood platters, each coming with a complimentary cocktail. She double checked Daniel's menu and saw that his was completely different. He was getting a tapas menu consisting of mini gourmet burgers, mac and cheese, and fries. And each of his courses was accompanied by a different ale. She could hardly believe the menus had been written specifically for them.

A violinist and cellist played beautiful music, including the pieces from the wedding, their first song, and Chantelle's choir pieces. Emily realized that everything down to the set list had been customized just for them.

"This is so incredible," she said, reaching out and stroking Daniel's hand on the table.

Everything felt so perfect. She didn't know such happiness was possible. But Daniel seemed suddenly distant. Emily frowned.

"Are you okay?" she asked.

"Actually, I wanted to talk to you about something," Daniel said. "And I'm a bit nervous."

"Oh," Emily said. She felt her stomach swirl with anguish. What if Daniel was about to reveal some past secret to her? She was always telling him to tell her more about himself but it still scared her.

"The bassinet," Daniel said.

Emily furrowed her brow, perplexed. "What about it?"

But then she realized what he was getting at and felt her stomach flip. Daniel wanted a baby? She'd expected him to want to wait for at least a year before bringing up the beautiful baby's crib he'd made and when they would plan to fill it. Was he really suggesting they start their family so soon?

"I don't want to wait," he said.

Emily's heart fluttered. She felt overjoyed, thrilled, excited. Daniel was offering something she'd wanted for years.

"Really?" she stammered. "You mean you want to start trying right away? Like, here?"

He nodded and a smile twitched on his lips. "It would be pretty neat to conceive on our honeymoon, don't you think?"

Emily felt a shift then in her perspective. She didn't understand why. It was something to do with him mentioning the honeymoon.

144

Suddenly the thought of actually trying for a baby made Emily nervous. It felt too real all of a sudden, too close. She hadn't been expecting it and it had taken her by surprise, making her flustered.

Emily sat there mute, not able to find the words. Daniel's expression changed at her continued silence. He frowned.

"Should I take that as a no?" he asked.

"I don't know," she admitted. She squeezed his hand across the table. "I want kids, definitely. And soon. But can we just enjoy the honeymoon first? Just have something for the two of us?"

The idea of rocking things when they were so perfect filled her with anguish.

Daniel looked crestfallen. "Sure," he said.

Emily felt compelled to reassure him. "Our lives have been crazy hectic. We still have the adoption to finalize. I feel like things have only just become settled. I don't know if I want to rock the boat just yet."

Daniel kept his gaze averted. "I get your point," he said stiffly.

"I mean, just think about the hormonal changes," Emily added, trying to unravel her own complex feelings about the situation. She'd gone from being tongue-tied to suddenly not being able to stop herself from oversharing the myriad of reasons why now wasn't the right time to try for a child. "If I stop taking the pill while we're on vacation my hormones will go haywire and I'll become a weepy mess! I don't want to spoil this once in a lifetime experience."

Her attempts to explain herself didn't seem to fly with Daniel. He looked hurt.

The dessert was delivered and they ate in silence. Emily's emotions were swirling inside of her, making her feel nauseous. She prodded her cheesecake with her fork, trying to work out why she was suddenly so reluctant. Was it because of what happened to Charlotte, the responsibility of having her own child and all the fear that came with that? Or was it because of her parents' divorce and the way in which it had altered her own life, caused her so much pain and difficulties over the years? She didn't think she and Daniel would succumb to divorce but she also knew children were a stressor in any relationship and she hated the thought of causing that kind of pain to her own children.

"Daniel, let's talk about this again once we're back home," she said.

Daniel nodded but he was so clearly dejected.

They finished up their meal and returned to their hotel, their hands limply clasped, the silence uncomfortable between them. As they dressed for bed, Emily felt worse than ever. The mood was completely opposite from how it had been for the last two nights, when they'd fallen passionately into one another's arms.

Emily got into bed, wishing she could turn back time to the moment Daniel told her he wanted a baby and instead of overthinking things, allowing herself to get caught up in the moment, in the romance of it. Because she'd much prefer to be making a baby right now instead of awkwardly pulling the covers over herself, feeling the distance between their bodies like a yawning chasm.

CHAPTER TWENTY TWO

The following day, Daniel and Emily strolled silently along the harbor's edge, taking in the sight of the amazing whaling houses. The baby-making conversation had left a sour taste in Emily's mouth and she couldn't help but find Daniel's attitude slightly riling. She felt a deep yearning for things to go back to how they had been.

"Would you like to go and see the church?" Emily asked Daniel.

He shrugged. "Sure, if you want."

Emily felt her insides tighten with grief and frustration. She hated it when Daniel became monosyllabic and she hoped he wasn't going to stay like this for the whole trip.

They visited the church, a beautiful old building that took Emily's breath away with its splendor. Outside on the streets there was a vintage-style ice cream truck. Emily discreetly purchased two cones, one for herself and one for Daniel. But when she surprised him with it, he didn't seem as overjoyed as she'd hoped.

"What's wrong, don't you like it?" Emily asked. "It's got real vanilla seeds in."

"The weather's still a bit cold for ice cream," Daniel replied. "That's all."

Emily's stomach sank with sadness.

They finished their ice creams and went into a gift shop to find more things for Chantelle. Emily wanted her to know they were thinking about her, even though every time they spoke to her it seemed as if Chantelle was having the time of her life with Papa Roy and had quite forgotten about them.

"What do you think about this?" Emily asked Daniel, showing him a necklace with a butterfly on.

"Don't you have enough necklaces?" Daniel replied.

"For Chantelle!" Emily laughed.

But Daniel didn't laugh back. "Oh. Yeah, I think she'll like it."

Her happiness dashed, Emily went to the till to buy the necklace. She caught up with Daniel outside the store.

"What do you want to do now?" she asked. "It's a little early for dinner but we could grab a long lazy one."

Daniel seemed to visibly tense at the suggestion. "And talk about what?" he said. "You said you didn't want to talk about kids until we got home."

Emily frowned. "I didn't realize that was the only topic of conversation," she said, defensively. "There are other things to talk about, you know? We share a whole life together, friends, family."

Her words seemed to get through to Daniel at last. He brightened a little and agreed that a long meal would be a good way to spend their evening. They walked hand in hand along the streets assessing the restaurants before selecting one. But Emily had exhausted herself trying to get Daniel to cheer up and now it was her turn to be a bit short and monosyllabic. She had to remind herself that it was all a bit raw at the moment. Daniel was coming back around. Things would be better tomorrow once the dust had had time to settle again.

*

The rest of the honeymoon was glorious and relaxing but that distance between them remained. When the time came to return home, Emily felt a pang of relief, finding herself eager to throw herself back into life and work.

Emily and Daniel returned to Sunset Harbor in the yacht, mooring it at the yacht club. They walked along the beach back home, dragging their luggage after them. When they reached the path that led from the beach to West Street, Emily felt a sense of relief. She always felt a strong sense of returning home, of being where she needed to be, whenever she saw the inn's roof loom into view behind the row of tall conifer trees.

They followed the drive and then climbed the porch steps and entered the inn. Everything was still and quiet. Emily had been half expecting a welcome party since they'd had such an awesome send-off. At the very least she was expecting Chantelle to come flying down the staircase and throw herself into their arms, for the dogs to come bounding out the laundry room to greet them. Instead, the only person around was Bryony, the website marketer. She was sitting in the lounge on her laptop, drinking coffee.

"Hey, guys," she said. She waved, making her bangles jangle, and pushed one of her dreads out of her eyes. "Nice honeymoon?"

"Yeah," Emily said, looking about her, bemused and distracted by the quietness. "Do you know where everyone is?"

Bryony looked guilty. She took a sip of her coffee and twiddled the large silver ring on her thumb nervously. "Serena and Lois went for a walk with Chantelle."

Now it was Daniel's turn to frown. He looked at the clock. "But they knew we'd be getting home at this time. Why did they choose to go for a walk when we were due home?"

Bryony's twiddling became more fevered. Emily got the distinct impression she was holding something back.

"They were hoping a walk would chill Chantelle out, you know?" Bryony said with a shrug.

Emily and Daniel looked at each other, their expressions mirror images of confusion. Just at that moment, they heard the distinct sound of a child's voice coming from outside, somewhere at the other end of the drive. It sounded like shouting. Angry shouting. And the voice was unmistakably Chantelle's.

They rushed out the door of the inn to see Chantelle at the other end of the drive, lying on the ground kicking and writhing. Serena was crouched over her, speaking in what looked to be a stern manner. Lois was looking around, flustered, clearly making attempts to get Chantelle to calm down.

"What the hell?" Daniel muttered.

Then he was bounding down the porch steps. Emily quickly followed, racing along the drive after him.

Lois turned at the sound of their approaching footsteps. She looked even more guilty.

"What's going on?" Daniel exclaimed, looking at the scene before him of his daughter throwing a tantrum.

Serena looked up, her eyes bright with emotion. "Nothing. Chantelle just didn't want to finish the walk so soon. Isn't that right, Chantelle?"

The child shot her a murderous expression. Emily gasped with shock. She'd never seen Chantelle like this, especially not with Serena. Usually the two of them loved each other dearly.

"Chantelle, get up off the ground," Daniel commanded. "This is no way to behave."

"No!" she screamed, kicking more ferociously. "I don't care about the stupid walk! I didn't even want to go in the first place."

Daniel looked at Serena, frowning, questioning. Serena sighed, her shoulders sagging.

"She's basically been like this ever since Roy left," she admitted. "The smallest thing sets her off. I don't know what to do."

Emily and Daniel exchanged a worried glance. Had Papa Roy leaving caused the meltdown?

Emily sat down on the gravel beside Chantelle. The child jerked away from her, but Emily knew her well enough now to expect it. She'd seen this before in Chantelle, the way her meltdowns caused her to block away everyone, to shirk away from comfort even when it was offered by people she knew loved her.

Emily touched Serena's arm lightly. It pained her to see her friend so overwhelmed by the situation. She felt guilty for leaving Chantelle in her care. She'd expected them to have a great time but instead Serena was looking harried and exhausted.

"We can take over from here," Emily told her.

Serena nodded and bit down on her lip. She was clearly fighting back tears.

Lois helped her to her feet and together the two of them returned to the inn. Emily could tell as they went that Lois was consoling Serena. She knew she'd need a long debrief with Serena later, to help bolster her friend and make her realize she'd done nothing wrong. But for now, her sole concern was Chantelle.

"You know, before Papa Roy said goodbye to me he said he wanted us to visit him for a vacation," Emily said breezily. She knew Chantelle well enough now to know that feeding into her emotions wasn't the best solution to the problem. Getting her to calm down was easier if she didn't pay a whole lot of attention to the meltdown. Chantelle would talk about her feelings at a later date when she'd calmed down.

"He has a house in Greece and a house in England," Emily continued in the same calm manner. "I don't know which one we'd go to. I've never been to either. What about you, Daniel? Ever been to Greece or England?"

Daniel looked at her suspiciously. He seemed shaken up by the whole situation and Emily thought he must be confused as to why she didn't appear to be. Little did he know that her heart was hammering in her chest, that she was almost shaking from the adrenaline of the moment.

"Neither," he said finally.

"I think Greece would have nicer weather. And food. So I hope we go there. But on the other hand we'd be able to make friends easier in England since we all speak the same language." She forced herself to chuckle. "And Papa Roy said the countryside is beautiful."

She peeked over at Chantelle. The child had stopped writhing. She seemed to be listening intently to Emily's words.

"He said there's a castle near him. Can you imagine that? A real castle. But then again, in Greece they have the coliseums, which are ancient!"

150

"How ancient?" Chantelle's little voice said. Her arms were wrapped around her face, muffling the sound of her words. Emily noticed she'd torn the elbow of her shirt sleeve.

"I'm not sure," Emily said. "We could do some research and impress Papa Roy with our historical wisdom."

Emily couldn't be certain but she thought she heard the sound of Chantelle hiccupping out a laugh. She looked up at Daniel, communicating silently with her eyes that things were calming down. Daniel looked shocked, like she'd just performed a baffling magic trick.

"I wonder," Emily continued, "what present Papa Roy got for us. Daniel and I never had a chance to open our wedding gifts before we left for the honeymoon."

"That's right," Daniel said, finally joining in with the strategy to coax Chantelle out of her breakdown. "And you know what Papa Roy's like with presents. It will be some kind of riddle. Or a key to a box that you have to find somewhere in the house."

Chantelle was suddenly sitting up, looking at Daniel, her eyes bright with interest. "I love riddles," she said. "Let's go and open it!"

Then she was on her feet, rushing toward the house. Emily sagged forward, letting out her tense breath.

"Well, that was all a bit dramatic," Daniel said. He helped Emily to her feet. "Was it Roy leaving that upset her so much, or us?"

"I don't know," Emily said, wiping the dirt off her jeans. "But let's not bring it up again today. We'll just open the presents and get back to being together, to normality. We can broach it another time."

Daniel nodded his agreement and together they went into the inn. Serena was at the desk, her eyes red with tears. Bryony was comforting her.

"I'm really sorry you had to go through days of that," Emily told her friend. "I promise you it wasn't your fault at all."

But Serena remained downcast. "I think I'm going to take the rest of my shift off if that's okay," she said glumly. "It's quiet here anyway."

"Sure," Emily said, but she felt awful as Serena left.

She went into the living room to find Chantelle and Daniel sitting beside the mound of gifts. Opening them was the last thing Emily felt like doing right now. She was reeling; from the way the honeymoon had fizzled out, from Chantelle's meltdown, from Serena's despondency. Added to that, she too missed her father's presence in the inn. She'd gotten so used to him being there. Now the place just felt empty.

But she put on a brave face for Chantelle and smiled as she sat down with the mountain of gifts.

"Let's open this one first," Daniel said, holding up a beautifully wrapped box. "Chantelle?"

He handed it to the girl and she peeled off the tape carefully, clearly not wanting to damage the pretty paper in any way.

"Who is it from?" Emily asked.

Chantelle checked the tag. "From Yvonne and Kieran." She removed the paper to reveal a glass teapot. Then she grinned. "It's so pretty!"

She placed it carefully beside her. Daniel handed the next gift to Chantelle. This one was from Suzanna and Wesley. Chantelle neatly removed the gift wrap and held up a photo frame with many windows for different pictures. They'd put photos in most of the spaces, of Daniel and Emily together, of Chantelle playing in the snow, of the family together at one of their parties dressed to the nines. There was one space left blank and Emily noticed that Suzanna had drawn a winky face on the white paper filling it. She knew what her friend was implying. It was space for a baby photo. Emily swallowed the lump in her throat.

"Look at this present!" Chantelle beamed, holding up the biggest gift of them all. "It's from Roman!"

Emily's eyes widened. Roman had already done so much for them, singing at their wedding, paying for the bar, pulling some strings so they could stay at the fanciest hotel on Martha's Vineyard, and now a gift.

"There's a card as well," Chantelle said. She handed the envelope to Emily.

Emily opened it up and read the message.

The Moreys

I wanted to get you something to express my gratitude for the time I spent at the inn. You all respected my privacy while I was here and that is something that is both rare and important for me. Never once did you pry into my business, though I'm sure you were curious as to why I was in Sunset Harbor. Well, I'll let you be the first to know that I have been searching for a house for a long time now, trying to find somewhere I can settle down. Thanks to you guys and the hospitality you've shown me, I've decided that Sunset Harbor will be the place for me. I've had to fly to LA for recording but when I'm back in town, in my own house, I'd like you all to come to visit. Chantelle, I will have a studio space installed in my

152

new house and would love for you to come and practice your singing there. You'll get on well with my vocal coach and I'm pretty sure she'll want to take you under her wing.

'Til I get to see you all again,

Roman x

Emily looked up, her mouth slightly agape. Roman was moving to Sunset Harbor? Thanks to *them?*

Any residue of Chantelle's tantrum had entirely evaporated. She was grinning impossibly widely. Daniel looked flabbergasted.

"We should probably make sure we don't tell anyone about this," Emily said, folding the letter and putting it away. "Chantelle, do you think you can keep this a secret until it's finalized? Roman would be disappointed if this information got to the press."

Chantelle mimed zipping her lips. Everyone laughed, still somewhat shocked by the news.

It was just what Emily and Daniel needed to break through the invisible wall that had started to grow between them after their disagreement in Edgartown. He looked more relaxed now, and Emily felt the family becoming more united again. She was quite giddy with relief and found that she couldn't pay as much attention to the gifts as she had done before, though her friends had given them some amazing things such as kitchen gizmos and state-of-the-art gardening tools.

"See, look," Daniel said, holding up a spinach-growing starter kit from Birk and Bertha. "You can grow the spinach to put in your juices." He tapped the juicer that Tracey had bought them.

"And drink them from the new tumblers," Chantelle added, pointing at the beautiful multi-colored glass tumblers from Jason and Vanessa.

After a while, the mountain of gifts shrunk down to just one.

"It's Papa Roy's gift," Chantelle said.

His had been buried at the bottom of the pile. Emily felt a hitch of emotion in her chest at the thought of her father. She missed him desperately.

"Everyone brace yourself," Daniel joked. "It's going to be something baffling."

Chantelle began opening the gift. The box was quite large, but when Chantelle opened it she laughed and pulled out two minuscule packages.

"That's a good start," Daniel chuckled.

Chantelle opened up the first box. Inside was an acorn. She frowned.

"There's a poem," she said. She cleared her throat. *"As you can see, this is the seed you'll need to grow your family tree."*

Emily's throat tightened with emotion. It was the perfect gift for them to begin their life together as a family. A tree they could plant together and watch grow bigger and stronger as the years passed.

"What's the other one?" she said, wiping the tears from her eyes.

Chantelle picked up the second box and opened up the lid. "I think Papa Roy forgot this one. There's nothing inside." She tipped it up to prove her point. Then she gasped. "Oh. There's a message here underneath."

"What does it say?" Daniel asked, his eyes sparkling with curiosity.

"It's just gobbledygook," Chantelle said.

She handed the box to her father. Emily watched as he craned his head one way and then the other, frowning. He passed it to Emily. She saw some words on the underside of the box written in thick black pen. It looked like half the message. She picked up the acorn box and turned it upside down. No message. Then she looked inside. There it was! The same writing in thick black pen. She laughed, delighted with her father's playful spirit, and carefully opened up the sides of the box. She laid it out flat in front of everyone, and added the other message to the side.

"Your other gift is hiding in something old and new, bought and sold." She frowned at Daniel and Chantelle. "Any ideas?"

Daniel shrugged. Chantelle tapped her chin, pondering. Emily shook her head and laughed to herself. How typical of her father to leave them with another mystery to unravel.

Just then, Emily heard her phone start ringing from its place on the hall table.

"You guys keep thinking," she said as she stood.

She went out into the hall and picked up her phone. The name flashing on the screen was Richard Goldsmith, their attorney. Emily felt a flutter of anguish in her chest as she accepted the call.

"Emily," he began, "I'm sorry to call you so soon after your honeymoon."

"That's okay. What is it?"

Emily couldn't help the feeling of dread growing in her gut.

"Sheila's attorney finally responded to the adoption petition. I'm afraid they're playing a slightly dirty game. Sheila has a doctor's note informing of her pregnancy diabetes and how she will soon need to be on bed rest. As such, the court date has been moved forward."

Emily gripped the phone tensely. "By how much?"

"It's tomorrow, Emily."

A feeling like ice swept over Emily. Had Sheila deliberately planned this to come when they were underprepared? Was she purposefully trying to sour her and Daniel's wedding joy?

Then another thought struck Emily. If the court date was tomorrow, that must mean Sheila had already made the journey from Tennessee to Maine.

"Is she in town?" Emily asked Richard.

"Yes," Richard confirmed. "Can you meet me in the morning?"

"Of course," Emily replied, her voice little more than a stunned whisper.

She hung up the call and clutched her phone to her chest, her breath rapid. There was no time to brace herself for Sheila. And rocking the boat for Chantelle right now when she was already so tender, it was the worst timing ever.

Emily put her phone down and headed toward the living room to break the news. The anticipation of the fallout made her stomach swill with nausea.

CHAPTER TWENTY THREE

Emily barely slept that night. She couldn't stop her mind from reeling through every eventuality, from preparing her for the worst. It made her sick with worry to think about an outcome where they lost custody of Chantelle, and she found herself breaking out in a cold sweat at the thought.

Daniel, too, tossed and turned all night in bed beside her. He was clearly having similar bad dreams. Emily desperately wanted to wake him so she at least had someone to share the burden of anxiety with but it wouldn't help their case if they both turned up sleep deprived to court the next morning. Better that one of them be well rested for the inevitable showdown with Sheila they would have to face in the morning.

At six, Emily gave up on catching any more sleep. She felt terrible, her head swirling as she got out of bed and headed downstairs. To her surprise, she found Bryony sitting in the lounge.

"You're here early," Emily said, rubbing her bleary eyes.

Bryony looked up at her, her expression somewhat wild. "Actually, I haven't been home yet."

Emily noticed the collection of empty coffee cups beside her. "You've been working all night?"

Bryony nodded. "I had to. My application for the website to be listed on the Maine tourist board's approved accommodation list was accepted at midnight. The site traffic has been exploding ever since."

Emily hurried toward her and peered over her shoulder at her laptop. There was a graph on the screen showing a huge leap in unique visitors to the page.

"I had to redesign the whole booking form on the website," Bryony explained. Emily realized she was buzzing from more than just caffeine, but excitement as well, at a successful job well done. "And move the site to a new server because it kept crashing. And look." She tapped some buttons, bringing up a new page on the site that hadn't existed the day before. "This is your live calendar. Makes booking ahead super easy. Green is vacant, gray booked. It's really quick for the customer to click on the room type they want with this drop-down menu. Then I installed an algorithm like the ones they use for selling plane seats. As demand gets higher, the price automatically hikes itself up."

Emily could hardly believe what she was hearing. Bryony had done all of this for her in such a short space of time. What an achievement!

"Wait," Emily said. "You said green is vacant?"

Bryony nodded.

"Then how come there's next to no green for the rooms on the third floor for June?"

Bryony grinned at her widely. "Because they're being snapped up! And I'm expecting the surge to continue."

Emily was shocked by what she saw. If she hadn't been so terrified about the upcoming meeting with Richard Goldsmith she would have been thrilled by the news. As it was, she felt daunted and overwhelmed.

The stairs creaked and Daniel appeared, heading down them.

"You've given up sleeping too, huh?" Emily said.

He nodded. They went into the kitchen for coffee and sat together at the breakfast bar.

"I feel sick with anxiety," Emily admitted.

Daniel nodded. "I know. There's so much at stake. What if we lose?"

Emily shook her head. "I don't even want to think about it. Chantelle is so fragile at the moment as it stands." She sighed heavily. "What are we going to tell her?"

Daniel shrugged. "I don't know. But we need to tell her that her mom's in town. It would be a far worse shock for her to find out by seeing her in town."

Emily was grateful that Daniel understood that. It seemed to have sunk into him at last that hearing bad news from the person you loved was better than finding it out for yourself!

"I should tell Miss Glass as well," Emily said. "If Chantelle acts up in school because of this they'll need to know why."

"*If?*" Daniel said, raising an eyebrow. "More like when. This is going to be hard."

With a heavy heart, Emily agreed. She went to the phone and left a message with the school receptionist to pass on to Miss Glass, explaining the situation. Then it was time to wake Chantelle up and break the news. Daniel headed upstairs to fetch her, while Emily cooked some pancakes. Daniel returned a half hour later, Chantelle it tow. They sat at the kitchen table and Chantelle tucked into her pancakes with a smile.

Emily sat with them and looked nervously at Daniel. She nodded at him, as if to say that the time had come to reveal what was happening. Daniel inhaled deeply.

"Chantelle, do you remember Richard Goldsmith, the man who is helping us with your adoption?"

Chantelle paused and looked at her father with a frown. "Yes."

"Well, Emily and I are meeting him this morning." He scratched his head, clearly struggling to find the right words to express what was happening to a seven-year-old. "After that we'll be meeting the people who will make the decision on whether you can be Emily's proper daughter."

Chantelle put her fork down. She sat motionless for a while, as if digesting his words.

"What if they say no?" she asked. "Will I have to go back to Tennessee?"

Emily reached out and grasped Chantelle's hand. "It's going to be okay, sweetie. Whatever happens, Daddy and I will always be here for you."

Chantelle's face began to turn red. Tears filled her eyes. "Is my mom here? Is she going to take me away?"

The panic in her voice cut Emily to the core. There was nothing she could say to reassure her, because she really didn't know herself. If the court ruled in Sheila's favor then would it be immediate? Would Sheila suddenly have the right there and then to pick Chantelle up from school and drive her back to Tennessee? The thought of it made her heart ache.

Daniel looked up at the clock. "We should probably go," he said.

But Chantelle was shaking her head. "No. I don't want to. If you drop me off at school how do I know that it will be you picking me up again?"

Emily stood and went to her side. She wrapped the girl up in her arms. Chantelle broke down sobbing. Daniel joined them too, and the family hugged each other tightly.

Finally, they were able to coax Chantelle onto her feet, not because she was resigned but because she'd exhausted herself from all the crying. They went out to the car, clipping her into the backseat. She pulled her knees up to her chin and wept bitterly into her arms.

The drive to school was tense and somber. Emily was half expecting to see Sheila on the way. The thought of her being in Sunset Harbor made her feel sick with dread. Knowing that she would soon be coming face to face with her again was horrible.

At the school gates, Emily saw that Miss Glass and Chantelle's counselor, Gail, were already waiting at the door. When they saw the pickup truck pulling into the lot, they both headed toward them.

Daniel rolled down the window and killed the engine.

"How is she?" Miss Glass asked him.

"A wreck," Daniel replied.

Gail peered into the back window. Chantelle was in the same curled up position, tears racking her body. Gail opened the back door.

"Hey, Chantelle," she said gently, her voice as soft as cotton candy. "I hear you're having a bit of a tough day today. Do you want to come to the safe room with me? We can play and draw."

The safe room was where Chantelle had her weekly sessions with Gail. Clearly the school had decided it would be best for the child not to be in her usual class. Emily hated the thought of her being separated from her friends and felt infuriated with Sheila for putting her through this anguish.

Chantelle raised her head from her knees. Her eyes were red and blotchy from tears.

"Sure," she said monosyllabically. She unclipped herself from her seat and got out of the car.

"Why don't you say goodbye to Dad and Emily?" Gail suggested.

But Emily could already tell Chantelle had put up an emotional wall. The child turned, her face impassive, and with a shrug, mumbled, "See ya." Then she took Gail's hand and walked away.

Miss Glass gave them a sympathetic look. "We'll take care of her. Let us know as soon as there's news. Good luck."

She left. Daniel turned to face Emily. He was pale. Her heart broke for him, knowing he felt what she felt. What if that was the last time they saw Chantelle as their daughter? What if that emotionless "see ya" were the last words she spoke to them? It was too painful to bear.

Daniel started the truck and reversed out of the lot. The drive to Richard's office was quick, but it felt like it dragged on for a lifetime. The anticipation was unbearable and Emily found herself gripping the edges of her seat on more than one occasion.

When they pulled up outside, Richard's receptionist was only just unlocking the door. Emily was grateful that he'd found time to squeeze them in at such short notice.

"He's on his way," the receptionist said. "Can I get you coffee?"

Emily declined. "My nerves are frayed enough as it is. I feel sick with it."

The receptionist looked at her sympathetically. "You've got a really strong case. I'm sure it will be fine."

"You don't know that," Daniel barked.

The door opened and Richard strolled in, his suit jacket already halfway off. He handed it to the receptionist without so much as a greeting.

"Come in," he said to Daniel and Emily.

They followed him into his office and took seats opposite his large table. Richard sat and got straight to work.

"So she's played this tactically," he said. "Hence the radio silence we've had since we issued the petition. Turns out she's been through a government drugs program for pregnant addicts. She completed it. It's a huge gold star for her."

Daniel sunk his head into his hands. Emily felt her stomach turn.

"Richard, be straight with me, is there a chance we could lose this?" she asked.

Richard steepled his hands. His expression was very grave. "There's a chance that now she's cleaned herself up the courts will look more favorably upon Chantelle being placed with the woman who raised her for the first six years of her life rather than the father who wasn't involved with her until a year ago."

"The fact Sheila concealed Chantelle's existence from me is going to be counted against me?" Daniel snapped. "How is that fair?"

Richard shook his head. "It's not fair. Not at all. Which is why I need to know. If it comes to drudging up the dirt on Sheila, do you give me your consent to?"

Daniel paused, looking at him. "What kind of dirt?" he said, frowning.

"I have it all," Richard said. "The stuff with her ex-husband."

"The one I put in the hospital?"

Richard nodded. "Yes. If they use that against you then I can counter with the fact she returned to him. Make it seem like she's unstable and was playing you two off each other."

"That's... that's pretty goddamn low," Daniel said, shaking his head. Sheila returning to her abusive husband was far more about his control over her than her instability or unsuitability as a mother. "Can't we keep it to the facts?" he asked. "The deprivation. The lack of a proper home and a school for the kid?"

Richard shook his head sadly. "She's sorted all of that out now. She has a home. She even has a school ready. Everything's in place."

"So the past doesn't matter then?" Daniel said with a huge sigh. "None of the damage she caused will be used against her?"

"All I can do is find a way to make the court question her current situation and the tenability of it. If we can show how she has a history or a pattern of cleaning up in the short term and then letting it all fall apart again, then we might stand a chance."

Daniel's jaw tensed. "You mean jeopardize the fact she's cleaned up?" he said.

Emily reached out and touched his hand. She could tell what was going through Daniel's mind, that making it seem like Sheila's success was temporary, that it would turn into a failure like it had before, was almost sadistic. Cassie was obviously on his mind, her failed rehab attempt and the effect it had had on his life. He knew firsthand how delicate and fragile that place was for an addict, how hard fought it was to become sober. He clearly would prefer Chantelle to have a clean mom in her life, even if that meant risking his chance at being her full guardian, than drag her through the mud and risk it causing her to relapse.

"You don't have my consent," Daniel said, sadly. He looked at Emily. "I'm sorry, but I won't do that to her. It's not fair."

Emily squeezed his hand. "You're doing the honorable thing, Daniel. The right thing. It only makes me love you more."

Richard nodded then, once, with finality. "That's it then. Are you ready to go to court?"

Daniel and Emily exchanged a glance. This was it. The moment they'd been waiting for. The moment that would decide Chantelle's fate, and the future of their family.

CHAPTER TWENTY FOUR

Emily found herself trembling as she and Daniel followed Richard Goldsmith up the steps to the court. The building itself wasn't as formidable as Emily was expecting, but that didn't stop her feeling overwhelmed and daunted.

Her emotions only intensified when she saw Sheila sitting on a chair in the foyer. Her frazzled blonde hair was now a darker, more natural shade, and she'd tied it back neatly into a bun. She was wearing a loose-fitting white maternity shirt and black pants. She looked younger, simple and innocent.

Emily gulped and looked over at Daniel. He seemed to be blinking in surprise at the transformation in Sheila. The sight of her pregnant belly seemed to bewilder him also.

Just then, Sheila looked up and caught Daniel's eye. Her expression was one of grief. She turned her gaze away.

"The judge is ready for us," Richard informed them.

He led them into the courtroom, which was more like an office than the large jury accommodating rooms that Emily was used to see on television. It looked more like the sort of place divorces were finalized, and Emily thought about how that was in a way what was happening; they were seeking to legally unbind Chantelle from her mother, after all.

There was one downside to the size of the room and that was the proximity with which they had to sit. Though the table between them was large, the space felt claustrophobically close for Emily. She could smell Sheila's perfume, see the beads of sweat collecting on her upper lip. It was far too close for comfort.

The judge entered last, a smartly dressed woman who looked more like a politician or businesswoman than a judge.

"Let's begin," she said, taking her seat. "Now, because of Chantelle's age, we wouldn't usually ask for her opinion on the matter. However, a note was passed to me this morning via Chantelle's counselor at school."

Emily looked at Daniel, surprised. The judge continued.

"I feel in this matter it would be worth expressing Chantelle's desires, since she is able to articulate herself quite clearly."

She unfolded a piece of lined paper. Emily noticed Chantelle's distinctive handwriting immediately. Sheila must have recognized it too because she gasped and burst into tears.

The judge cleared her throat and began to read the letter.

"Dear Judge, please tell my mommy Sheila that I love her. I don't want her to think that I hate her. I don't want her to be sad but I want to stay living with my daddy and Emily, and Mogsy and Rain our dogs. I love Sunset Harbor. I love my school and Owen the piano man who teaches me to sing. I love our big house and being close to the beach and when daddy takes me fishing in the boat. My best friends are Bailey and Toby and if I move back to Tennessee I don't know when I will be able to play with them again and that makes me sad. My mommy wrote me a letter once and told me she was having a baby so I know she won't be lonely if I don't go back to her house. If the baby is a boy I think she should call it Roy which is my granddad's name. He's the kindest person I know. If it's a girl then she can call it Chantelle if she wants, I don't mind."

Sheila began to sob uncontrollably, folding forward so her face was completely obscured by her arms. It was heartbreaking to watch. Emily herself felt close to breaking down. Chantelle's letter struck a chord deep inside of her. She was so aware of what she was asking for, of what she would be giving up. That she cared about Sheila's well-being at all, Emily struggled to comprehend, but it was in Chantelle's nature to be caring to everyone.

The judge paused, looking at Sheila's heaped form.

"Would you like a moment?" she asked.

Sheila looked up, her bottom lip sucked in, and shook her head.

The judge nodded. "There's only a little more." She continued reading aloud. "I hope that you will make it so that I can stay with Emily and daddy forever. When I think about having to leave them it makes me very upset and angry, and then I am mean to people like Serena which I don't like doing. I want to be adopted by daddy and Emily because I think once that has happened I won't cry at night anymore with worry. Chantelle."

The judge folded the letter away. She looked at Sheila and gave her a sympathetic smile. Sheila's expression immediately changed to one of defeat.

"It would be foolish of me not to pay heed to Chantelle's wishes," the judge explained gently. She tapped the large ring binder stuffed with paper on the desk in front of her. "And having reviewed everything else that's been presented to me by your attorneys—medical histories, employment histories, criminal records—I'm going to make my final decision to grant Mr. and Mrs. Morey full legal custody and guardianship over Chantelle." She looked at Daniel and Emily. "You can apply for her to have the same surname as you if you wish. There are some forms for that."

But her last words were drowned out as Emily and Daniel both let out involuntary cries of delight. They leapt out of their seats and clasped each other tightly, both sobbing in earnest. Richard Goldsmith stood also, and clapped a hand on Daniel's shoulder. His eyes were misty with tears.

"Thank you," Emily said to the judge. "This means the world to us."

The judge nodded.

But the win was bittersweet for Emily, because their success meant Sheila's failure. Their dream come true was her waking nightmare. Emily couldn't help herself from empathizing with Sheila, pitying her for all the terrible decisions she'd made in the past and the repercussions they'd brought on her today.

The judge turned her attention to Sheila, who was weeping bitterly.

"This isn't the end of the process," she explained gently. "I'm going to grant you written communication rights. That means you can send Chantelle cards and letters via the solicitor. If Chantelle wishes to read them she can; however, she is under no obligation to do so, or to respond to them if she does. That being said, Mr. Goldsmith will be legally obligated to send updates on her welfare, including updates about school grades and significant milestones. We'll review the situation when Chantelle reaches eleven, which is the age we usually start taking the child's views into consideration. If she wants contact with you then it can begin, but not before." She closed her ring binder with finality. To Sheila's attorney she added, "No contact from this moment forth. To do so would be in breach of the order. Are we in understanding?"

The attorney nodded. "I'll debrief my client fully."

Just then Sheila stood up. She flashed a vicious look from Daniel to Emily and back again.

"I'll make you pay for this," she snarled in her thick southern accent. Her voice was filled with venom. "Both of you better watch your backs."

Sheila's attorney leapt up and spoke sternly under her breath in a desperate attempt to get her client to shut up. The judge narrowed her eyes at Sheila, looking unimpressed with her outburst.

"Do I need to remind you that it is illegal to make threats of violence? Probably not the best idea to do so when there's a judge to witness it."

Sheila glared angrily at everyone, shooting hatred from her cold eyes. Finally, she sat back down.

"In that case," the judge said, "I call this matter closed with a review date for four years' time. Mr. and Mrs. Morey, I wish you the best of luck for the future."

She shook each of their hands then left, striding away with the same purpose with which she'd initially strode in, off to decide the fate of other people's lives.

Daniel grasped Emily's hand and discreetly they left the courtroom to continue their celebrations away from Sheila's hate-filled eyes.

*

Emily rang the school ahead so that Chantelle would be ready for them to pick her straight up. When they pulled into the lot, they saw her playing on the jungle gym with Miss Glass and Gail supervising. Chantelle looked up at the sound of the pickup truck and her face burst into a smile. She ran, full pelt, down the path toward them.

Daniel flew out of the truck, leaving the door hanging open, and swept her up into his arms. They twirled around in circles, hugging tightly. Emily joined them, throwing her arms around them both.

Miss Glass and Gail reached them. Both seemed overcome with emotion, smiling and crying simultaneously.

Emily's heart swelled with joy. She knew this was a moment she would never ever forget for as long as she lived. She felt as euphoric as a new mother holding their baby for the first time. Because that's what she was now, Chantelle's mom.

"Congratulations," Miss Glass said, her voice cracking.

Emily looked at her, smiling through her tears of joy. "Thank you."

Chantelle lifted her tear-stained face from Daniel's shoulder. She reached out and wiped Emily's tears from her cheeks.

"I have an idea," Chantelle said. "To cheer you up."

"I'm not sad, sweetie," Emily told her. "These are happy tears."

"Even so," Chantelle began. "Papa Roy told me that the best use for tears is to water the plants."

Emily laughed with abandon. That certainly sounded like the sort of thing her father would say!

"You want to get things for the greenhouse?" Emily said.

Daniel set Chantelle down on her feet. She grinned but shook her head. "I think you and Daddy should go and choose some plants after you drop me home. I'll get everything ready in the greenhouse and you can see what me and Papa Roy did while he was here. I think you'll really like it, Mommy."

Emily froze, her heart leaping into her throat. Chantelle had called her Mommy and it felt like the most perfect thing in the world. Tears began trickling down her cheeks again.

"Quick, Daddy," Chantelle said, tugging on their hands, pulling them toward the truck. "You need to go to Raj's and buy some plants before Mommy wastes all her tears!"

CHAPTER TWENTY FIVE

Emily felt elated, like she was walking on clouds. The bell over the door to Raj's nursery tinkled as she floated in, Daniel just behind.

"You guys look happy," Raj said from behind the counter.

"We are," Emily gushed. "We won the adoption!"

Raj beamed from ear to ear. "That's amazing news, guys! And you're celebrating with plants? What a wonderful idea."

"It was Chantelle's idea," Daniel said.

"I think we should get the brightest flowers we can," Emily said.

Raj nodded. "I'll fetch a selection from the greenhouse for you to choose from."

He disappeared out the back and returned a few moments later with a basket filled with vibrantly colored flowers. "Fuchsias. Sunflowers. Petunias. Which ones do you like?"

"All of them!" Emily exclaimed. "We'll take the lot."

They paid for the plants and loaded them into the back of the pickup truck. As Daniel drove them back to the inn it looked like they were transporting a rainbow. Chantelle would just love it!

But when they reached the inn there was a commotion out in the driveway. Serena and Lois were shouting at a man that Emily didn't recognize. The argument looked very heated.

Daniel parked, his expression one of panic. Emily rushed out the car and up toward Serena and Lois.

"What's going on?" she demanded.

But then another figure came rushing out of the inn. When Emily realized who it was, she went cold all over. It was Sheila, and she was dragging Chantelle out by the arms. The composed Sheila she'd seen earlier in the courthouse had evaporated, replaced by the wild-eyed Sheila she'd first met all those months ago.

Chantelle screamed bloody murder as Sheila battled with her, yanking her across the porch steps despite her best efforts to fight back.

"Jimmy, help!" Sheila shouted at the man.

He barged past Serena and Lois, knocking them out of his way, then grabbed Chantelle around her waist.

"Put down my daughter!" Daniel bellowed.

He rushed the man and punched him square in the face. The man went down like a lead weight, Chantelle falling with him into a

167

heap on the gravel. She started crying. Daniel picked her up, cradling her in his arms.

"Assault!" Sheila started shouting at Daniel. "You knocked out my boyfriend and there are witnesses! I'll get you sent to prison where you belong you… you kidnapper!"

"Get out of here!" Daniel yelled at Sheila, distraught. "You're jeopardizing your visitation rights by coming here. Didn't you listen to the judge?"

Sheila looked deranged, like she was beyond caring.

"I don't want you visiting me," Chantelle shouted at Sheila. "I don't want to ever see you again! I have a new mommy now. Emily's my mommy. So leave me alone!"

Sheila looked stunned, like she'd been slapped in the face. She seemed to suddenly realize then that she'd blown it with Chantelle, that she'd broken the last bit of faith the child had in her. Gone was the Chantelle in the letter, the girl who didn't want her to be sad, who wanted her to have a happy life with her new baby. In her place was a girl who wanted nothing to do with her.

From the ground, Jimmy stirred and started to wake up. His nose was bloody. Sheila crouched down and grabbed his hand, yanking him to his feet. He wobbled, dazed from the force of Daniel's blow.

"Let's get the hell out of here," Sheila said, flashing angry eyes at Daniel, Emily, Serena, and Lois. She looked lastly at Chantelle. Bitterly, she uttered her parting words. "Good luck with your new life."

*

Emily ran to Daniel and Chantelle, tears streaming down her cheeks from the shock of the altercation.

"Sweetie," she gasped, wiping the tangles of hair from Chantelle's eyes. "Are you okay?"

To her surprise, Chantelle was not crying. In fact, she seemed completely fine.

"You guys saved me," she said. "You really are my daddy and mommy."

They held each other tightly.

"Yes," Daniel soothed. "Forever and ever."

He set Chantelle on her feet. The child looked up, the fear that had been in her eyes moments earlier now completely gone. Instead, she looked confident in her belief that this was her home now, her family, that the law had spoken and she was where she needed to be.

"When you next see the judge, can you tell her I don't want to be Sheila's daughter at all or ever again?" she said.

Emily realized that she'd demoted Sheila. She no longer viewed her as her mother. As far as Chantelle was concerned, Emily was her mom now.

"We won't be seeing the judge until you're eleven," Emily said. "That's a long time. Lots will change in that time."

"I won't," Chantelle said confidently. "Even if Sheila and Jimmy send me pictures of the baby I won't change my mind. I don't want to see them ever. They're not my family. You guys are."

She clutched both of their hands. Emily drew strength from Chantelle, from her sudden unflappability. She herself felt very shaken by the event, nauseous, and feeling like all she wanted to do was sleep. Daniel gave her a look of concern.

"I think the stress is taking its toll on Emily," he said. "Let's get her inside."

They walked slowly into their home, Chantelle looked up at him.

"You mean Mommy," she said. Then to Emily she added, "Don't worry. We'll get you a glass of milk and a coloring book. That's what me and Gail do when I'm stressed. You'll be feeling better in no time."

Emily smiled, feeling blessed by the turn of events, happy and relieved that Chantelle was indeed her daughter, and it was looking like that would never change.

CHAPTER TWENTY SIX

SIX WEEKS LATER

Sunshine streamed through the glass of the greenhouse. Emily wiped her brow. Summer was nearly here and with it came a slightly uncomfortable heat. Usually Emily loved summer but she'd recently found herself overheating and feeling a little sick from dehydration as a result.

The greenhouse was looking fantastic. Chantelle had led the way over the last six weeks, following in Roy's footsteps and finishing the work he had started. The vibrant rainbow of flowers Emily and Daniel had purchased from Raj's looked splendid. It was like a tropical paradise. And more, Trevor's fruit trees were starting to flourish. Emily thought of the juicy fruit they would soon be bearing, once summer was truly here.

Daniel and Chantelle were busy digging a hole.

"Is that deep enough?" Chantelle said.

"I think so," Daniel replied. "Do you have it?"

Chantelle nodded and took something out of her pocket. The acorn from Papa Roy.

Emily came over and the three of them peered into the shadowy hole. Then Chantelle dropped it in.

"I hope our family tree grows so tall it bursts out the roof of the greenhouse."

Emily looked up. The greenhouse was incredibly tall, but if they nurtured their family tree well then it might just grow big enough to reach the top.

Just then, Bryony rushed into the greenhouse, bringing her incense scent with her. "Guys!" she exclaimed, jumping up and down. "I have news! We're fully booked!"

Daniel and Emily exchanged an excited glance.

"For the weekend?" Emily asked.

Bryony shook her head, her eyes twinkling with excitement. "For the entire summer!"

Emily's mouth dropped open. "Are you kidding?"

Bryony shook her head. "Nope. And you have three hundred people on the waiting list."

Stunned, Emily took a seat on the garden bench. Her excitement was taking the form of nausea and dizziness. She looked up at Daniel.

"We'll have to expand," she said. "We can't accommodate all those people. And we'll need more staff."

He nodded. "It's time to get new people in anyway, don't you think? I think Lois and Serena are ready to move on."

Emily agreed. Neither of them were trained hostesses. It was time to treat the business with the professionalism it deserved, not just relying on friends and college kids and expecting everything to tick by.

"We should meet with an architect," Emily said, still feeling dazed. "See about having some of the outbuildings redone."

"First things first," Daniel said. "We need to celebrate! How about a picnic on the beach?"

Chantelle punched the air with excitement. Emily felt too sick to think about consuming anything, but she was also too stunned by Bryony's news to protest and was willing to be swept away to the beach by Daniel and Chantelle.

*

Emily watched as Chantelle sprinted along the beach, waves lapping at her bare feet. Mogsy and Rain chased after her, yapping at the water as it broke on the shore.

Daniel placed the picnic hamper down on the ground. "I'm going to go and prep the boat," he said. "Wanna come help?"

Emily lay out the blanket and shook her head. "I think I'll stay here with Chantelle. Have a rest." She was feeling tired and put it down to all the stress they'd been through recently.

"I won't be too long," Daniel told her, before walking the short distance to the harbor.

With the promise of summer approaching, some of the locals had begun to lower their boats back into the water ready for sailing. Emily knew Daniel was excited about the new season and she watched him, smiling to herself, as he began tending to his boat.

Chantelle ran over to Emily then.

"Look what I found!" she said. She held out her hands. Resting in her palms was an array of shells.

"Here," Emily said. She tipped the small tub of blueberries onto a paper plate and handed the now empty tub to Chantelle. "Why don't you fill this up with the best shells you can find?"

Chantelle beamed and rushed off to start her collection.

A little while later Daniel came back from preparing his boat.

"Are you okay?" he asked sitting beside her on the blanket. "You look distracted."

"I'm just thinking about the inn," Emily said.

"Of course you are," Daniel said with a chuckle. "When aren't you thinking about the inn?"

Emily feigned mock affront. "Sometimes I'm thinking about how sexy you are," she said. "And how cute kittens are."

Daniel laughed again. "So? What's on your mind?"

Emily took a blueberry and placed it in her mouth. She chewed slowly. "Trevor's house. We should turn it into part of the inn. It's the only thing that makes sense. If we keep growing we're going to need more rooms, a bigger kitchen, somewhere for the staff to have a break."

"You're sure you want to use Trevor's house for that rather than the outbuildings?"

Emily thought of the empty swimming pool in which Charlotte had died, lying there abandoned for close to thirty years. Then she thought of Trevor's house, the home in which she'd watched his life fade from him. The thought of renovating either of them made her heart ache. But clinging onto the past wasn't healthy. Sooner or later she would have to make that decision and move on.

"I'm sure," Emily said.

Daniel nodded his agreement. "Well, in that case, we ought to celebrate the future of the inn. Champagne?"

He leaned forward and took the bottle out of the cool bag. But Emily shook her head.

"Actually, I think I'm going to give up drinking," she said.

Daniel frowned. "What? Why?"

Emily felt her nerves grow. "Because I think I should start taking care of my body. Preparing myself. Getting healthy so I can conceive."

Daniel's eyes pinged open. "You want a baby?" he gasped.

Emily nodded. She could tell from his expression that this was a good revelation. She hadn't put him off thoroughly from her behavior on their honeymoon then.

"I do," she said. "And I'm sorry it took me so long to come around to the idea. I don't know what came over me. I think I just got scared, or daunted because of the adoption. But I'm not getting any younger. We should start sooner rather than later."

Daniel looked over the moon. He put the champagne bottle back in the cooler bag.

"You can still celebrate," Emily told him, laughing.

But Daniel shook his head. "No way. If you're sacrificing champagne and cocktails to make my baby, the least I can do is give them up too!"

"That's very sweet of you," Emily said, touched by the gesture. She wrapped her arms around him, feeling delirious with happiness. "But I draw the line at you taking prenatal vitamins, okay?"

Daniel laughed at her joke and planted a soft kiss on her lips. "Deal."

*

On their way back from the beach, they decided to walk through Trevor's house and think about ways it could be altered. As they stepped inside, Emily felt a terrible grief wash over her, so strong it made her feel faint and trembly.

Daniel reached out and took her arm. "Okay?" he said, supporting her.

Emily nodded. "I'm sorry. It's just stressful thinking about this. I don't want to erase him."

Daniel brought her hand up his lips and pressed a kiss upon it. "He wanted you to have the house. It's yours to do what you want with. He'll be proud of you for making this decision."

Emily's spell of faintness passed. She felt like Trevor was with them, looking down, approving of their plans. It gave her strength and rejuvenated her. For the first time she felt strong enough to look around the whole of Trevor's house, not just the hallway that led through the kitchen and laundry room into the greenhouse. Now she could go upstairs, thinking of the luxurious suites they could install, inspired by their honeymoon experience. Trevor's sparse, clinical style was the opposite of what Emily envisaged for the place. The whole thing would need to be changed.

She came back downstairs and walked through the kitchen.

"We could knock this wall through," she said to Daniel. "Make the kitchen and dining room one huge space. Then the living room could be a restaurant which is open to everyone, not just guests at the inn."

"That sounds ambitious," Daniel said. "I don't know if Parker and Matthew would be able to handle that kind of responsibility."

"I'll be hiring more chefs, of course," Emily said.

Daniel looked at her proudly.

"Do you think this is a supporting wall?" Emily said, knocking on the wall that separated the hall from the living room. "I think open plan would be amazing, don't you? We could have a proper pizza oven here." She gestured with her hands. "Then there would be a desk, like the one in the foyer. I'm sure Rico had more."

Just then, Chantelle clicked her fingers. "The foyer desk!" she said.

Daniel and Emily looked at each other and frowned with confusion.

"Huh?" Daniel questioned the girl.

"I've cracked Papa Roy's riddle!" she exclaimed. "Something sold because Papa Roy sold it to Rico, something bought because Mommy bought it back off him. Which makes it old *and* new, as well. An old bit of junk for Papa Roy and a new bit of treasure for Mommy. That must be where the final wedding gift is hidden!"

Emily's eyes widened with excitement. The three of them ran out of Trevor's house, buzzing with anticipation. When they reached the foyer desk, Chantelle began pulling open all the drawers, drawers that had once been hospital beds for Emily's dolls. She smiled to herself as the memory her father had given to her resurfaced.

Finally, Chantelle pulled open the last drawer. And there, resting upon the same silky fabric Roy had used to wrap Emily's locket, was a tiny painting of the sun setting above the harbor. It was so small it looked like it belonged in a doll's house. Emily assumed it was a replica and wondered if there was yet another riddle involved, or some hidden meaning from her father. But when Chantelle reached out and lifted it up carefully it was clear the tiny painting was an antique.

"There's a note, too," Chantelle said.

She fished it out. Emily noticed the same black pen her father had used to write the poem and the riddle on the boxes. He must have had a grand old time arranging all this for them.

Chantelle read aloud. "This won't look that impressive hung up in the inn. A bit on the small side if you ask me. The artist is named Rosa Hooper. I've been hiding this for just the right time. Use the proceeds however you wish. Here is the number of a good appraiser."

Emily laughed. Her dad clearly meant for them to sell the painting. Perhaps they could fund their vacations to Greece and Cornwall from the money raised.

Chantelle handed her the slip of paper with the appraiser's phone number. His name was Sid Carson.

"I'd better give this guy a call," Emily said. "Find out how much this piece of treasure is worth!"

CHAPTER TWENTY SEVEN

To celebrate the new plans for the inn, Emily decide to host fireworks for all the guests and staff. The inn was filled to the brim with guests so it was a loud, happy, bustling affair. With the jazz band playing in the living room and Alec behind the speakeasy bar, the place was alive with joy.

Outside, bright fireworks burst in the darkening sunset. Emily decided to call Amy to tell her about her expansion plans and the fact that she and Daniel were going to start a family.

"Em, guess where I am," Amy said when she answered the call.

Emily narrowed her eyes in contemplation. "I haven't a clue. Where?"

"Sunset Harbor."

Emily was so surprised it knocked her off guard. "You didn't come all this way just for my fireworks, did you?"

Amy laughed. "No. I'm not coming to see you at all actually."

"You're not? But then why…" Suddenly it dawned on Emily. "Are you with George's brother? What was his name again? Harry?"

"Maybe…" Amy said coyly.

"I don't believe it!" Emily exclaimed. "Tell me everything!"

Amy didn't need prompting. Straightaway she began speaking at a million miles a second, gushing. "We've been dating ever since the wedding. So about two months."

"Are you kidding?!" Emily squealed.

She could tell by the tone of Amy's voice that she was smitten. It wasn't like how she'd been with Fraser, it was a million times more gooey.

"I think I'm in love," Amy finished.

"What are you going to do?" Emily said. She couldn't imagine Amy coming to Sunset Harbor for a man, but at the same time she knew George had strong family ties to the place and assumed Harry would be the same.

"I don't know," Amy said. "But the long distance is killing me. Maybe I'll move to Sunset Harbor. I mean it's working out pretty well for you."

Emily could barely contain her excitement at such a prospect. She was amazed that her life here was only getting fuller and fuller.

But she forced herself to temper her enthusiasm. Amy had rushed into things with Fraser, maybe she was just doing the same with Harry. Still, she was thrilled for her friend. She hadn't heard her sound so happy in ages.

So stunned was Emily that she completely forgot to tell Amy about her news. And after hanging up the call, she didn't have time to call back because an eccentric-looking man was hurrying up the path toward her.

"Sid Carson," he said, holding out his hand.

The appraiser her father had recommended? What was he doing here?

"I thought our meeting was tomorrow," Emily explained. "We're in the middle of a party!"

"Was it tomorrow?" Sid replied in a rumbly voice. "Goodness, I am sorry. Date-keeping isn't my forte."

Emily laughed. He was just the sort of guy she'd expect her horologist father to be acquaintances with.

"No problem," she said. "You're here now, you may as well join in."

She took him to the bar for a cocktail, and he settled on a red velvet stool. Emily went and fetched the sunset painting.

"Oh my," Sid said as he took the fragile painting in his hands. He placed an eyeglass on his right eye. "This is an original Rosa Hooper, I can tell you that."

"I'd expect no less from my father," Emily said.

"Ivory plate. She used discarded piano keys, you see." He looked up and smiled, then removed his eyeglass. "The museum of fine arts in Boston would be very interested in this for their American miniatures collection. I think you'd be able to get fifty thousand dollars for it."

Emily was winded with shock. Her father had assured her he'd never taken any of his possessions to pay for his life abroad, that he'd left everything to her, the diamonds, this very house. Here was proof. She knew her father would be aware of the painting's true value, that he could have sold it and lived comfortably for a year or two. But instead he'd left it for her, for her family, for their future.

Emily thanked Sid and invited him to stay for the rest of the party. Just then, Daniel came into the speakeasy looking for her.

"I thought you'd given up alcohol," he teased.

"I have!" she said. "I was having a meeting with Sid Carson." She pointed to the eccentric-looking man dancing in the corner of the speakeasy, cocktail in hand.

"The appraiser?" Daniel asked. "What did he say?"

"Only that painting is worth fifty thousand dollars!"

Daniel looked as shocked as Emily herself felt.

"Are you sure?"

She nodded enthusiastically. "There's a museum we can sell it to. Then we can put the money toward renovating Trevor's place!"

Daniel beamed widely and swept Emily into his arms. He spun her around in a circle. Emily squealed, elated by the good fortune her father had given them.

When Daniel set her back down on her feet, they saw Chantelle rushing into the speakeasy.

"There you are!" she said when she spotted them.

"Is everything all right?" Emily asked.

Chantelle looked somewhat wild-eyed.

"Yes!" she said, nodding. "I had an idea and I wanted to tell you right away."

Daniel and Emily both looked at her curiously.

"You said there was an outbuilding with a swimming pool in it that never got finished," Chantelle said. "Well, I think you should turn it into a spa. Like the one where we had the bachelorette party. Then I can have my toenails painted all the time. And when it's summer and there's no school I can have my fingernails painted too!" She beamed with pride.

Emily looked at Daniel. The thought of changing the outbuilding had made her uncomfortable before, much in the same way the thought of gutting Trevor's house had. But the same sensation of strength washed through her at Chantelle's suggestion. She knew that it was Charlotte's spirit giving her her blessing, approving of transforming the place into something of joy rather than leaving it as a place of misery.

"I think that's a great idea," Emily said.

Chantelle grinned and hugged her parents tightly.

"Although," Emily added, "we'll have to have a talk about how often you can have your nails done. I don't think a child your age should be pampered all the time."

Everyone laughed.

Chantelle finally released them.

"I think it would be a shame to waste this sunset sitting on the porch," Daniel said. "Why don't we go and watch it from the harbor?"

"But what about the fireworks?" Emily said.

Daniel grinned. "They'll look just as spectacular from the view on the boat." He held the keys up of his boat and twiddled them around his finger.

Chantelle's eyes widened. "First boat ride of the season!" she cried, jumping up and down and clapping. "Can we, Mommy? Can we go for a sail?"

How could Emily refuse such a request from the little girl who now called her Mommy?

"Of course," she said.

Hand in hand they left the inn, the music from the jazz band floating after them. It followed them all the way down to the beach and along the sand. It was only as they reached the harbor that the sound of sloshing waves against the dock was loud enough to drown out the distant sounds of merriment.

They clambered aboard the boat for the first time that year, united as a family. Daniel got the engine going and drove them out into the blackening ocean, just as the last sliver of sunlight disappeared over the horizon. A blanket of stars took its place. They stood united, watching the explosion of colorful fireworks above their inn.

Emily sighed, content. It felt like heaven.

EPILOGUE

The evening grew chilly so Daniel sailed them back to the dock. When they arrived, they discovered the doors of the yacht club were wide open. It was having its own party to celebrate the new season, with a fireworks display to rival Emily's.

"Shall we grab something to eat?" Daniel suggested.

Everyone agreed it was a good idea and they piled inside. There was a friendly crowd gathered, and posters on the wall advertising Sunset Harbor's upcoming Memorial Day Weekend events. It was just next weekend, Emily realized, surprised at how fast time seemed to be passing her by.

The sounds and smells of the restaurant assaulted Emily. She found them overwhelming and found herself a bit wobbly on her feet as they walked over to a spare table.

"I think I lost my sea legs over the winter," she said. "I'm feeling quite shaky."

Daniel took her by the elbow to support her. "That's not the first time you've felt faint," he said, sounding a little concerned. "You were dizzy at Trevor's house as well." He reached out and touched her forehead. "You don't seem hot but I wonder if you're coming down with something."

Emily shrugged. "Maybe. I'm just going to use the restroom."

She was starting to feel a bit hot in the bustling yacht club, and the smell of fresh seafood was turning her stomach. She only just made it inside the restroom when her nausea rose and she threw up into the nearest toilet.

Her heart began to beat with shock. She rested her head against the cubicle wall, trying to calm her breath. It wasn't like her to get seasick.

Then a sudden thought hit her. Her period was late. She hadn't had one since the week before the wedding, almost two months ago. Could she be pregnant? But she hadn't yet stopped taking her contraceptive. She couldn't be!

Emily rummaged in her purse for the pregnancy test that lurked at the bottom. She'd taken to carrying one with her ever since a scare during college that had happened while she was hiking with her friends and had no access to a pharmacy. The anguish it had caused her not knowing for those weeks had been horrible, and she'd carried an emergency test with her ever since just in case.

She took it out of her purse now, checking to make sure it hadn't expired. Was she being crazy? There was only one way to find out. And that was to take the test.

*

Emily walked back to the table where Daniel and Chantelle were sitting. It was right by the tall floor-to-ceiling windows that looked out onto the beach and the perfect view of the fireworks. Emily sank into her seat opposite them.

"Mommy? What's wrong?" Chantelle said, concerned as she looked up at Emily.

Daniel looked at her too, a worried expression on his face.

Emily heard her voice formulating the words in her mind, but it seemed like someone else's words, like she was dreaming. Somehow they found their way from her mind to her mouth, and suddenly Emily was speaking them, committing her thought into a reality, into a sudden realization.

She looked from Daniel to Chantelle and then back again, her voice a breathless whisper.

"I'm pregnant."

COMING SOON!

FOREVER, PLUS ONE
(The Inn at Sunset Harbor—Book 6)

"Sophie Love's ability to impart magic to her readers is exquisitely wrought in powerfully evocative phrases and descriptions….This is the perfect romance or beach read, with a difference: its enthusiasm and beautiful descriptions offer an unexpected attention to the complexity of not just evolving love, but evolving psyches. It's a delightful recommendation for romance readers looking for a touch more complexity from their romance reads."
--*Midwest Book Review* (Diane Donovan re *For Now and Forever*)

FOREVER, PLUS ONE is book #6 in the bestselling romance series The Inn at Sunset Harbor, which begins with book #1, For Now and Forever—a free download!

35 year old Emily Mitchell is still reeling from the surprise news that she is pregnant. Just married, she and Danielle have no time to process the news as they are thrust into doctor appointments, preparing for the baby's arrival—and, in a surprise party, the revelation of their baby's gender.

Summer has finally returned to Sunset Harbor, and Emily and Daniel have their hands full with the overflowing inn, their gut renovation of Trevor's house, the building of a new spa, and Chantelle's reacting to the baby news. They barely have time to settle into life as newlyweds when Emily gets a call from her dad: he wants them all to visit him in England. Surprising herself, Emily agrees.

A life-changing trip to England culminates in shocking news, and Emily finds herself reeling. Daniel withdraws, and as summer comes to a close and her pregnancy develops, she wonders: will she ever be able to settle into this new life?

And will life with Daniel ever be the same again?

FOREVER, PLUS ONE is book #6 in a dazzling new romance series that will make you laugh, cry, keep you turning pages late into the night—and make you fall in love with romance all over again.

Book #7 will be available soon.

"A very well written novel, describing the struggle of a woman (Emily) to find her true identity. The author did an amazing job with the creation of the characters and her description of the environment. The romance is there, but not overdosed. Kudos to the author for this amazing start of a series that promises to be very entertaining."
--*Books and Movies Reviews*, Roberto Mattos (re *For Now and Forever*)

Sophie Love

#1 bestselling author Sophie Love is author of the romantic comedy series THE INN AT SUNSET HARBOR, which includes six books (and counting), and which begins with FOR NOW AND FOREVER (THE INN AT SUNSET HARBOR—BOOK 1).

Sophie would love to hear from you, so please visit www.sophieloveauthor.com to email her, to join the mailing list, to receive free ebooks, to hear the latest news, and to stay in touch!

BOOKS BY SOPHIE LOVE

THE INN AT SUNSET HARBOR

Made in the USA
Middletown, DE
03 August 2019